The Villagers

DI Claire Falle series

Lonely Hearts

Home Help

Death Bond

Dr Harrison Lane series

Preacher Boy

The Horsemen

Dark Order

Holy Man

Writing as Gwyn Garfield-Bennett

Islands

404

PLEASE NOTE: SPELLINGS USED IN THIS BOOK
ARE BRITISH ENGLISH.

PREACHER BOY

1ST IN THE HARRISON LANE MYSTERY SERIES

GWYN GB

CHALKY DOG
PUBLISHING

1

Dr Harrison Lane pulled into Felton Woods car park and put the Harley's brakes on, just in front of the uniformed police officer who stood there, palm forward, ordering him to stop. The young officer looked intimidated but stood his ground with the briefest of twitches, acknowledging the twenty or so colleagues who swarmed all over the area behind him. Harrison took his helmet off and an earbud out, cutting Metallica off in their prime.

'This car park is closed, sir,' the officer said. 'I need you to leave immediately.'

Harrison said nothing but reached inside his leather jacket and pulled out a Metropolitan Police ID card. He handed it to the officer with the raise of an eyebrow and the whisper of a smile. The card read, 'Dr Harrison Lane, Ritualistic Behavioural Crime Unit'.

The officer looked at it and then at the face of the man in front of him. Harrison watched as a wave of recognition, then suppressed inquisitiveness, swept across the man's features. Without another word, he stepped aside and handed the ID back. Harrison took it with the hint of a nod, replaced his helmet, and slowly rode his motorbike into the car park, aware of the young man's eyes following him.

There was no apparent urgency to Harrison's movements. Around him buzzed a swarm of activity. Police officers and Scenes of Crime personnel rushed from vehicles into the woods that formed an embrace of brown and green around the top half of the parking area. He got off his bike and stopped to take in the scene, his eyes scanning every inch.

They had taped the car park closest to the woods off and it was empty except for a single car, a black VW Golf, almost directly in front of him. To his right a pale-faced man was talking to two police officers, a bored-looking Spaniel at his feet. Near them stood a huddle of white-suited forensic officers sorting small plastic boxes and bags at the back of their van. Three paths broke the line of trees and bushes, the middle one guarded by a uniformed officer. You didn't need to be Sherlock Holmes to realise there was a body in those woods.

Harrison already knew this; he'd received the call at 6.30 a.m., and it had taken him just forty-five minutes to get across town and out here. After running a hand through his short dark hair, he unzipped his jacket. He closed his eyes, breathing deeply so his muscular chest strained rhythmically at the white T-shirt underneath.

He pulled the scent of the place into his nostrils: earthy, the autumnal signature of decaying leaves. A dampness was in the air; that was good. The early morning dew would act as a canvas on which any physical disturbances could be read.

Behind him the young police officer watched transfixed as the solid bulk of Dr Harrison Lane stood planted in the middle of the car park, not moving.

Finally, his eyelids flicked open, revealing a deep look of concentration that sharpened the brown pools of his eyes. After placing the white forensic boots and suit over his clothes, he started a slow journey towards his target.

As Harrison walked, he examined the ground and bushes. The investigating team's feet had stamped and churned the path, but that didn't stop him from looking. He knew even the minutest clue could turn the direction of the case.

A forensic photographer came down the path in the opposite direction, brushing past. Harrison's concentration remained unbroken.

The path led to a small clearing, a breath of sky that broke the canopy of leaves. At the edge stood two women who stopped talking and turned to watch him, but Harrison didn't acknowledge their presence. He only had eyes for what was in front of them.

At his arrival, the older woman, a plain-clothed police detective in her fifties and clearly in charge, motioned to the forensics team to stop what they were doing and stand aside.

Harrison stepped closer to the centre of the clearing. A body lay amidst the mud and leaf debris. It was too small to be an adult. Pale waxy skin glistened with dew in the thin white light of the morning. He stopped and drank in the scene in front of him. Position. Cover. Conditions. Trees rose all around the clearing, forming an impenetrable circle, broken only by one entry and one exit path. Mature oaks and beech were interspersed with fir and horse chestnuts. Their trunks, skirted by elderberry bushes, were entwined with ivy that reached up towards the branches as though shackling the trees to the forest floor. Where there wasn't ivy, the cracked brown roughness of the bark was upholstered with furred green moss and lichen.

Other than the paths, the wood was a suffocating darkness made more impenetrable by the occasional grey barrier of stone ruins that rose like drowning sailors from the undergrowth. To those who stood in the clearing, this didn't seem like a place to go for a stroll, or perhaps it was the focus of their visit that lent the woods their sombre, ghostly edge.

Slowly Harrison moved forward, turning his attention back to the ground as he walked.

He was upon it now. The body of a boy, around seven years old. He looked like he had just fallen asleep, but the rotting leaves upon which he lay were his grave.

Harrison stopped on the forensic platform placed around the boy's body, and dropped to a crouch. The boy's thin upper torso was uncovered, and across his chest, "V R S N S M V–S M Q L I V B" was written in black marker.

He turned to examine the roughly made wooden cross behind the boy's head. It looked upside down. The arm—fixed by what appeared to be a length of wool—crossed the vertical bar around one-third from the bottom. Four candles were pushed into the earth at each corner. They had been lit and mostly burned down. In the boy's left hand was what looked like a small torch.

As Harrison turned his head, he exposed the small brown eagle tattoo on his thick neck to the group of bystanders who all stood watching silently. Even the birds had exited the clearing, as if in respect for the intensity of his concentration.

He stood up and moved around the body, studying the ground beneath the stepping blocks laid out by forensics to protect the evidence. He almost sniffed at the air. There was something raw and animalistic about this man and the way he moved. All his senses focussed and alert.

Harrison gave one last scan around the area just as from behind him the sound of crashing footsteps heralded the arrival of someone new into the clearing.

'So the Witch Doctor's arrived!' A blond mid-thirties police detective walked up to the two women and nodded toward Harrison, smirking.

'Shut it. Don't start now,' the older woman snapped at him, not taking her eyes off the scene in front of her. The younger woman, an attractive brunette, shot him a look of contempt, which he failed to notice.

Harrison took another walk around the body, and then his face softened. The concentration slipped from him. He gave one last look to the boy, this time with compassion in his eyes, as if seeing him as a child for the first time.

2

Detective Chief Inspector Sandra Barker held out her hand in greeting. 'Harrison,' she said, smiling.

'Detective Chief Inspector.' He nodded back, grasping her hand with warmth. She had short dark blond hair that had turned white at the temples, giving it a streaked look. "Maturity highlights," she called them. A feathered fringe sat above eyes that could bore into the most hardened criminals but also soften when focussed on a victim. When she smiled, creases appeared at the corners of her mouth and eyes. Her lips weren't full, and people often mistook her resting face for one that was hard and stern. Harrison, however, knew better.

'This is Dr Tanya Jones, our crime scene manager,' DCI Barker introduced the young woman next to her. 'Dr Jones, Dr Harrison Lane, Ritualistic Behavioural Crime Unit lead. You both know Detective Sergeant Jack Salter.' She nodded at the new arrival.

Harrison offered his hand to Dr Jones, who took it, not taking her eyes away from his. She wore the working uniform of a crime-scene investigator, a white microporous coverall and blue PVC overshoes, the same as every one of them in the clearing. The hood on Tanya's suit was pushed off her head to reveal long hair tied up in a ponytail. With her hair scraped back from her face, it was easier to see her high cheekbones and pale complexion. In her left hand she held her mask and the blue nitrile glove she'd taken off the hand she offered to Harrison.

'It's a pleasure to meet you. I've heard a lot about your work,' she said as his big hand enveloped hers.

Behind them, as they talked, the rest of the forensics team worked to put up a protective tent around the boy's body. The painstaking collection of evidence would continue once they'd secured the crime scene from all the elements, and long after the detectives had left the woods.

Keen to get on with the police work, DCI Barker cut short the introductions. 'Are we looking at some kind of satanic cult?'

Harrison shook his head. 'Definitely not. It's one man obsessed with religion.'

'No way you could just tell that by looking,' DS Salter butted in.

Everyone ignored him.

'There was no ritual. The boy didn't die here. He was brought and placed here. The woods were once part of Felton Abbey's grounds. You can see part of the ruins.' Harrison turned and nodded towards the grey stones that poked above the undergrowth.

'Any idea what the letters are on his chest?' DCI Barker continued, taking out her notebook. Its blue cover carried the Metropolitan Police logo. She flicked through pages of notes to find a clean space in which to write.

'It's the satanic exorcism prayer of Saint Benedict. Latin. *Vade Retro Satana, Numquam suade mihi vana. Sunt Mala Quae Libas, Ipse venena bibas.* Step back, Satan, never tempt me with your vanities. What you offer me is evil, drink the poison yourself.'

DCI Barker looked up at Harrison and thrust her notebook towards him. 'You'd better write that down for me. You think he was poisoned?' She squinted at him as he wrote.

Harrison shook his head again. 'I don't think so. Obviously the postmortem will confirm that. It's not meant to be a literal meaning, and there's no obvious sign of poisoning. He looks too peaceful.'

DCI Barker's frown turned to sadness before her face resumed its professional mask. 'So what's with the upside-down cross and the candles? Isn't that the cross of the Devil?'

'It is,' Harrison said, 'but I don't think that's what he intended. The man who found the body, his dog probably nudged it when he walked up to the boy to sniff him. It's only loosely fixed. The paw prints stop right next to it before retreating. The candles could represent the light of Christ; but with what I think is a torch in the boy's hand, it's more likely to be the fact your man is afraid of the dark and didn't want to leave the boy alone without light.'

DCI Barker wrote that in her notebook.

DS Salter shook his head.

'There's something in the boy's mouth,' Harrison continued. 'Could be a protective talisman. I think the man who brought him here is worried the Devil's going to take him or has taken him. I believe he's been trying to teach him, save him if you like. The prayer suggests he might have killed him, thinking he was possessed. Or that he blames the Devil for his death.'

'How can you say he's been teaching him? There's no way anyone could tell that!' DS Salter tried to be a part of the conversation. This time he spoke more forcefully.

Harrison turned and considered him for the first time. 'Have you looked at his right hand? The boy has been writing incessantly for days. His index and middle fingers are inked and rubbed raw from constant use. His wrist carries abrasions where it had been dragged across a surface as he wrote.'

DS Salter wished he'd taken a closer look at their victim before opening his mouth. This guy was a smart arse.

DCI Barker took back control of the questioning. 'So who we looking for?'

'A lone killer, obsessed with the teachings of the Church and the battle with evil...'

'No shit, Sherlock!' DS Salter muttered. The three of them looked at him as though he was a complete idiot.

'His struggle with it would have started in childhood,' Harrison said. 'Perhaps he had a strict upbringing, and the punishment was being left alone in the dark. He'll be a loner, on the edges of society. He or his family are regular churchgoers, but he might have stopped attending recently. Something triggered this. People may have noticed his absence. He's shorter than average, around five foot four or five, and of slight build. I'd say he brought the boy here four or five hours ago, and you should search for a small van, not a car.'

DCI Barker nodded. 'Thanks. That gives us a few leads to work on until forensics get us more information.' She looked at Dr Jones, who'd been listening to the conversation in awe. 'In the meantime, I've got to get through the Saturday shopper traffic to the Phillips family and tell them we've found their missing son before the press gets a hold of this. You got a spare crash helmet on you, Harrison?'

'Of course. No problem. It was a pleasure to meet you

Dr Jones,' he said, looking at her and gave a smile that energised his eyes without barely moving his lips. He turned and started to walk from the clearing. As he passed DS Salter, 'Later,' was all he said without even a glance.

Salter scowled after him and turned to DCI Barker. 'Look, there's no way he can know it's just one person, let alone what he bloody looks like,' he said in a barely hushed voice.

DCI Barker put her notebook away, 'Have you ever heard of the Shadow Wolves?'

DS Salter shrugged and looked perplexed.

'Google them, Jack. He was brought up by one of their best.'

'What the...? And what's with the whole "Later" thing?'

'He means now isn't the time or place to tell you what a prick you can be. Drop the macho humour and try just being yourself, can you?'

DCI Barker walked off. Behind her Jack Salter couldn't hide his annoyance, and Dr Jones had to turn away so he couldn't see the smirk on hers.

As Sandra Barker left the clearing, she heard Salter's mobile ring.

He sighed to himself and answered, 'Marie...'

She paused for a moment to turn and watch him, the irritation melting into a flicker of concern. Then she followed Harrison to the car park, where he stood staring at the ground in the taped-off area.

'Definitely van tyres, but not a big company van—a private one. Small business, maybe. The tyres are different and quite worn. A fleet vehicle would likely have all the same tyres.'

'Definitely his vehicle?' DCI Barker asked.

'Yup. While his tracks are mostly obliterated on the

path, it's the same footprints as we saw around the body. Here, carrying the boy towards the woods, and then lighter imprints on his return. The dog walker is in trainers, but a different sole pattern.' Harrison pointed out marks on the ground to the DCI, who looked but, try as she might, couldn't see what he saw. She nodded anyway.

'I'll get the guys on it.'

Once she'd briefed her team, DCI Barker returned to Harrison, who'd taken a spare helmet out of his Harley Davidson saddlebag and was waiting for her.

'Any excuse,' she said as she came to stand next to him, admiring the Harley, 'but it'll be a lot quicker with you than going by car.'

Sandra Barker took the hand he offered and swung a leg over the seat. Riding pillion had never been something she'd expected to get into in her fifties. She'd seen too many motorbike accidents in her career, but with Harrison she felt safe. He had that effect on people. She also had another motive for wanting to get him on his own.

THEY PULLED up outside an ordinary house on an ordinary street, except in this home, the misery inside was anything but ordinary.

DCI Barker was relieved to see they were the first to arrive. 'The vultures haven't got here yet, that's good. Bloody Twitter has a lot to answer for.'

They both looked at the house in front of them, the curtains half drawn across the sitting-room window. An attempt to keep the world out.

She sighed for the job ahead and got off the bike. She was about to walk away, then remembered. 'Harrison, he's a good cop you know, even if he's a prat sometimes.'

He knew exactly who she was talking about.

'He's having a tough time right now. Marie's struggling with motherhood, and he's finding it hard. Cut him some slack, would you? Please? I need you both working together on this.'

'Sure.'

DCI Barker nodded in thanks, then turned and headed up the path. As soon as she was through the gate, a woman's face appeared at the window. Within seconds, the front door had opened.

Harrison watched as DCI Barker went inside. He caught a glimpse of her through the sitting-room window, and then she disappeared from his vision. He didn't need to see her, though, to know what she was saying. Harrison heard it. The wailing, gut-wrenching, heart-breaking, guttural cry of a mother who had just been told her worst fear.

3

_____

Sally Fuller looked at the scene around her kitchen table and smiled to herself. Their two children, three-year-old Sophie, and seven-year-old Alex, had just finished eating a bowl full of Coco Pops each and were now excitedly bantering about swimming. They both sported chocolate moustaches from where they'd drunk the milk left in their bowls. What she loved was the sibling bonding that was taking place across the breakfast debris.

'I'll teach you to swim, Sophe,' Alex said, his face beaming with big-brotherly pride. It was a trait Sally loved about him. He'd never been jealous of his new sister's arrival; instead, he loved being two instead of one. Increasing their family size had been hard won. They'd tried for three years to give Alex a sibling, and there had been four false starts, miscarriages that had ripped at her heart with each failure. She'd begun to think Alex would remain an only child, when they were finally blessed with a successful pregnancy and Sophie came along.

Although three had been in the original game plan, they'd stuck with two. Not only could they not face another round of potential miscarriages, but having kids proved to be more expensive than they'd realised. Sally needed to go back to work, but with the cost of childcare that wasn't financially viable until both children were at school. Even then, she wondered how they would manage the school holidays. The result was that her husband, Edward, did as much overtime as possible to keep them afloat.

This Saturday was a rare one when he didn't have to go into the retail warehouse where he worked. They were going to make the most of this family time together. Sally had decided that with all four of them at home, it was a good enough excuse to take the big steak pie out of the freezer. It was a luxury one, some famous chef's brand, and out of her usual budget, but she'd bought it at a reduced price because the packaging was a bit damaged. It had been in the freezer for a few weeks, waiting for a day that was worthy of their eating it. Today was that day. They could have chips and frozen peas with it, and maybe she'd make a rice pudding. The kids loved that. To top it off, she put a bottle of Pinot Grigio in the fridge and already had earmarked a movie to watch later.

Alex had earned his ten-metre swimming badge last month, which he'd pinned to the corkboard in his bedroom, along with tickets from Alton Towers, the Warner Brothers' Harry Potter Tour, and a merit certificate from school. He'd been the fastest in his class, so he'd also won two free tickets to their local pool. He was desperate to share his new skill with his sister and his hard-earned prize with them all. While Sally wasn't a particular fan of indoor swimming pools, she knew the kids would love it, so they'd agreed that today's treat would be to go for a swim. The one advantage was that it wouldn't require driving in the car. They could walk, which would save a frustrating journey, sat in traffic with two impatient children, and the nightmare of trying to find parking.

'Can I wear my Elsa costume?' Sophie pleaded.

'Yes,' Sally replied.

'Can we go to McDonald's after?' chimed in Alex, looking from his father to his mother and back again.

Edward had been finishing his toast and coffee at the end of the table and looked at Sally with a wink in his eye. 'We'll see,' he replied.

'Is that a yes?'

'That's a "We'll see",' he replied to Alex's cheeky grin.

Alex mimed a jubilant cheer at his sister, and she copied him. His little apprentice.

'Go clean your teeth,' Sally said, gathering the bowls.

'Elsa?' Sophie added.

'Yes. I'll come and find your *Frozen* costume in a moment. Now go on.'

Fifteen minutes later, Sally was in the hallway, sorting out coats. She hadn't had time to fill the dishwasher yet, but that could wait. The priority was having fun as a family. The dishes would still be there when they all got home.

'Alex, where's your coat?' she shouted up the stairs.

There was no answer, so she shouted again.

'Coming,' shouted Sophie, her little feet running along the carpeted hallway upstairs.

'Edward, is Alex up there?' Sally called up to her husband.

She heard him go into Alex's bedroom; the door opening, then shutting.

'Not up here,' he replied, coming to the top of the stairs and looking down at her. Sophie wriggled underneath his arms and came down the stairs on her bottom, bump-bumping down one step at a time.

'Alex?' Sally called again. 'Alex?'

She heard the back door open and shut. Alex, already coated, wandered into the hallway.

'Where were you?' Sally asked.

'Giving Snowball and Squeaky their breakfast,' he replied, 'You were all taking so long to get ready.'

'Go wash your hands,' Sally said, aware Alex usually forgot to after feeding the guinea pigs.

Edward came down the stairs just behind Sophie, who'd finally bumped to the bottom step, a big beaming smile on her face.

'You'd better get used to that, son,' he told Alex.

'What?' Sally asked.

He smirked. 'Waiting around for you women to be ready.'

4

DCI Barker's team worked out of Europe's largest purpose-built police station in Lewisham High Street. It had its advantages over her last office at one of the traditional stations that had since closed. The fact that it was a new purpose-built, modern building was one. The canteen floor tiles weren't covered with countless spilt drinks and unrecognisable food smears, which would have taken forensics a year to decipher. Plus, the toilets and locker rooms weren't straight out of a 1980s horror movie scene. It also still had the buzz of a working police station, unlike Jubilee House in Putney, where some of the other Major Investigation Teams worked. Here they had the largest custody suite in the Met, with a noisy, smelly melee of suspects with whom she could still get her adrenaline fix if she needed a break from the mundaneness of office bound work. Plus, there were a couple of added bonuses. If she was stressed, she could go stroke one of the horses in the mounted division stables. Their big, patient faces would look at her while she wound down from her latest case. She loved the smell in the stables. That mix of hay, horse, and leather. The station was open 24/7. Crime didn't stop, and neither did they.

In their incident room, the status board was already updated. This was no longer an abduction case, but a murder enquiry. The photo of a smiling Darren Phillips— which had been in every national newspaper that week— was now accompanied by a shot of his final resting place. A map with a triangular line connecting his home, abduction point, and Felton Woods sat between the two. The fresh-faced boy beamed out from the board, reminding everyone in the room exactly why they were about to spend the next week and more putting in overtime.

The office was packed with personnel and computers, plus a good dose of used coffee cups and fast snacks. DCI Barker had twenty-one detectives, a police sergeant, and two civilian staff on her team. She was three detectives down from her full quota, but finding experienced officers wasn't easy. She had just one detective inspector, Tom Goodman, whom she'd asked to be SIO on a stabbing on Wandsworth High Street. He was also due in court soon for another case they'd worked on last year. Add to that a suspicious death in the homeless community that she was SIO on, plus a potential lead in Portugal for an attempted murder from last year, and their caseload was full. She also had a vacancy for a detective sergeant and had been told a new recruit would start any day. She hoped he'd be ready to hit the ground running.

Her boss, Detective Superintendent Robert Jackson, had promised extra cavalry from one of the other MITs if they were overwhelmed. This was their highest-priority case right now, and she'd make damned sure she used every available resource she had.

It was why she'd requested Harrison Lane's help. DCI

Barker had worked with him before and knew his specialist knowledge would give them a head start. She'd been relieved when he'd said he was available. His reputation was spreading beyond the Met. Last she'd heard, he'd been helping the Manchester police with a particularly complicated case, and the team up there had made a series of arrests after getting nowhere for months. While there were some who still steered clear of his slightly maverick ways, plenty of others knew his results spoke for themselves.

Harrison was a unique blend of psychologist, ritualistic crime expert, and tracker. It was a potent combination at a crime scene. He wasn't one to share much detail about his life, but he'd told her that when he was young, he and his mother had lived with a Native American tracker, who'd been part of the elite Shadow Wolves. They helped patrol the Mexico/USA border looking for drug runners. His stepfather, Joe, had taught Harrison tracking and survival skills. DCI Barker worked for the first time with Harrison a couple of years ago. It had been that unique combination of knowledge which had ensured they caught a paedophile who would have otherwise got away. The man was a wealthy banker with a private jet lined up ready to get him out of the country. Luckily Harrison had seen through the man's attempt to frame someone by saying they had an occult motive, and when he went on the run, could find him quickly. The man was now languishing at her Majesty's Pleasure for a few years, and would be on the sex offenders register for life. Harrison definitely helped get the right results. She hoped he was going to do just that again on this case.

In the incident room, most of her team were now either on computers or phones or milling around, waiting for the briefing to start.

Into the hubbub walked DS Salter, talking animatedly on his phone. 'Of course I will. I promise. Yes, I'll call. Look, I have to go. You too. Bye.'

He pocketed his phone just as Sergeant Steve Evans spotted him. 'Salty, how's that boy of yours?' he asked in his unmistakable Welsh accent.

Jack checked himself for a fraction of a second, then sloughed off the gloom, and his face returned to its usual cheeky grin. 'Taff, mate. He's doing great. Soon be teaching that bunch of Welsh schoolboys a thing or two in the Six Nations.'

'In your dreams!' Evans replied, slapping him on the back for good measure.

Behind them, Harrison Lane entered and nonchalantly pulled off his leather jacket. At least half the women in the room—and a couple of the men—couldn't help stop what they were doing to watch him and the solid biceps that stretched the cotton sleeves of his T-shirt.

'Here he comes,' snarked Jack to anyone who'd listen. 'Managed to park your broomstick, doc?'

Harrison ignored him and crossed to the back of the room, where he found himself a quiet spot to lean against the wall, just as DCI Barker came out of her office. She wasted no time with pleasantries. Every minute was precious. The room instantly fell silent.

'As you all know, Darren Phillips's body was found this morning in Felton Woods,' she began. 'We don't believe this is where he was killed. Indications are he wasn't sexually assaulted and just one man was involved. You should all have read Dr Lane's initial notes about the nature of the crime scene, as well as the profile of Darren's killer. Darren was missing for over a week. He was kept somewhere, and we need to find out where. I want every frame of CCTV, every building in the area checked. If you've already looked at it, give it to someone else; I want it looked at again. I want every family member and friend re-interviewed. And I want every church and religious group visited. Sergeant Evans will dish out tasks, so get to it. I don't need to tell you the media will be all over the story. No one is to discuss this with anyone outside of the team.'

The mute button was instantly released, and the hubbub resumed as the team jumped into action. Any fresh case brought a surge of adrenaline, but when it involved a child, the effect was even stronger. At least half the officers felt a sense of failure at not having been able to save the boy. They'd been searching for him for a week; it had been as though he'd disappeared into thin air, and now he was dead. Their numbers had been bolstered by colleagues pulled off some of the other cases, and they needed to be briefed on what had been done and found to date. It was a race against time. The longer it took to find the killer, the colder the trail would get. DCI Barker was throwing everything she had at this.

DS Salter and Harrison followed the DCI into her office. She liked to be in among her team, so it tended to function more as a conference room than a private office. If she ever shut her door, then you knew not to disturb her. There was a long table down the left side, and DCI Barker's desk was in front of the door as you entered, with a couple of filing cabinets topped by a sickly-looking aloe vera plant. She tried to keep the space uncluttered and tidy; in fact, she was a little obsessive about keeping it tidy. If things piled up, it was as though their doppelgänger piled up in her head. The decor and furniture were modern utilitarian, but she had one vice besides the old, worn leather desk chair that squeaked as she sank into it; her waste bin was already displaying her colourful addiction. Around six chocolate wrappers lay at the bottom of an otherwise-empty bin. The DCI sighed, and her hand subconsciously went straight to the top drawer of her desk.

'I need to speak to the press bureau, get a media statement out before the papers start making it up.' She unwrapped a purple Quality Street and popped it into her mouth, chewing for a moment while she thought. 'Jack, you're acting as deputy for me on this one, but I need you out there following any leads the team brings in. Make sure Harrison gets all the interview transcripts, would you? I'd like you to take a look through everything we've collated so far, Harrison. You might spot something we didn't.' She threw the screwed-up empty wrapper into the bin along with its spent colleagues. 'And Jack, I want you in charge of the re-interviews with the family.' She studied him more carefully. 'Is Marie all right?'

Jack looked slightly embarrassed at the question and threw a glance at Harrison. Before he could answer, there was a knock on the open door, and a young detective constable stepped over the threshold.

'Ma'am, Dr Jones said there's something you and Dr Lane should go see straight away at the Greenwich mortuary. They're just starting the post-mortem on Darren.'

'That was quick,' the DCI said. 'Knew we could rely on Nicholas. Please let this be something good. Jack, you carry on while I'm out. Anything crops up, just call.'

DR TANYA JONES was waiting for them with the pathologist, Dr Nicholas Aspey, who was showing her something in one of the exhibit trays. He had on a blue hair cap and white mask, with his blue hospital scrubs covered by a plastic apron and his hands protected with latex gloves. Only his ears and eyes were visible, and these held glasses to his face. He clearly had just started the post-mortem but not got very far. Harrison was glad they hadn't got round to opening him up. He had a fairly tough stomach for most things, but even he found the stench that came from a person's entrails less than comfortable.

All the furniture in the room, from the wheeled trolleys to the cupboards and shelving, was gleaming stainless steel. At every station, the bright white rectangles of lighting in the ceiling were also enhanced by examination lamps. Harrison found the gleaming steel created an icy chill feel, which was a completely irrational concern, seeing as anyone who had to lie on one of the examination tables was already dead and stone cold.

Darren was the only occupant of the steel room. The critical need to ensure no contamination meant the other team of morticians would have to work in another room, but as this was the weekend, it wasn't an issue.

The body of Darren Phillips lay, much as they'd found him, only this time he was on a metal table, not a forest floor. He looked like a sleeping angel. One of the lab technicians was photographing him from every angle as though it were a macabre modelling shoot. In the air was the hint of cleaning fluids combined with the slightly pickle-like odour of formalin.

As they walked in, Dr Jones looked up. 'Ma'am, we've literally just brought Darren in, but I think you should see this now. It confirms what Dr Lane suspected.' Tanya's eyes skipped quickly from the DCI to Harrison and away again.

As they drew closer, they saw a ball of paper sheets in the tray. Some had been partially unrolled and were covered in small writing crammed across their surface. Dr Jones stepped back so Harrison and the DCI could get a closer look, but not before her hand had accidentally brushed against his. She wondered if he too felt the tingle of electric energy that transferred between them. It was possible. She'd seen his eyes look to her at their touch, but maybe he'd simply been about to apologise. The pathologist brought her back to business.

'His mouth was full of them. There's more,' said Dr Aspey. 'Looks like biblical texts.' He handed a pair of tweezers to Harrison, who, after putting on gloves, took them and carefully looked at the most accessible sheets. After a few moments, he looked up at DCI Barker and nodded.

'Before or after death?' she asked the pathologist.

'I'm not sure. I need to find out the cause of death first —that's still not apparent—and open him up. Those you're looking at now, I'd say after, but I'll confirm that for you in the next hour or so.'

Harrison crossed to the examination table, where he contemplated Darren's body before bending down towards the boy's head.

'There's a faint smell, like acetone, perhaps paint. I caught it in the woods. Hair soaks up odours,' he said.

'We'll be taking samples. I'll see what I can find,' Dr Aspey replied.

'So does this confirm your theory?' DCI Barker asked, watching Harrison closely.

'I need to see which passages he's written. That might give us some more clues as to the state of his captor's mind, but from what I can see already, yes. Why he felt Darren was possessed or needed to be protected from the Devil, I don't know. Did he know Darren? Or was it just "wrong place at the wrong time"? Something has definitely triggered this behaviour, pushed him over the edge. Someone out there must have noticed something.'

'We'll get the sheets processed asap,' Tanya said. 'If

they're not too damaged, we should have at least some of them across to you by the morning.'

'Okay, good.' Harrison nodded and walked out of the room.

'Sociable, isn't he?' She raised her eyebrows and turned to DCI Barker.

'He's what you call the strong, silent type. You'll get used to him. When he's concentrating on a case, he's not one for chit-chat, and it takes him a bit of time to trust someone. It'll come.' She turned to Dr Aspey, 'Thanks for coming in on a weekend at such short notice, Nicholas.'

'Not a problem. You know me—I'd far rather spend my time helping this young man than get dragged around Selfridges or Waitrose. Jackie said we need new cushions for the living room. We've got people over tonight, and she's stressing. Some old school friend she hasn't seen in ages, although why Jackie thinks she'd be coming to judge our cushions I don't know.'

Sandra and Tanya both smiled knowingly.

Dr Aspey moved over to where Darren lay and gingerly sniffed the air. 'I didn't smell anything chemically or like acetone,' he said, and moved closer to the boy's head, 'although now that he mentioned it...'

W hen Harrison needed to think, he did one of two things. He either disappeared out of the city and headed for the wide-open countryside and nature, or he sought the silence and safety of his own space where he could control the environment and allow his mind to think and digest. As he was working a case in London, that meant the only option right now was his office deep in the basement of the Metropolitan Police headquarters, New Scotland Yard on Victoria Embankment.

In one sense, being shoved below ground level with no natural light was an anathema for Harrison. He was a man who'd spent years in the fresh air and sunshine, but given the option of a spare desk in a busy incident room, he found solace in the gloom of his underground bolthole. The office was mostly used as a repository for his files, research, and the various spoils of cases—as well as his technical assistant, Ryan.

Ryan wasn't in residence when Harrison arrived. The door was locked, and it was a relief to open it and know he could spend some precious time alone. The image of

Darren's pale white body was etched into his retinas. He had to clear his head and assess what he already knew and what he needed to find out in the hunt for his killer. Darren had to be put to rest.

As the door opened into the dark office, light from the hallway shafted inside. To the left was a neat desk surrounded by bookshelves and filing cabinets; but it was what covered the walls and sat among the books that would make the unsuspecting jump. Grimacing death masks and painted skulls leered from the shadows, while roughly sewn voodoo dolls, red-painted devils, Ouija boards, and bone runes huddled on the shelves, cluttering every space. Copies of *The Journal of Haitian Studies* and *The African Studies Review* sat alongside *The Satanic Rituals*, *Pagan and Christian Creeds*, the Old Testament, and *Demonology and Devil Lore*. In the half-light and at first glance, it looked like the cave of a sorcerer, but as Harrison flicked on the light switch, the room showed its modern face. Computer screens and a small tea-making station broke up the foreboding menace of the occult and all it whispered.

He crossed straight to the kettle and filled it up at the sink, relieved to see his mug washed, ready for a fresh tea bag. There'd been some issues with cleaners in the past, the odd one not caring for his choice of decor and refusing to go into the room. Harrison had tried to talk to them, but it was blind fear and that meant potluck on some days as to whether the place had been cleaned. Harrison knew that until everyone saw through the hocus-pocus of it all, he'd still have a job mopping up the results of crimes conducted in the name of so-called magic and spiritual beliefs—as well as washing his own mug.

While he waited for the kettle to boil, he took off his leather jacket and stretched. It had been a long morning, and riding the bike and focussing for extended periods

meant he needed to release the tension in his neck and
shoulders. His back was broad and muscular, like the rest
of him. For a few minutes he stretched the muscles,
rippling his back and shoulders, pulling the tension from
them and rubbing his neck. As it was Saturday, and he
hadn't planned on being in today, it was going to turn into
a long week. He had to ensure he was in top form.
Somewhere out there was a man who'd taken and
murdered Darren Phillips. Harrison wanted him caught
and put away so he could never touch a child again.

As he sat down at his computer to read through the
material gathered by the team, the decidedly pleasant face
of Dr Tanya Jones interrupted his thoughts. A brief sliver
of time had come into his mind, their hands touching in
the post-mortem suite. It had thrown him off his
concentration then and did so again now.

She was attractive: blue eyes with a heavy curtain of
lashes and a sculptured face that contained full lips and a
perfectly formed nose. She was also intelligent, a fellow
scientist who relied only on facts and evidence. Harrison's
kind of woman. But he couldn't let himself get distracted,
couldn't risk the loss of focus. He had to put her out of his
mind and concentrate on what mattered: finding Darren's
killer and continuing the hunt for the man who had
murdered his mother.

The incident room was quieter than earlier. Those who weren't out interviewing and searching were tapping away on computers. Some were on the phone taking calls, following the appeal for information, or setting up interviews. The atmosphere was also more subdued. The morbid black humour that, for most of them, was a necessary mental-protection mechanism, was turned off when a child was involved. There were few things off limits for emergency services in-house humour, but the murder of a child was one of them.

DCI Barker stood in front of the incident board, one arm across her body, holding the elbow of her other arm as she rubbed her cheek in thought. DS Salter walked across and stood next to her.

'Good chance it could be someone he knows from school, church, or a club—or even a neighbour or family friend,' she told him.

'We've found some partial fingerprints on the torch, but so far nothing's coming up on Ident1. The torch is with forensics still. See if they can get anything more. They're checking for DNA too.'

'Something tells me we won't have him in our systems. Harrison said this guy has flipped for some reason, but why?'

'Could the suspect be a woman? It wasn't a violent killing.'

'Definitely not the mother—you can't fake that reaction—and anyway Harrison's convinced it's a man.'

Salter didn't reply, which prompted DCI Barker to look at him. He was clenching his teeth, the muscles in his cheeks taut with the effort of not voicing what he was busting to say.

'How are you getting on with the interviews? You know the stats. It's most likely to be a family member.' She changed the subject.

'Double-checked the family's alibis and they're sound. Working on friends now.'

Salter's mobile rang; it was on silent, but there was no mistaking the buzz from his inside pocket. He took it out and looked at the screen. It read, "Home."

'Go on. And make sure you buy her some flowers later.' DCI Barker was getting seriously concerned about Jack's home situation and his ability to focus on the job. She'd hate to do it, but maybe she should tell him he needed to take some time, step away from this case, and let another DS take over. They sure didn't need to lose the manpower right now, and he was her most senior DS, but his family was more important, as was his sanity. Besides, it might not be a bad thing if he continued to rub Harrison up the wrong way.

Jack looked relieved and went to take the phone call, just as Sergeant Evans walked up to them.

'Ma'am, reception's just called. A convicted

paedophile, out on parole and living in the same street as Darren's family, just walked in. He walked straight up to the desk and said he wanted to confess.'

'Really? This easy?' Delight lit up DCI Barker's face.

'I'll get on it now, Taff,' DS Salter replied, cancelling his call.

'I'll go with you, Jack, and bring DC Johnson with us. I'll get Harrison too. Taff, can you let the desk know we're heading down now?'

'Sure, boss,' he replied.

'And Taff, don't advertise this to the whole team, all right? I don't want them to ease up. This investigation needs to keep going full throttle.'

An hour later, Harrison Lane walked into the small observation room next door to one of the interview rooms at Lewisham Police Station. DCI Barker was already in there, and she gave him a nod in greeting as he entered.

'He's refused representation,' she told him, indicating the man on the video screen in front of her. 'Handed in his laptop as well. They've swabbed him and taken his clothes. Just waiting on the shoe results. He didn't complain.'

A balding man in police-custody issue trousers and top sat expectantly staring at the two police detectives in front of him. He looked calm.

Harrison took his place, standing next to the DCI. Both of them had their arms folded. She was a fit fifty-four-year-old but not skinny, probably the result of her chocolate habit. She wasn't short either at five nine, but the large muscular bulk of Harrison beside her made her look almost petite. He dominated the room, but she didn't feel uncomfortable. He wasn't like some big men, who, aware of their size, used it to their best advantage against everyone they encountered, including women. Harrison was always mindful of another's personal space, and she'd seen him somehow make himself appear smaller if the situation required it. She guessed that went with the territory of being a psychologist. He knew how to approach people to get the best out of them and when to make himself less intimidating. She'd also seen him take the opposite strategy. He might have a doctorate, but he was a man few people would pick a fight with, and even fewer would come out all right if they did.

Both of them stood eagerly watching the screen, waiting to hear what the man in front of DS Salter and DC Johnson would say.

'So do you want to tell us what happened?' DS Salter asked the man. This was standard interview technique. Let the suspect tell their story—if they wanted to. Sometimes they didn't; it would just be met with "no comment". Usually they would tell their own version of a "story" even if it was just to say, "Weren't me, Guv". If they were guilty and didn't want to admit it, it would be an elaborate fabrication that the interviewer would then pick apart and find inconsistencies in. In this case, the man wanted them to know he was guilty, so he sang like a canary.

'I'd been watching him, playing in the street with his friends. There's a few of them that ride bikes or play football. He kept going back and forth past my house on that bike of his. I wanted him. I wanted to invite him in and talk to him. I wanted to get to know him.'

DCI Barker's stomach bile reacted to his words. At this stage in her career, most crimes were just part of the day job and the criminals were clients you had to endure. However, there were always some cases and some individuals who could still break through the professional wall she had built around herself. The officers they lost most frequently were those who worked the child abuse shifts. Despite the artificial-intelligence software built to grade images on a computer so people didn't have to trawl through every single sickening one, there was still the need to review material. Safeguards were in place. Officers had time-outs scheduled to ensure it wasn't continuous exposure, but it was often just a question of time before the depravity ate through to their soul and twisted their view of the world. You couldn't un-see some things, no matter how hard you tried.

The man continued with his story, uninterrupted. His face was calm, and he almost smiled in parts, as though he was forgetting where he was and recounting a holiday memory.

'I knew it was a matter of time before I got pulled with my record, so I did him in and took him to the woods. I laid him out, made it look like it had been some satanist who done it. You know, put a cross upside down, candles, stuff like that.'

'We've not released that information,' DCI Barker told Harrison. He didn't reply, but she knew he'd heard because his eyes narrowed as he listened.

The man finished telling his story then looked up at DS Salter and DC Johnson expectantly. Next, Jack would start to nail him down to a timeline, get the facts in order, and see how that stacked up and if there were any inconsistencies. He started in reverse order, with leaving Darren's body in Felton Woods.

The change was imperceptible, but Harrison noticed it. Within a couple of questions, the man was fidgeting.

'What time did you arrive at Felton Woods?' DS Salter asked.

The man scratched his neck and rubbed his chin.

'Not sure. I wasn't exactly looking at the clock. I had other things on my mind.' He might have sounded cocky and sure of himself, but his body language told a different story. He had shrunk slightly in his chair, and his eyes flicked from Salter to Johnson.

'He's lying. We're wasting our time,' Harrison exclaimed and turned away from the screen to look at DCI Barker.

'He knows how Darren was found,' Barker said quizzically.

'He's too tall, too heavy, and too vague in his story. There're no details to substantiate. The initial phase of the interview was pure fantasy. He was retelling a dream. He probably had thought about doing it, but he didn't. Now he's been pulled out of that fantasy mode. He's got to think about what he's saying, make sure he gets things right. Now he's nervous. Whenever Jack asks a direct question about the murder, he's evasive. If he really came in here because he wanted to confess, he would have maintained that calmness, been more controlled with his answers, even under questioning.'

Barker nodded. She had her reservations too, but it didn't add up. 'How does he know about the satanic stuff?'

'No idea, but he's scared of something. Look how he sits curled up, and it's not the fear of being arrested and charged that's doing that.'

DCI Barker thought for a moment then picked up her mobile and typed a message in text. In the interview room, DS Salter's mobile buzzed. He pulled it out of his pocket and looked at the message.

'Tell him you don't believe him and you're going to send him home.'

DS Salter was a little surprised by the command, but he was a professional. Nothing showed on his face. He placed his mobile facedown on the table and did as told.

'I don't believe you, I don't think you had anything to do with Darren's death.' He stared hard at the man in front of him. Tiny pinheads of sweat were erupting all over his face, and his eyes widened at Jack's words. With a quick glance at his colleague, DC Johnson, to encourage him to follow his lead, Jack picked up his notes and phone, 'We're letting you go.'

The man visibly paled. He looked like he might be about to vomit. White-knuckled hands clutched at the table as though he would refuse to leave, and his legs shook and jiggled.

'No, please, no. They're going to lynch me. They know about my record…'

DS Salter stood.

'Okay, okay. I didn't touch him, but I wanted to. I've got pictures on my computer. Check it out. You need to arrest me. I've broken my licence conditions.'

DS Salter terminated the interview recording and walked out of the room to the sound of the man's begging shouts.

When he came out of the interview room, DCI Barker and Harrison were already in the corridor. Jack's face, as he walked out, reflected their own thoughts.

'Little scrote, wasting our time. Just worried about his own skin,' he fumed at them.

'But how did he know about the way the boy was laid out?' DCI Barker questioned, as much to the air as to the three men in front of her. 'Hand him over to the Child Protection team, will you? He's not going to help us with our enquiry, but if he's been breaking his parole and is re-offending, they'll want him off the streets as much as I do.'

'I can do that, ma'am,' DC Johnson replied. 'I'll take him down now.' He turned around to reenter the interview room.

'Well, we did think it was too good to be bloody true.' DCI Barker sighed. She started back towards the incident room, annoyed that they'd wasted time away from the investigation. 'Perhaps we need to make it public that Darren wasn't sexually abused before we get every paedo in the area, nervous of being lynched, filling up holding cells.'

They hadn't gone far before her mobile rang, 'What now?' she muttered when she saw who was calling. 'All we need is a PR issue on top of this.'

The name read 'Danny Payne.' He was an earnest twenty-seven-year-old with impeccable grooming. Unfortunately, he'd inherited his immediate boss's desire to control every possible element of the Met's public persona. As soon as DCI Barker answered her phone, she could tell something had upset him. His voice was taut.

'DCI Barker,' he said, 'Have you seen the online news? I've sent you a link via email.'

'No. Hang on,' she replied, opening her emails and clicking on his name. The link was to a national online news site; right in front of her was the headline 'Satanic Murder of Seven-year-old Boy'. Alongside Darren's angelic face was a photograph of the dog walker with the caption 'How I Stumbled Upon the Demonic Murder'.

'The shit,' Barker swore. 'I asked the dog walker not to say anything. Jack, get someone to pull him in and tell him he could have compromised our enquiry. Make sure they put the wind up his greedy, money-grabbing arse. Perhaps send Taff. Uniform will work better, and I know how passionate he gets about unreliable witnesses. I hope they paid him enough for his story because he's going to feel like crap once we're done with him.'

7

The Fullers walked along the busy street towards the swimming pool. Sally held on to Sophie's hand as she babbled away excitedly about nothing in particular, from swimming to her little friend, Katya, and what they were going to have for lunch. Edward walked a couple of paces in front of them while Alex skipped a couple of feet ahead of him.

They'd left the house with Alex and Sophie walking together, but he had soon got impatient with her progress. Three-year-olds weren't the fastest walkers, and halfway into their journey, Sally realised why they tended to travel by car. There had been a stop to inspect a dead pigeon, and they'd had to wait while she stared at a bus-stop poster advertising the latest Disney movie. Sophie had entered into a debate with nobody else about the merits of the costume being worn by the main character. Sally's mind had wandered to tomorrow and the list of things she knew needed to be done. There was Alex's school uniform that had to be washed and dried before Monday, and the house needed a good clean. She'd have to get up and get on with it in the morning and not do what they'd done last Sunday, which was lie in bed and have the kids join them for cuddles that ended up being another hour of snoozing.

'Come on, Sophie,' Alex shouted back to his sister.

They were nearing the pool; it was just around the next corner. Sophie didn't know that, but she knew she wanted to be with her big brother, so she wriggled her little hand out of her mother's and tried to run after him. She did okay for a few steps, then went flying, tripping over her own feet, which hadn't yet mastered the speed of her older sibling. A great wail rose up. She'd fallen flat, banging her knees and bumping her chin.

Sally and Edward stopped and crouched to pick her up and see if she was hurt. People walked past staring, making Sally feel self-conscious. Edward brushed Sophie down, rubbed the dirt from her little pink hands, and kissed them better. It broke Sally's heart to see her little face all crumpled and sad after she'd been so excited about their trip out.

'If you're big and brave, I promise we can go to McDonald's after swimming,' Edward told her. It achieved the result of subsiding the sobbing.

She was fine. The tears had been more shock than anything else.

'You know she can't walk that fast, Alex,' Sally said. 'It's not fair to expect her to keep up. She's only three.'

There was no reply.

'Alex.'

She looked up scowling, expecting to see him standing there.

There was no sign of him.

'Edward, where's Alex? He'd better not have tried to cross the road on his own,' she said to her husband as she took Sophie's hand again and they set off.

Edward hurried around the corner, calling out, 'Alex! Alex!'

When Sophie and Sally joined him moments later, there was no sign of Alex. Just his swimming bag in the middle of the pavement. Edward reached down and picked it up. His face said everything Sally felt.

8

H arrison throttled down his bike to a slow rumble
and eased it along the street where the Phillips
family lived. The road looked completely different from
this morning. It reminded him of a python he'd seen once,
which had swallowed a small sheep. The contents of the
road had swollen with a large bulge of activity midway
along. Outside the Phillips's house, a pack of reporters,
photographers, and two camera crews had gathered,
blocking the road and pavements. Along the front garden
wall lay a multicoloured row of teddies, flowers, and cards.
A small audience of local well-wishers trickled along to pay
their respects—or be on the local TV news.

Harrison revved the bike, causing a female reporter
to jump and swear while recording a piece to camera.
He'd little time for reporters after the way they'd
described his mother after her death. It might have been
almost two decades ago, but he'd never forgotten or
forgiven. He knew he shouldn't assume every reporter
was the enemy, and the young woman he'd just startled
would have been a child when his mother was being

pilloried in the press; but it was just another part of that time he couldn't and wouldn't let go. At least not until he'd got justice.

Harrison edged his bike past her and the crew who mumbled some expletives at him, and parked it right outside in the hope it was in as an annoying position as possible for their camera shots. Then he walked up the path, discreetly showed his ID to the guard officer outside, and knocked.

The family liaison, an Asian woman PC with hair as black and shiny as a raven's feathers, opened the door. She recognised him. She'd been at the briefing earlier and he'd noticed her, thinking how she could moonlight for shampoo commercials. Behind him he heard a flurry of clicks as photographers fired off in case they missed something. It sounded like a swarm of locusts in flight, their wings clicking and clacking as they prepared to devour everything in their path.

The family liaison showed Harrison into an empty sitting room, the one he'd seen DCI Barker enter earlier that morning. She went off to tell Mrs Phillips about her guest and Harrison was left alone.

The house had taken on the hushed silence of a home in mourning. No loud noises, no music, no chatting. The energy had been drained from it, sucked into a sinkhole of grief that had opened up at the very heart of their home. All Harrison heard was the occasional loud whisper, sniff, or murmur. The air hung, dust particles suspended, as though afraid to breathe for fear of being sucked into the vortex of grief. The living had been put on hold for the dead.

Harrison was there for one reason: to find out as much as he could about the family and Darren, hoping to see some connection with his killer. If he worked out why he

might have been chosen as the victim, that could lead them
to his murderer.

Although the sitting room was tidy, a thin layer of dust
had settled over everything. It had been nearly a week since
Darren had been snatched.

The furniture was all modern, not rock-bottom prices
but certainly not luxurious. Louise was a single mum who
in more normal times was house proud but broke.
Harrison didn't need to meet her to know that. In the
hallway, he'd seen two different sizes of boys' shoes side by
side. He wondered how long it would be before she could
bear to start putting away Darren's things.

In the sitting room there were the usual photographic
memories of a family, Darren's baby smiles, him sitting
with his big brother, the family on a beach somewhere. On
the bookshelves were a collection of various bestsellers,
every day novels interspersed with children's books. The
obligatory Harry Potter and Philip Pullman sitting next to
Jodi Picout and Liane Moriarty and the black spine of
Twilight. There was no copy of the Bible or any sign of
religious icons. Nothing to suggest they were regular
churchgoers.

The sound of sniffing heralded the arrival of Louise
Phillips. She dragged herself into the living room; her face
swollen and blotchy from hours of crying.

'They've already interviewed me,' she told Harrison,
her voice fragile, as though there was nothing but broken
glass left inside her.

'I know, Mrs Phillips, and I apologise for disturbing you
again. I won't be long—just a couple of questions.' His
voice was calm, gentle, reassuring.

Louise half collapsed onto the sofa and gazed up at
him. Harrison sat next to her, bringing himself to her level.

'I'm so sorry for your loss,' he started.

She nodded and dabbed again at her eyes with the crumpled tissue in her hand. Louise was a thin, probably underweight, woman with shoulder-length brown hair. She didn't wear any make-up, but Harrison guessed that was more to do with the situation than habit. Louise had lost one of her children through kidnapping and murder. She was in shock. The likely anger and extreme emotions of losing a child in this way hadn't yet set in. Everyone reacted differently, but Harrison knew Louise could face years of depression and anxiety. Elisabeth Kübler-Ross's five stages of grief were a good framework for those who had lost someone under "normal circumstances," but murder was a whole extra level of emotion.

'I work in psychology, helping profile offenders for the police,' Harrison said.

'I'm trying to understand if there are any links between Darren and the man who did this. To do that, I need to understand Darren better. Is that okay?'

Louise nodded.

'First, I want to ask if you attend a church. Did Darren or his father?'

'No. We've never been religious. His dad certainly isn't.'

Harrison had already read up on the family. The parents were divorced, and Ralph Phillips had remarried and moved to Liverpool. He'd been contacted, but he'd not even seen Darren in eighteen months. Police up there were checking alibis and doing some digging, but it didn't look like he was in the frame at all.

'The vicar's been round, though,' Louise continued quietly. 'I don't know what to do for the funeral...' She trailed off.

'Do you have any family or friends who are or were regular churchgoers?'

'Not really. My mum goes at Christmas; that's about all. Suppose it will look hypocritical to bury him in the churchyard then, won't it?' She looked up at him again. A lost woman.

'You put him wherever you want. Don't give a second thought to anyone else. He's your son. And there's no rush. Do it in your own time. Don't feel pressured.' Harrison knew that Darren's body wouldn't be released for burial just yet, but he wasn't going to mention that to Louise now. Time would become an illusory concept anyway. One day would replace the next with no meaning while she came to terms with the horror of her loss.

Louise closed her eyes for a moment and gently nodded. 'I want him to be at peace. I want to believe I'll see him again in a heaven where he's safe. I want to, but I can't. Is that wrong?'

'There's no right or wrong,' Harrison said, 'and faith is an individual choice. What I do believe is universal love. Each one of us has to find our own way to grieve. You need to allow yourself time to work through your emotions. You'll know what's right when the time comes.'

'I hope so.'

Harrison paused for a few moments, allowing her to gather herself. He felt so sorry for Louise, having to not only deal with these emotions in private but also to have a street full of media and neighbours watching every move she made. He remembered his own grief reaction after his mother's death. Anger had been the dominant feeling, along with self-destruct mode, but he also hadn't wanted to be around anyone. He'd craved solitude, and having to answer police questions and deal with media intrusion was the last thing he'd been equipped to do. He needed to get his questions done and leave Louise in peace.

'Did Darren go to any clubs or societies?'

She shook her head. 'Nothing but us and school.'

'Friends? Did he play outside often?'

'Just around the road with a couple of mates from school. He never stayed out long.'

Harrison knew it was at the end of the road, while playing on their bikes, that the killer had snatched him. One minute he'd been there; the next he was gone; and all that was left was his bike, the back wheel still spinning on the ground. His friends had seen nothing, no one. Just that Darren had been laughing and joking with them one minute and not the next.

'What kind of personality was Darren?' Harrison deliberately left the question open, not wanting to lead her answers.

'Quite, shy, not very confident really.'

'What was his relationship with his father like?'

Despite the shock she was in, at the mention of her ex-husband, Louise tensed up. She sat up a little taller, balled her right fist around the tissue, and pursed her lips—all subtle signs that most people wouldn't even have noticed. Harrison did.

'He hasn't seen him for over a year, and he was only five when he left, so it's distant.'

'Did Darren ever talk about him or ever seem upset?'

'Not really. No.'

'Did Darren spend time at anyone else's house? A friend's or neighbour's?'

'No,' She looked almost annoyed at the question. 'He enjoyed being at home. He'd always come straight back from school. Darren's been too young for sleepovers. He must have been so scared being away from us all this time.' Louise started to cry again, and Harrison gave her time to gather herself.

'How about his brother? Were they close?' he asked.

Louise looked up at him, her eyes searching his face for
the motivation behind the question. 'Yeah, they were good.
Noel's devastated,' she replied. Harrison saw the tiger
mother preparing to defend her remaining son. He moved
quickly to explain.

'Would I be able to have a few minutes with him, with
you present of course? As his brother, he might have a
different perspective on anything that was bothering
Darren, something he'd been doing or someone he'd been
seeing... but perhaps was afraid to tell you about it.'

Louise looked away again with tears welling up.
Swallowing hard, she scrubbed at her right knee with the
palm of her hand. Harrison knew the thought her son
might have kept something from her was hard.

'I'm not sure. Like I said, he's very upset.'

'It would just be two minutes, and I promise to stop if
you think it's distressing him,' he replied softly.

She thought a moment longer, then nodded. 'I'll go get
him, he'd want to help,' she said, heaving herself from the
sofa.

Harrison heard her footsteps tread heavily up the stairs
before returning in stereo a couple of minutes later. A
young teenager followed her into the sitting room. There
was no mistaking he was the boy in the photographs with
Darren, but since that time he'd started to morph into the
young man he would be. His face had lost its puppy fat; the
eyebrows thickened; his hair was styled; and he was now
taller than his mother. But he hadn't just physically aged
from the printed version on the shelf; he looked as though
he'd had the energy of youth drained from him overnight,
leaving just a ghost of the boy. Harrison's heart went out
to him.

'This is Noel, Darren's brother,' Louise said.

Noel barely looked at Harrison. He guessed that at the

best of times—like most teenagers—his social skills were underdeveloped, and he lacked the confidence to engage in direct eye contact. Now it was a hundred times worse. Noel just couldn't stand allowing another human being to see the raw emotions his eyes betrayed.

'Hi, Noel,' Harrison said. 'I'm Dr Harrison Lane, how you holding up?'

Noel shrugged and still didn't look up.

'I won't keep you long because I know this is a tough time. I'm a psychologist working with the police to catch the man who took your brother, and you might be able to help. I wanted to ask if there was anything different you'd noticed about Darren's behaviour. Anything he'd said to you in the days or weeks before he went missing.'

Noel shook his head.

'It might be something really small, or it could be something he asked you not to tell your mum, but you know it's important now to share anything at all that might help us catch who did this to him, right?'

Noel lifted his head and looked at Harrison. 'Yeah, I know,' he said, his voice a broken whisper, the combination of emotion, lack of use, and hormones.

The house phone rang, making Louise jump at the noise and halting their conversation. She let it go to the answering machine, and all of them stopped and listened to Louise's cheerful recorded voice telling whoever that she couldn't come to the phone right now. It was a woman from another time, a woman who bore no resemblance to the one she was today. There was a beep and then a pause before they all heard, 'Louise, it's Mum. We're packed and just getting ready to leave.' Louise jumped up and grabbed the phone off the charger.

'Mum, I'm here,' she said, and walked to the other end of the sitting room to carry on the conversation.

Harrison took his chance to ask some more questions
—questions Noel might answer differently without his
mother listening.

'Did the two of you hang out much?'

Noel shrugged, 'Yeah, you know, at home and stuff.
He's quite a bit younger than me, so we didn't really do
much outside, like.'

'What kind of things did Darren like to do?'

'Ride his bike, play *Minecraft*, usual stuff,' Noel replied.

Harrison was aware of Louise watching them from a
few feet away, but she was still talking on the phone.

'Was there anything bothering him? Did he mention
someone in particular?'

Noel shook his head repeatedly. 'No. No, there was
nothing.'

'How would you describe your brother's personality?'
He'd already asked their mother that question, but he
needed to know if Noel agreed.

Noel shrugged. 'He was quiet.' Then he realised he'd
talked about his brother in the present tense, and his eyes
dropped to the floor.

'Quiet? More quiet than other boys his age?'

'Yeah, shy, you know.'

Harrison heard Louise winding up her phone call.

'Noel, is there anything Darren, or you, didn't want
your mum to find out?'

Noel shook his head, but his eyes stayed firmly fixed on
his feet.

'You won't get into trouble. Whatever it is, wouldn't be
your fault. If you tell me, it'll help your brother.' Harrison
almost whispered this, giving Noel the chance to say
something his mother wouldn't pick up on. He studied
Noel's face, looking for any telltale twitches or tension. He
saw only sadness.

'No, seriously, nothing,' was all Noel said, and he finally looked up.

'Okay. No problem, thank you. I'm going to leave my card, so if you think of anything, or hear anything, please call me.'

'Sure.'

'And Noel, don't think you're being strong by holding this in. The toughest thing is to let it out. That's what real men do,' Harrison said. 'You and your mum need each other, and that means taking care of yourselves.'

Noel nodded and looked at his mother as she returned to their conversation before leaving the room.

'Thanks,' Louise said to Harrison; she'd caught what he'd been saying.

'The victim support team will offer some specialist counselling for Noel. Make sure he goes. Even if it's just for a couple of sessions, they'll be able to keep an eye on him and check he's handling everything okay.'

Louise nodded. Harrison watched Noel slump up the stairs. He didn't think he was hiding anything. He knew the research would say teens were the best and most prolific of liars, and it was often hard to tell, but under this huge emotional stress and with such big stakes, he believed him. He'd have expected to see some cracks in the deceit, if there were any. Instead, what Harrison saw was a young lad rocked to the core by his brother's murder. He also saw that he was trying to be strong, almost certainly felt like he should be the big man of the family and look after his mother. Noel might even feel guilty that he hadn't been able to help Darren. While the police tried to catch Darren's killer, it was important that the living were taken care of too. Harrison made a mental note to double check the victim support team had him on their radar.

Louise looked exhausted, and Harrison didn't think

he'd learn much more from her. What he needed to do next was get to know Darren a little better through his own things.

'Would you mind if I looked in Darren's room?' he asked.

'The police have already searched in there, but if it helps catch...' She ground to a halt, unable to say the words.

'Thank you. I won't be long,' Harrison replied, saving her the agony of continuing.

He left her collapsed in a heap on the sofa. She didn't even look up as he left the room.

It wasn't difficult to find Darren's bedroom. A sign on the first door on the right said, DARREN'S ROOM—KEEP OUT, with a collection of LEGO movie character stickers dancing around it. Before he went in, Harrison took a few moments. He needed to clear the emotion from his head, to focus. Louise Phillips's grief was overwhelming, and he wasn't going to help her unless he did his job properly. He closed his eyes and concentrated on his breathing, the rhythm, the feel of the air going in and out of his lungs. Slowly, he regained his focus. Tuned in all his senses. Only then did he allow himself to open the door and go inside.

It was everything he'd expected from a young boy's bedroom, a *Toy Story* duvet cover and *Superman* curtains. There were posters from comics on the wall and a small desk in the corner with an opened school exercise book on it. Harrison looked at the imagery. It was all harmless stuff, no theme, no threat or anxiety thread. He flicked through the exercise book on the desk. Nothing but spelling practice and sentence constructions. No doodles that could give away an internal fear. No cries for help.

Harrison knew the importance of seeing and not just

looking. He also knew young boys hid things from their parents. If anyone inappropriate had been trying to befriend him, they would have told Darren to keep it a secret.

After looking through the rest of the ephemera and clutter of the room, Harrison started to hunt.

Under the bed was the first obvious place, but there were many others: under the mattress and the bottom side of the desk, inside his pillowcase and tucked behind the bed headboard. He checked every drawer and cupboard, inside books and boxes, even in the lining of the curtains and under the carpet. He checked each toy for secret compartments and pockets and even looked behind the posters. The only thing he found was a tracing of Superman, half coloured in, folded, and tucked inside his dressing gown pocket. The irony wasn't lost on Harrison.

In some ways it was a disappointment—no easy answers. In others, it was reassuring. Darren had just been leading the life he was meant to lead. Perhaps it really had been just "wrong place and time". The problem was, it threw no light on who might have taken him or why.

He needed to get back to the station and see if anything new had come in from the teams that were out collecting statements and evidence. As Harrison reached the bottom of the stairs, he glanced into the kitchen. The family liaison was just handing a cup of tea to the uniformed officer who'd been standing outside. The kitchen worktops were piled with bouquets of flowers, and he saw that several vases had already been filled. Louise Phillips would hate the smell of cut flowers for the rest of her life.

She was still in the sitting room and got up when she saw him.

'Thank you, and once again I'm sorry for your loss,' Harrison said.

She gave a weak smile and went to open the door for him to leave. As he was about to pass through it, she grabbed his hand.

'Catch him, won't you?' she said, the raw emotion in her words.

There was a whirring clicking, and the flash of a camera hit her face at its most vulnerable. She recoiled as though slapped. A photographer had broken ranks and was on the doorstep, taking advantage of the absent police officer. Harrison pounced. His calm face erupted in anger as he got between Louise and the photographer, squaring up to him like an angry bear. The skinny, stubble-faced young man in front of him clearly hadn't been expecting a six-foot-two rock of muscle—or the expression on Harrison's face. He stepped back in shock, twisted his foot, fell, and dropped his camera onto the pavement. There was a satisfying cracking sound as the giant lens hit the concrete and snapped off.

Harrison closed the front door behind him, protecting Louise from any further intrusion and upset. He stood over the photographer, who was scrambling to get up and out of his way.

'You're trespassing,' he told him, before kicking the broken lens towards the squirming white-faced rat on the ground.

Behind Harrison, the uniformed officer had flung open the front door to find out what was happening. He stood on the front doorstep, unsure what to do and whom he should be protecting.

'Do you have a mother?' Harrison asked the photographer who by now had risen to his feet and was backing away towards the rest of his pack. He nodded.

'Then imagine how she might be feeling if something happened to you.' With one final stare, he walked past him. The pack of reporters and photographers parted like the Red Sea as he headed through their midst to his bike and rode away.

The incident room seemed to have switched into fast-forward despite it being the time when most 'normal' offices emptied out for the day. The place was packed with officers on the phone, meeting in huddles, tapping away at computer screens, or watching CCTV replays. In the middle of it all, DCI Barker and DS Salter stood looking at the incident board.

Harrison walked in and headed towards them. It didn't take him long before he realised what the commotion was about. There was another young boy's face on the board next to Darren's.

'Another boy's been snatched,' DCI Barker said the second he reached them. He saw the flicker of fear in her eyes, almost tasted her desperation. She was a mother too, and it was her responsibility to save another family's child. They'd already failed one mother; they couldn't fail another.

'When?' he asked.

'Just over four hours ago, a mile from where Darren went missing. The officers who attended contacted us as soon as the similarities became apparent.' DS Salter filled in the information. He didn't like the feeling, but he couldn't help the sense of satisfaction that he was at last telling Harrison something he didn't know.

Someone had already plotted the map on the board, and the new name alongside Darren's read, 'Alex Fuller.'

'Are the boys connected?' Harrison asked.

'Not that we can tell at this stage. We're not even sure it's the same offender, but the MO looks the same,' Barker replied, 'One minute he was there in the street, and the next he was gone. Parents searched everywhere. They were on their way to the swimming pool and there was no reason for him to run away. His swimming bag was found abandoned on the pavement. We're going through every CCTV camera we can find in the area. One of them must have caught something.'

Harrison nodded.

'They look similar. Both around the same age, slightly built and brown hair,' he added.

'Exactly,' DCI Barker replied.

'Any breakthroughs with Darren?' Harrison asked.

'We've had a witness come forward, said he saw two men in a Land Rover going into Felton Woods last night about ten thirty,' said DS Salter.

Harrison looked at Salter then at Barker. 'It wasn't two men—it was one—and he drove a van. He didn't take Darren there until the early hours.'

'You can't know that for sure,' Jack replied forcefully.

'I can and I do,' Harrison said. He'd only just calmed himself down after the photographer episode and wouldn't allow DS Salter to question what he knew to be a fact.

'We have to follow up on every potential lead,' Jack said.

'You'll be wasting time.'

Tired of their sparring, DCI Barker decided to interrupt. 'Both of you stay focused. We've a little boy out there. We need to work together and find him before his body ends up on our post-mortem table with Darren's.'

'Talk to him. I'm going to find those two men,' DS Salter replied, nodding at Harrison and not attempting to keep the venom from his voice.

Harrison gritted his teeth as Jack walked off. DCI Barker waited until he was out of earshot.

'You went to the Phillips's house alone, and without telling the rest of the team you were going, or getting official clearance. You find anything, or do something, and you don't have a police officer with you, it could jeopardise a conviction. You make sure Jack knows where you are at all times if it has anything to do with this case.'

'I just…' Harrison tried to come back.

'Okay?' is all DCI Barker said. Her raised eyebrow was enough.

Harrison nodded. Quite apart from the fact she didn't look like a woman who would be challenged, he knew she was right.

'Did you get anything?' she asked.

He shook his head.

'What do we know about Alex Fuller?' he came back, changing the subject.

'Nothing much yet, but obviously early days. What we know so far is he and Darren went to different schools and the families are unrelated.'

'The only connection is the killer himself,' said Harrison.

DCI Barker turned away from the board to look at him. 'What do you mean? Apart from the obvious.'

'I think he's taking boys who resemble him when he was their age.'

'Okay, go on.'

'He definitely lives locally, and he'll have been cruising around, looking for the right boy.'

'Why now?'

'A life-changing event such as divorce or bereavement. It could be one of the parents, or maybe both have died. He's trying to relive or put right something from his childhood.'

'So we could look at recent deaths in the area?'

Harrison nodded.

'If you're sure, I'll put Mark, our analyst, onto it. He likes nothing better than hunting for clues in data. In the meantime, I want you and Jack to speak to the parents. Do you think you can manage that without killing each other?'

'Of course.'

'Good. And Harrison? I heard about the photographer.'

'I didn't touch him and he was out of order.'

'I know you didn't touch him, but you certainly looked threatening. Right now the media don't tie you in with us, but that'll change the more high-profile cases you work on. I don't get it. I've seen you keep as cool as ice when you've been goaded by some of the nastiest scumbags out there, yet now and then, you flip. You let emotion get the better of you.'

'I was in control. I didn't touch him,' Harrison looked at her, 'but I get how it could have looked.'

'Especially in front of a bunch of headline-hungry journalists and cameras! Look, if I got aggressive with every piece of shit I came across in this job, I'd have been locked up years ago. Come on, Harrison, you know the score. I want you to keep a low profile. I don't want your maverick status impacting my investigations, and I certainly don't want to lose your expertise, but if you overstep, it'll be taken out of my hands. You understand?'

Harrison nodded.

'He's apologised to the family. Apparently, a rookie freelancer trying to make his mark. The papers won't publish the shots of Louise, and if it's any consolation, it cost him an arm and a leg with that lens breaking.'

Harrison felt a small internal victory whoop at that news but didn't show it.

Feeling like a chaste schoolboy, he started to head out of the incident room. He was only halfway out when the TV news came on and footage from outside the Phillips's house appeared on-screen. The reporter was the woman Harrison had interrupted earlier.

'Emotions ran high today as friends came to pay their respects to Darren Phillips's family...' The footage showed Harrison just after he had stepped out of the house and as the photographer fell to the ground. Murmurs of support rippled around the MIT officers watching the TV, as they saw Harrison squaring up and the photographer scrambling backwards.

DS Salter, working at his desk, looked up disdainfully and shook his head.

'That sorted the parasitic dick wipe,' Harrison heard one detective mutter as he left the room. He'd just gone up in the team's estimation.

DCI Barker was listening and watching. 'Bloody good job he doesn't wear a uniform and the press are too thick to ID him, so don't go getting any ideas,' she shot back at them. The last thing she needed was a problem with discipline. Harrison was a valuable asset, but he was also a civilian advisor, and if the brass decided he was a liability, they'd cut him loose. She didn't need that either.

A cross London in a dingy flat that had seen better days, an old flat-screen TV was broadcasting the news report from outside Darren Phillip's house. Someone had frozen the picture. It was rewound before being stopped on an image of Dr Harrison Lane as he walked towards the camera, jaw set.

In the gloom, a woman in her mid-seventies, with skin that had lived a life of too much sun and drugs, sat on a dirty old sofa staring at the screen. Her eyes weren't kind. There was a steely hardness to her thin bony face, framed by long white hair.

'Well, well, after all these years,' she said to the TV, 'the prodigal son has returned.'

D S Salter walked along the basement corridor of the New Scotland Yard Metropolitan Police headquarters. He always got a heavy feeling when he ventured this far into the bowels of HQ. Down here was the evidence from decades of unsolved cases, stored in boxes and files in the hope that one day the victims would get restitution. The weight of responsibility in each of those files far outweighed their physical state. Salter used to think working on cold cases would be boring. None of the live pressure you get from fresh crimes like their current one. But he'd changed his mind over the years. He knew a detective must have got a great deal of satisfaction when they solved one and could move it into the *completed* storage areas. Trouble was, there were always fresh boxes and files to take their place, no matter how hard they all tried.

Updates in science and technology certainly helped, and he loved the idea of someone who'd been living their life happily thinking they'd got away with a crime opening their front door to find the police on their doorstep. The thought that someone could masquerade as a pillar of society while hiding a dirty secret of rape or murder wound him up. Every single success was a victory—and one more victim avenged.

Of course, there were some cases where new DNA techniques couldn't help because they were too far down the annals of history and evidence contaminated beyond use, or lost, and all witnesses long since died. One of the most famous cases of them all was Jack the Ripper. Down here in the basement was a letter he had allegedly written. It wasn't in the 'unsolved' case room, but part of the Black Museum, the Met's collection of criminal memorabilia, gathered from prisoners and investigations since the 1800s, and used as a teaching collection for police recruits. It was a private museum, only open to police officers, and if Jack was honest, it gave him the creeps.

He'd found himself down there alone one evening as a young officer. There'd been a talk in the museum for new recruits and afterwards, he'd been too engrossed in looking at the exhibits to realise that everyone else had left for the pub. For a moment he'd thought they'd locked him in. Suddenly all the death masks and morbid exhibits like Dennis Nilsen's stove where he had cooked his victims, or the hangman's nooses and plethora of evil weaponry, had started to suffocate him. He'd nearly hugged the curator when he'd walked back into the room after being in the toilet.

That night, Jack went straight home in a sweat and questioned if he'd done the right thing by becoming a police officer. He and Marie were already living together then, and on seeing his face when he returned, she thought he'd been attacked or seen a murder. It was her who'd brought him back to himself and reminded him how much joining the force meant to him. By the morning, he was fine again, but he avoided the Crime Museum after that and told no one why.

Jack had to walk past the door to the Black Museum to reach the office of Dr Harrison Lane, another place that gave him the creeps. He'd only been there once before, briefly, but it had stuck in his mind.

He was searching for him so they could go together to see the Fullers. Initial statements had been done, but they needed to conduct a more in-depth interview. It annoyed him that he needed to hunt him down. Every minute was precious in this investigation and he was wasting his time. What did Harrison even need to be there for, anyway?

When he reached Harrison's office, he wasn't at his desk. Jack stepped into the room, trying not to take any notice of the decor, but it made the hairs on his neck bristle with anxiety. He liked to think he was pretty grounded, but down here, surrounded by all this stuff, it got to him.

The only saving grace was that he wasn't alone. On the opposite side of the room from Harrison's desk was his technical assistant, Ryan Chapman. His desk was evidence that they were very much in the modern world. It was buried under three computer screens and a mound of empty crisp packets, cans, bottles of fizzy drinks, chocolate wrappers, and sweets.

When Jack arrived, he could only just see Ryan behind his wall of screens and junk food. An overweight twenty-something with thick glasses and the palest skin he'd ever seen, Ryan was the classic computer nerd. As with his boss, social skills weren't his forte, and trying to engage him in conversation was like attempting to get a group of cats to do the can-can.

Jack went and sat on top of Harrison's spotless desk. 'Where is he? I need him to come out with me urgently.'

'Dunno.'

'No idea at all?'

Ryan shrugged. 'He got a call from someone in Child Protection and had to go see them. Said he wouldn't be long.'

Jack figured Ryan wouldn't tell him even if he knew. He was as loyal as an old hound to Harrison. He stood back up and looked at Harrison's desk. On top was a mug, half filled. It didn't contain tea or coffee. Jack picked it up and sniffed it.

'Christ, what is this stuff? It's weird. Have you smelt it? Oi, Ryan, does he mix his own potions and drink them?'

The only reply he got was a daggered look from around the computer screens.

'Come on. You must lift your nose out of those computers at some point to see what he's up to. This isn't normal.' Jack sniffed at the mug again just as Harrison walked in.

'Ah, the man himself. So, Dr Lane, what is this stuff? Is it legal?'

Harrison said nothing. He walked past Jack to where the kettle sat and picked up a box. He chucked it onto his desk right next to Jack. It was a packet of Waitrose camomile, limeflower, and lavender tea bags.

'Help yourself.'

Jack looked slightly embarrassed but brushed it off by going on the attack. 'I've been waiting for you. You weren't answering your phone. We have to interview the family of Alex Fuller as soon as possible. See if we can avoid another dead boy.'

He didn't wait for Harrison to reply or explain. He stomped out the office and back up to street level and the fading daylight.

12

H arrison looked at the dirty breakfast bowls stacked at the side of the sink and thought about how different the Fullers' day had started. Sally and Edward Fuller sat at the kitchen table. She wore a glazed, shocked look, her eyes clouded. Harrison doubted she'd retain much information they told her, and she probably couldn't offer too much either. Edward was pumped with adrenaline, like an angry wasp trapped inside a jam jar. Guilt was almost certainly one of the driving forces—that and the desperate need to do something despite feeling completely impotent. He was doing his best to comfort his wife, but Harrison could see they were travelling at two different speeds in their emotional journeys.

DS Salter led the interview. 'Anything you can tell us at this stage will help us find Alex. We're exploring several lines of enquiry,' he said.

Sally looked up at him as though suddenly remembering something. 'What about that other little boy, Darren. He was kidnapped. Could it be...' Her throat strangled the rest of her question.

'One of our lines of enquiry is to consider if there's a connection between Alex's kidnapping and the recent abduction of Darren Phillips.'

Sally's hand shot to her mouth as though pulled there by the gasp that escaped her lips. 'My God, that poor boy's just been found dead, hasn't he? Oh, my baby, my little baby boy.'

Edward took her hand away from her face and rubbed it, but he said nothing. The battle to keep the tears and emotional tidal wave back took up all his capabilities. Harrison noted he had calloused hands which, combined with his physique, suggested he did a manual job—but not the building trade. His skin was white; he clearly rarely spent time outside. Harrison was grateful their alibis and the CCTV from the time Alex disappeared meant neither parent was a suspect. They didn't need to establish whether either of them was lying.

'Mrs Fuller, it's only one possibility,' Jack said. 'We don't know if the two cases are connected. I know this is an upsetting time, but we have to explore if there are any possible links between your son and Darren.' His voice was quieter and calmer than his usual tone. Harrison saw a different side of him when he was working like this. He'd always trusted DCI Barker's instincts, and now he could see for himself that underneath all the rugby bar buffoonery, Jack was probably a decent detective. He also was a man under stress, and that wasn't just the job. His eyes were bloodshot, with dark circles beneath them. Add to that the fact it had been a very long day for all of them, and it was surprising either of them were functioning at their best.

Both parents shook their heads in response to DS Salter's question.

'No, Alex didn't know him,' Edward said. 'Definitely

not. We were all watching the news the other day when the story came on.'

'There's no possibility they were at any clubs together? Scouts or a sports club? Anything like that?'

DS Salter knew to keep pushing the point. Witnesses were unreliable at the best of times, but especially when in shock.

They both shook their heads again.

'Do you have connections with any churches?' Harrison asked.

'No, we're not churchgoers. Alex doesn't do anything like that. He'd have said if he knew the other boy.'

'Does he have access to a computer?' Jack questioned.

'He's allowed to use mine,' Edward said, his voice thick with emotion. 'It's supervised and for schoolwork. He doesn't have an email account or a mobile phone.'

The questions continued, one after another. Each one a dead end for the investigation. They were getting nowhere. It was just like it had been with Darren. Their boy had been there one moment and gone the next. No apparent reason or motive. No answers.

When they'd first arrived, Harrison had looked around the house and kitchen. They were a family of four. Most of the photos showed a pretty little girl beaming at the camera next to Alex. The Fullers looked tired and frustrated, so he changed the subject to ease the pressure.

'How old's your daughter?' Harrison asked.

'Three,' Sally answered, looking up at him.

'Pretty little thing.' Harrison smiled back. 'Is she upstairs asleep?'

'No, my mum came and fetched her,' Sally replied. 'She was getting too upset because she saw we were. She doesn't understand where her brother is. I'm hoping if she stays with my mum for a couple of nights, by the time she's home he'll be back too.'

Her words, so ripe and full of desperate hope, hung between them. Pears on an autumn tree, ready to drop to the hard ground beneath.

Sally looked up at them both. 'Darren was missing for about a week, wasn't he, before being... found? What happened to him during that time? Where was he?'

'We're still investigating,' DS Salter replied, shifting slightly in his chair.

Sally looked even more upset at his answer.

'Darren appeared to have been looked after. There was no sexual assault,' Harrison's voice broke through the emotional tension. Jack looked at him angrily, but it was clear what he'd said brought some relief to Sally and Edward.

'Thank you,' Sally replied in a whisper.

With little more to be gleaned from the Fullers, Harrison and Jack looked in Alex's bedroom, then called it a night. They'd found nothing that could give them any clues as to who had taken the boys and why.

They'd just said their goodbyes to his parents, Harrison was the last to leave the kitchen, when Sally tugged his arm. She pulled a photograph off the fridge door. It was the four of them, all laughing at the camera with Alex centre stage.

'Please. When it seems impossible, look at this picture and remember Alex should be here with us. That he's loved. That he'll be terrified. Please, please bring him home safely to us.' She shoved the photograph into Harrison's hand and turned back to her tears.

As Jack and Harrison walked down the path from the house, Salter rounded on him.

'You shouldn't tell people information about an ongoing case,' Jack said.

'It was nothing that could jeopardise a conviction. They're parents whose son has been taken. It gave them some relief. You're a father, aren't you?'

For once, DS Salter didn't reply.

Harrison and Jack drove home, both of them with dry, tired eyes. They were spent. Behind them they'd left a couple who wouldn't sleep that night except for the odd fitful hour, jerking from broken dreams that ranged from happy reunions to shallow graves. Just a mile away, in another home, another mother was grieving with the knowledge her son would never be returning home to her.

13

J ack pulled up outside a semi-detached house in a neat, modern close of family homes on the outskirts of London. It was a TV-soap representation of suburbia. Fake hanging baskets gave some colour to the white walls, and in front was a neatly manicured garden, designed for easy maintenance. The windows gleamed with cleanliness, and the front door looked newly painted. A perfect exterior. The neighbouring houses looked similar. Nice cars parked on the garage ramps. This was a place where professional people lived. People with good jobs and enough money to afford a reasonable mortgage and nice standard of living. The kind of neighbourhood that Deliveroo and supermarket drivers visited regularly with takeaways and food deliveries for busy occupants. Neighbourhood Watch stickers could be seen on various windows, and apart from the blanket of general traffic hum, which shrouded the entire area, it was quiet. But Jack didn't see any of that; his mind was elsewhere.

He got out of his car, walked up to the door, and hesitated. Listening. There was the sound of a television inside. As he looked at the key in his hand, his eyes glazed over as though he didn't recognise what it was for. He realised he'd forgotten to stop off for flowers like Sandra had suggested. Too late now. A moment later he snapped out of it, plunged the key into the lock, and opened his front door.

As soon as he did, a crescendo of noise hit him. The TV was on full volume and somewhere was the sound of a baby crying. The kind of distressed cry where the pitch had reached its peak, and the sound was strangled frustration. He threw the keys onto the hallway table, shoved the front door shut, and rushed into the sitting room. On the sofa was his wife, Marie, curled up fetal-like, her arms hugged around herself. She was staring at the television in a trance. Next to her was a monitor through which they could hear the sounds of a hysterical, crying baby.

'Marie? Marie?' Jack shouted, but he got no response. He left and ran up the stairs at break-neck speed towards the room where he knew he would find Daniel.

He pushed open the door. There in the cot, purple faced, and croaky from exertion, was their son. Jack rushed across to him and picked him up tenderly. The baby felt hot and damp in his hands, his body rigid. It took a few minutes for the sobbing to subside, but finally, at the sight of his father and the feel of his arms around him, the baby gradually stopped and reduced his noise to gulping sniffles and whimpers.

'I'm here. Daddy's here, little man,' Jack told him. He held his son against his chest, rocking back and forth, kissing his head gently, taking in the scent of him. It brought tears to his eyes. The fear and guilt he'd carried around with him all day. He hadn't been here when his son had needed him. And Marie?

'Let's go get you something to eat, shall we?' he whispered to Daniel.

The baby looked up at him with his puffy, tear-filled eyes as they headed downstairs, where the TV was still at full volume.

'Marie, Marie...' Jack called to her as he walked in and switched off the TV. She wasn't watching it. She sat, tears pouring down her face, unable to look up at him.

He stood in front of her, holding their son. Behind her, on the wall, was a photograph from their wedding. Six years ago he'd married his beautiful, vibrant fiancée. The camera captured the sheer joy of the day on their faces. They were mid-jump, like two kids. He remembered the moment as if it was yesterday. The photographer had stolen them away from the reception to take shots in the gardens, and they'd had fun. The stress of wedding planning had eased now that the ceremony was over, and they were Mr and Mrs Salter. Marie was stunning. Her eyes alight with love and happiness, cheeks flushed, skin perfect. Her long black hair expertly pinned up to showcase the face Jack loved so much. They were best friends.

Then, a year ago, they'd decided to add to their happiness and have a child—only it didn't work out like they'd planned. The pregnancy hadn't been plain sailing, and the birth was traumatic. Marie endured nearly forty-eight hours of labour before the doctors announced they'd have to intervene and drag their son from her. She lost a significant amount of blood when she'd haemorrhaged. Jack found the whole thing traumatising, and he'd just been a witness.

Marie spent three days in hospital before being sent home to carry on her recovery. They'd encouraged her to breastfeed, but she'd been too exhausted, so Daniel had gone onto a bottle straight away. It meant Jack was able to help with the feeds, but the whole situation seemed to decrease the opportunity for Marie to bond with her son. Even when she was stronger and able to nurse him, she'd done so as little as possible. Then the depression set in. She refused help. Wouldn't let Jack call on their mothers or friends. Refused to go to the doctor. He had no idea what to do.

Slowly Marie looked up at Jack and Daniel. The dark circles under her eyes accentuated her pale skin, and her hair hung limply onto her shoulders. There was no vibrancy, no joy on her face.

'Please, Marie, help me,' Jack said to her.

She stared back at him as tears poured down her cheeks.

'Marie, I don't know what to do. I don't know how to help you. Please talk to me.'

An hour later, Jack had fed and changed Daniel, who was asleep, exhausted in his arms. He carried him back upstairs and gently placed him in the cot. He'd dreamt of these moments, imagined the bond of love that he felt now when he looked at his sleeping son. He'd never dreamt it could turn out like this. Their reality was nothing like the movies or TV ads. Jack had no idea how to make it right.

He closed the baby's door and crept across the hallway. In their bedroom he could just make out the head of his sleeping wife on the pillow, the bottle of sleeping pills silhouetted by her bedside. He made a mental note to put those away later when he went to bed—somewhere she wouldn't think to look.

It was already past nine pm, but Jack hadn't had the chance to change yet, and he was hungry. He went downstairs to the kitchen and looked in the fridge. It was virtually empty, just a few eggs, some cheese, and milk, and a half-empty bottle of wine. He grabbed the wine and some eggs, poured himself a glass and downed it in one before finding the frying pan, a bowl, and putting together an omelette. He hadn't managed to pour the mix from the bowl into the hot frying pan before the baby monitor lurched into life behind him. Jack closed his eyes for a moment and took a deep breath. Then he turned off the hob and took the empty pan from the hot ring before he headed back upstairs to Daniel.

14

The incident room was empty, apart from one detective who was putting his jacket on to leave. The main lights had already been turned off. A couple of the computer screens were left on, soft white rectangles glowing in the gloom. A beam of light shone from the open door of DCI Barker's office. The detective walked towards it. Inside she was still working, frowning at the screen in front of her, writing notes on the pad of paper on her desk.

'Good night, ma'am,' he called to her.

'Good night.'

'Not got a home to go to, ma'am?' he asked jovially.

'Good night,' is all he got back with a firm voice. He got the message and left.

DCI Barker was filling in the day's decision log. It gave her the chance to go over what they'd done that day and reflect on why she'd made the choices in the enquiry that she had. It was one of those paperwork tasks that could so easily just be a chore, an audit trail that had to be completed just in case their enquiry came under review.

But for her, it was more than that. After a busy day on this investigation, followed by catching up with what was happening in their other cases, it gave her mind a chance to focus and look at the bigger picture in peace. More often than not, it prompted notes on her to-do list for the next day as she saw potential gaps or directions the enquiry hadn't travelled. Tonight her to-do list looked decidedly sparse. They needed a break. She couldn't believe that nothing had been picked up on CCTV. The killer was out there somewhere, and she intended to find him.

ACROSS TOWN, Harrison's flat covered the top floor of a converted warehouse in the Docklands. Sparsely furnished, with a big empty open space, wooden floors and large windows, it looked out over the Thames. It was one of the earlier conversions from when the docks had shut, and the area become derelict. A blend of ultramodern and traditional, which gave it a stylish vintage look. The flats were a lot bigger and cheaper back then, before the new Canary Wharf had been built and the financial crowd and trendy digital businesses moved in.

There was just one side lamp on in the living space. The glow of the properties across the water, a twinkling light show on the surface of the river, provided a backdrop across one window-filled wall. In the open-plan kitchen, the timer on the built-in fan oven showed five minutes left. The cardboard sleeve of a Marks and Spencer meal-for-one lasagne on the side, accompanied by the soft hum of the oven, told of a dinner almost ready to be served.

The walls, painted brick, carried artworks and ephemera. Only these weren't so random as those in Harrison's office. No eclectic mix of cult and religious icons. These had been carefully chosen. Images of an ancient people hunting buffaloes; black-and-white photographs of wrinkled, wise Native American faces; a headdress, colourful and bursting with spirit, amid the blank white space.

In front of the kitchen was a dark-grey leather sofa and matching chairs with a glass coffee table. Harrison wasn't sitting on the furniture; instead, he was cross-legged on the floor. On the table some herbs smouldered in a metal dish next to a photograph of a young woman. She looked to be in her early thirties, dancing and laughing at the camera. Long blond hair and a flowery dress. Hippie style.

His eyes were closed. Hands rested on his thighs, palms upward. Not a muscle twitched. His breathing was so shallow and slow you could barely see his chest rise and fall.

Harrison's mind was focussed. As toned as his muscles. Winding down from one day and preparing for another busy one tomorrow.

15

I n DCI Barker's office, three half-drunk takeaway cups of coffee sat on the big meeting table, along with a bottle of spring water. Barker, Salter, and Dr Lane sat reading a report, the highlights of which were being read out by Dr Tanya Jones. Clearly none of them had caught enough sleep, but Jack's eyes looked the worst. They were bloodshot, his face creased like a tired puppy.

'The cause was asphyxia, most likely environmental suffocation. No marks on his neck. He just ran out of air,' Dr Jones began. 'They found nothing in Darren's airways or lungs, and there were no other injuries to suggest he was forcibly held down, as you'd expect on a victim's wrists or neck. It wasn't a violent death. No signs of a struggle or defensive injuries of any form.'

'That's one small mercy,' DCI Barker muttered.

'He'd been dead between six and eight hours before we found him,' Dr Jones carried on. 'Which would put the time of death at just before or after midnight.'

'So, he could simply have run out of air wherever he was being held?' DCI Barker confirmed.

'It's looking like that. Certainly, it's what Dr Aspey has concluded.'

'He must have been kept in some kind of enclosed space. Anything to suggest where or what he was held in?'

'Nothing unusual on his clothes, apart from what appears to be traces of teak oil. He'd eaten, but not much, and it was standard stuff, cereals and bread. All items that are easily obtainable. He was a bit dehydrated.'

'So he did attempt to look after him, sort of.' DCI Barker voiced her thoughts out loud. 'And no evidence that he'd been gagged?'

Tanya shook her head.

'Teak oil could suggest a garden shed,' Jack said. 'But with no gag he'd have to be somewhere where he knew Darren couldn't be heard if he shouted for help.'

Sandra Barker nodded. 'Perhaps he shoved him in a trunk or box of some sort when he went out. Throws up the possibility he might not have meant to kill him then.'

'It's a possibility,' Tanya agreed.

'So where did he go, or what was he doing while Darren was dying?' Jack asked.

'Indeed, and it's worrying in itself, isn't it? For Alex Fuller, I mean, because it could suggest the killer hadn't completed whatever it was he'd taken Darren for. What about any other evidence, fingerprints from his captor?' Barker questioned.

'Only partials and we've no matches,' Tanya said. 'We're obviously waiting on the DNA. I'm on their backs to turn it around fast. I've also got someone working full time on the *Bible* scriptures. All definitely put in after death. The writing is Darren's. His mum sent in some samples and that fits with the condition of his right hand.'

Jack gave a quick glance to Harrison, who was never one to gloat. While he felt Jack's eyes on him, he didn't look up. In all honesty, he'd been avoiding Tanya more than anything. Her perfume was in his nostrils, and he'd found himself wanting to look at her, but it wasn't the content of what she was saying that grabbed him. Her lips carried a subtle rose-pink shimmer that made their soft fullness catch his eye, but it was her eyes he wanted to avoid. Their blue depths pulled him to her, plunge pools that made him want to dive straight in. It broke his concentration, and right now he needed to focus.

'I've got a team on CCTV,' said DCI Barker with a hint of desperation. 'Both boys seemed to disappear into thin air. The killer has got to have made a mistake somewhere. Any thoughts, Harrison?'

He shook his head, more disappointed in himself than anything else. 'I've been to both the boys' houses, spoken to the families, and looked in their rooms. There doesn't appear to be any connection, no signs of prior grooming. These aren't straightforward cases. They're not sexually motivated or money motivated. I don't believe he's a psychopath. I think he's a young man with a repressed character and personality disorder. His problems stem from childhood. He'll be fairly quiet, keep to himself. Probably never had a proper relationship. He comes from a very religious home and lives fairly locally to the boys. I'd say he knows the CCTV black spots, and Fenton Woods was definitely the outer extremity of an area he's comfortable with. As I said last night, these boys are likely to represent his own childhood. They look similar and most probably look as he did at their age. Something traumatic happened to him back then, and now it's been reawakened by another trigger event.'

'So we have a thirty-mile radius to search.' Barker sighed. 'Better get back to it then.'

. . .

HARRISON RETURNED to his basement office, where Ryan was already munching his way through a family-size pack of bacon crisps.

'Yo, boss. Wondered when you were going to show,' Ryan greeted him.

'Ryan.' Harrison nodded and walked over to his desk.

'I've got something new come in for you. Reports of some satanic graffiti at a cemetery, less than a mile from where Darren lived.'

'Probably just kids. When?'

'Last night,' Ryan replied. 'Nunhead.'

'Nunhead?' Harrison's interest suddenly piqued. Ryan took the cue and handed him an iPad with the location and screenshots from the social media posts he'd been reading.

'Probably not connected,' Harrison replied. 'But I'd better check it out. The killer could have been out and about late last night.'

He scrolled through, handed the iPad back, and walked out.

'You're welcome,' Ryan shouted after him, but he smiled at his back. Harrison's social skills could be better, but that didn't mean he wasn't appreciative.

It didn't take Harrison long to get to the cemetery. Much as he hated London traffic, he was adept at weaving in and out of it and spotting the tiniest gaps. Nunhead Cemetery sprawled across fifty-two acres, with huge Portland stone pillars that held cast-iron gates and railings all the way round the perimeter. Inside lay the remains of around 250,000 people, most of them buried from 1840 until they abandoned the site in 1969. It was Victorian London's homage to its dead at its finest, originally called All Saints' Cemetery and one of the Magnificent Seven in the capital. Unfortunately for Nunhead, it didn't boast

Karl Marx or George Michael like Highgate, or Emmeline Pankhurst like Brompton, and it had fallen into disrepair, not reopening its gates or receiving attention until the 1990s. Harrison knew all this because he'd been here before.

When he was at university, a few of them came to an open-air concert held in the chapel. It was a Gothic chapel with no roof, a victim of some vandal's fire-raising during the neglected period, but it created the perfect dramatic concert venue on a summer's evening. The evening was memorable, not for the concert, but because he realised it wasn't his first visit. When they'd arrived, he'd got a strange feeling of having been there before. The symbol on the huge cast-iron gates, of an hourglass framed on one side by a devil's wing and the other a wing of an angel, brought back a distant memory of him holding his mother's hand as they'd passed it.

Harrison and his university friends walked around the grounds. His friend, Sam, played the joker, frightening the girls they were with by jumping out from behind a stone angel or making bushes move in the darkness, when all that could be seen were the ghostly shapes of overgrown headstones. Harrison was older than the rest of the group by around two years, but a decade in maturity. The two years he'd lost, and the reason he'd lost them, were enough to age anyone. He knew most of the undergraduates found him boring. Too intense. He tended to hang around with the Taekwondo crowd or the studious types. That night his friends had been drinking, so they were out to have a laugh.

The further Harrison walked, the more a feeling of unease had overtaken him. They'd wandered deep into the site where the restoration teams hadn't reached. Past the catacomb to where the graves were overgrown and unloved. The others dared one another to tell ghost stories and spooky facts about the cemetery. Harrison tried to join in, but the wash of memories from his earlier visit there, and the riptides that dragged them from him took all his focus.

Eventually they came across an area where the Gothic monuments melded into the undergrowth. An obscene prosthetic addendum to nature, decayed religious effigies intertwined with fresh green life. Here the feeling of déjà vu almost overwhelmed him. In his memory, everything was bigger; there had been others there besides him and his mother. The swish of black material, murmuring voices, a tension in his mother's hand as she held his.

Back then, in his university days, he'd still been angry. Not the all-consuming, self-destructive anger he'd felt at first, but an ember that stayed lit in his belly, waiting to be triggered. At Nunhead he'd found that trigger. He'd grasped hungrily at the snatches of memories it invoked, but his hunger frightened them away. He'd been too eager to see something that wasn't and too blind to see what *was*. There were also things his mind wouldn't let him see. A darkness his mother had run from. A darkness buried with the corpses all around him.

What Harrison *had* remembered was that after that night he and his mother went to America and the endless dry heat and sun of Arizona. While they were there, that cool grey evening at Nunhead, with the smell of damp decay everywhere, came to him in snatches. Large holes existed in the memories, holes that frightened him in the darkness of his bedroom at night, and he'd resisted them. Gradually his mind buried it altogether, only to reawaken when he'd returned as an adult.

Before then, graveyards hadn't frightened him. If anything, they'd made him feel jealous—not of the living, but of the dead. He'd read the messages of love left by family members who grieved their passing. He'd placed his hand on the cold grey headstones and imagined he could feel the spirit of the grave's occupant pulsing up from the ground and through the stone, like electrical currents that talked to him through touch. His loneliness had sought a little of their family love.

He no longer felt jealous of the dead at Nunhead. Most of the Victorians, who'd long ago been buried with such ceremony, had no one left to mourn them. The angels and headstones might have looked impressive, but people just walked past, occasionally reading a name, wondering about a life they had no concept of. Forgotten. The generations had moved on, but the dead had nowhere else to go. Nunhead was a final resting club for the privileged, where once you could be sure of meeting the right class of person over the graveside, but now even the mourners were ghosts.

Today, as Harrison walked in, quite a few people were strolling in couples. He thought how Nunhead had probably been quite an effective pickup joint in Victorian times. You'd be guaranteed to find a widow or widower, with a good inheritance, feeling lonely. More effective than many of the modern dating sites.

He walked past the Gothic chapel and the lime trees that lined the gravelled path. Away from the neatly restored area and towards the section Ryan had mentioned earlier. That same feeling he'd had all those years ago ran down his spine. Grainy images flickered in his mind. Why did he feel drawn here? What happened that night that was different from all the other nights? Had his mother taken them to America to escape it?

Harrison walked between two large, pillared mausoleums. One carried the downwards-facing Greek torch that represented life extinguished. That same symbol was at the gates—and in his memory.

The gravel ran out, and he found himself walking on a dirt path. To one side was an open space where the sunlight lit up new gravestones of white and shiny black marble, machine etched with gold lettering. Modern graves, some well looked after. Then a neatly mown, boxed hedge section of white carved stones. All the same. All standing straight. Regimented. War graves. To his left it became dark. Thick undergrowth and trees crowded around ancient gravestones, barely discernible in the gloom. Green lichen camouflaged the headstones so only a pale ghostly shadow of them could be seen. Through a break in the trees, Harrison saw the dome of St Paul's Cathedral in the city below. Farther on, darkness settled on both sides. Occasional tombs rose from the undergrowth, overlooking clusters of shadowed headstones. It was here that Harrison found what he was looking for.

The satanic symbols were easy to spot, black daubed graffiti amid the green lichen and pale weathered stones. Crude pentagrams covered faded words of tribute and love. He stopped and looked. It was too familiar. He knew this was the same area inside his mind, the same place he'd stood trying to pull the memories from his head that night of the concert. He had to concentrate, to disassociate himself from the emotions threatening to distract him. Harrison closed his eyes and focussed on his breathing. He was here to investigate, not reminisce.

When he opened his eyes, he turned his attention to the ground. Leaves—golds, browns, reds, yellows—covered the ground, and there was evidence of several shoe prints. Straight edges on crushed leaves, broken twigs and underneath, the prints of trainers in the mud. Using a stick, he searched in the debris and found several cigarette butts. They were still bright, freshly dropped, not like the older weathered and discoloured ones he'd seen on the path earlier. They also looked like one of the cheaper brands, thinner, and the paper wasn't such high quality. His suspicion was confirmed when he spotted a crumpled packet discarded in the bushes. The evidence and the graffiti itself confirmed his supposition that kids were responsible. Modern satanists used the inverted pentagram; this one was the correct way up, and there was a badly spelt slogan on one stone: *'Satan takes your babys'*. Teenagers with nothing better to do.

As he stood there, a bearded man walked down the path purposefully, from the same direction Harrison had come. He stopped and looked at the graffiti.

'It's not the first time we've had this happen here,' he said by way of a conversation starter to Harrison, who nodded. 'Of course, no one saw anything. You a reporter?' he asked as Harrison took a couple of photographs on his phone.

He looked at the man. He judged him to be in his late sixties, perhaps even early seventies. Kept himself relatively fit and active and was used to being outdoors from the look of his clothes and skin. He also wore a badge that said, "FONC, Friends of Nunhead Cemetery." Someone who helped look after the place.

'No,' Harrison replied. 'I work with the police in ritualistic crime,'

The man's face changed.

'It's okay,' Harrison said. 'This is nothing serious.'

'Just kids, I reckoned,' the man said, as he came to stand next to him and looked at the large pentagram.

'Yeah. Definitely not anyone who's a serious satanic follower,' Harrison reassured him. 'They've not inverted the pentagram for one thing. Schoolboy error.'

The man nodded. 'I thought so. Ah, well, we'll soon have it cleaned off. As I said, it's not for the first time. I came by to make sure it was just surface damage.'

Harrison nodded his goodbye and waited a few moments until the man left. Satisfied the graffiti was unlikely to have anything to do with Darren, he allowed himself a few personal moments. This was definitely the same spot he'd been before. What was it about this area? These graves? He read each headstone individually, looking for a clue to explain why he'd been there with his mother and why this area had now fallen victim to satanic graffiti.

They were all ancient, *Henry Joseph Brown, beloved son of William and Elizabeth Brown who died 3rd January 1902, aged 29 years*. A column carved to be broken and represent a life cut short, said, *In loving memory of Ronald Robert, infant son of Charles and Harriet, 1871*. There was an Alice, *beloved wife of Henry, who'd died in 1892, aged just 31*. She lay there alone in her grave. Where was Henry, lying next to a new wife somewhere else in the cemetery? Or maybe he'd died a pauper's death, wracked with grief. No one to mourn his loss and no marker to show his passing. Was one of these people linked in some way to an old satanic cult, perhaps? If anyone had been officially suspected of witchcraft, it would have been highly unlikely that they'd have been buried in consecrated ground. Perhaps they were victims. Harrison took photos of each gravestone with his phone. None of the names meant anything to him.

After the last time he'd been here, he'd tried hypnotism to see if it could retrieve his buried memories. The hypnotist wasn't even able to get started. Harrison's mind had become so self-controlled it wouldn't let him in. Wouldn't let anything else out either. His mind was locked.

Whatever he did, he seemed to get no closer to his mother and the answers he sought.

He looked around him again. Perhaps it wasn't the graves but the place. Maybe even before the cemetery was built, it had been an isolated spot where pagan rituals took place. Or perhaps it was one of the places where witches were hanged or executed. Nunhead was surprisingly high up, looking over central London and the Thames; it would have once been far outside the city walls, far enough away for unsavoury things to have taken place. Harrison used his phone again to mark the spot with his GPS. He'd get Ryan to see what he could find.

He turned his attention to what was around the headstones. One tree totally dominated the area, and it was surrounded by younger trees and bushes. They wouldn't have been there when he'd been a child, but the tree definitely would have been. It was a huge oak with giant sloping arms that reached to the ground. Harrison wasn't an expert on trees, but he knew they could live up to a thousand years. He peered through the branches of the younger, protective barrier that had grown up around it. The trunk of this oak was ancient, with gnarled crevices and craters in the calloused bark. It was the width of a car, firmly planted, a home to millions of flora, fauna, and insect life. An entire forest microcosm. It had to be at least five hundred years old, just from what he knew about other trees he'd seen like it. That was Henry the VIII's time. Definitely long before they built the cemetery around it. The huge branches of the oak, dark and skeletal, protected an empty clearing beneath them. Its towering presence prevented anything else from growing in its shadow. Flashes jumped into his head. Him as a small boy standing on the edge of that small clearing.

Claustrophobic under the canopy.

The roughness of the bark on his hand.

Flames.

Moonlight on metal.

What did it all mean?

Harrison stepped back for a moment. His heart was racing. He wanted to dive in there and face up to it, but there was no way he'd get beyond that undergrowth without some cutting tool. It was too dense. He'd have to come back, but not yet. This secret had waited for him a long time. Alex Fuller needed him now. He'd already wasted enough time.

Harrison started walking back towards the gate. The sky had turned from pale-blue and white to a pewter grey that dimmed the light of the day and threatened rain. It gave the walkers a greater urgency, and people hurried past him, heading for their destinations before the skies opened.

He was just within sight of the gates when he came alongside an elderly woman sitting on a bench.

'We've met before, haven't we?' she asked him.

Harrison nearly missed what she'd said, but he stopped and looked at her. She was dressed in a black overcoat with a green woolly hat, and a wrinkled, haggard face peered from underneath. It wasn't a warm face. The eyes were hard, the bone structure severe. There was something about her, but he couldn't place it, so he tried to judge whether she suffered from dementia or was just mistaken.

'I don't think so,' he replied politely and went to move on.

'Oh, I know we have. A long time ago. Sit with me a moment, would you? I think I can help you.'

He hesitated, not wanting to waste time and also not wanting to engage in conversation with a woman it might be difficult to extricate himself from, but something made him stop and walk over to the bench to sit down. Perhaps he did know her, or maybe a hidden memory was trying to surface.

'I don't sleep too well now. My hips ache no matter how soft the mattress,' she said, not looking at him but staring away into the distance. 'Anyways, I looked out my window last night and saw them, a bunch of teenagers it was, with cans of spray paint. They were heading into the cemetery. That what you wanted to know?' She turned to him, watching his face. Her eyes seemed to bore into his skin.

Harrison couldn't make her out. Did she just want to chat or was there something more?

He looked at her, trying to glean further clues from her appearance. Her face was a mask, her eyes shutters on her soul. He didn't like what he saw, and his gut instinct told him to leave.

'Thank you.' He waited a few beats then stood to go, eager to get away from her. She made him uneasy. Was it her voice? Did he recognise it from somewhere?

'You don't talk much, do you?' the old woman continued.

'I prefer to listen,' he said with hesitation.

'Still miss your mum, do you?'

Harrison had been contemplating his escape route. He could just see the entrance gate from where they were, but he spun round to look at her.

'What?'

'I said not my idea of fun... what them kids did.'

He was sure that wasn't what she'd said. Alarm bells sounded inside him, but he couldn't work out why.

'I need to get back to work,' Harrison said, starting to back away.

'Goodbye, then. I'll see you again sometime soon, I

hope.' She watched him, smiling as though she'd just made a joke and it was on him.

When he looked up, the cemetery entrance was no longer clear. A black-cloaked figure stood in the middle, staring at him. For a few moments, Harrison thought he was seeing things. He was shocked. After all this time. The years of searching. This time there could be no confusion. He knew exactly where he'd seen the figure before.

The man saw him watching and spun round quickly to leave. Harrison wasn't going to let him escape. Not this time. His feet skidded on the gravel as he launched into a sprint.

The man ran too; he was surprisingly fast. Light on his feet. And he had a good head start.

Harrison flew through the gates and onto the street outside. Left. Right. He just caught sight as the man disappeared round a corner towards a block of flats.

Harrison's stomach had lurched so hard when he'd seen him that for a moment he'd worried he wouldn't be able to breathe. Wouldn't be able to run.

He belted along the road. If the man reached cover, it would be easier for him to hide.

A car came round the corner. Harrison swerved out the way—just in time, but he'd nearly tripped up the kerb.

Every molecule in his body screamed. Every fibre of his being was focussed on one thing: catching this man.

Harrison pulled himself to a stop underneath the flats. It was a concrete patio area. No people in sight. He spun round to the sound of a door as it slammed shut. The glimpse of a black cloak.

He was off.

He yanked the door open. A young woman with a pushchair was about to come through. She looked startled. He hurtled through the door so fast he had to grab hold of the frame to stop himself from falling onto the pushchair. He garbled an apology but didn't stop. More valuable seconds lost.

The lift had a sign stuck to it: OUT OF ORDER. There was nowhere else the man could have gone except up. But which floor? He launched himself up the stairs. Two steps at a time. One flight. Two flights. He stopped and listened. Laboured breathing and footsteps above him.

The sound of a door closing. Then again. Another door?

He ran up. His chest pounded. What flight was he on?

The sound of his breathing rushed from his lungs to his mouth and roared in his ears.

Through the window in the door on the next floor, he saw an elderly man bent double. He was leaning on a stick, struggling with some shopping bags. Shuffling along the corridor with tiny steps.

There had been two doors closing. Had the cloaked figure gone to the top? Was there another way out?

Fourth floor. Nothing to be seen.

Fifth and he'd reached the top.

Where was he? He could see no sign of the black-cloaked figure.

Harrison ran out onto the walkway which covered the length of the block of flats. Could the man have gone into one of the flats here? He started trying the doors out of desperation, but they were all locked.

Someone opened their flat door.

'Oi, what you doin? What you want?' a gruff bald-headed man shouted at him. Harrison pushed past without a word and ran back the other way. This was ridiculous; the man couldn't just disappear. He had to have gone into a flat.

He peered over the balcony, trying to scan the floors below. Down to the ground.

The only people he saw were the young woman with the pushchair and the old lady from the graveyard at the bus stop in front of the flats.

The lift machinery started behind him. The sound of whirring and clunking as it screeched and whined its way down the shaft.

Then it stopped.

Harrison bent over. He felt sick. He'd lost him.

The realisation hit. The lift was supposed to be out of order.

He peered over the balcony again. Down below him the entrance door opened and an old man with shopping bags walked out. It was the old man he'd seen in the corridor below, only this time he wasn't shuffling—he was striding. Striding towards the bus stop and the old woman who stood smiling at him.

The penny dropped.

Harrison thumped the railing and headed back to the stairs. He had to get to them before the bus arrived.

He slipped and flew down the stairs. Not worrying about the burning sensation on his hands from the rail, or when he'd rammed his shoulder into the wall, which sent the breath bursting from his chest.

In the entrance lobby, he stole a glance at the lift door. The sign had gone. Then he was outside.

He ran towards the bus, but it was already pulling away. That would not stop him. This was the first chance in fifteen years that he'd got anywhere near close to him. He had to catch that bus.

For once Harrison was grateful for the London traffic.

He raced down the road, trying to dodge pedestrians. The bus was ahead of him, turning the corner. If he could make up some ground, he'd catch-up with it at the next stop.

He ran, his breathing laboured with exertion. He would do it.

Once he rounded the corner, he could see the bus. It had stopped at a traffic light and was in a queue, wedged in between a black cab and a delivery van. He was going to catch them.

Adrenaline coursed through him; he ran into the road. The pavement, too cluttered with people, slowed him down. A driver beeped at him. A cyclist yelled something, but he didn't hear or care.

The bus pulled away again, starting to get some speed up. It indicated; it was pulling into a stop.

The last couple of hundred metres.

Harrison watched as no one got off, but a few people were gathered around the bus entrance waiting to board. The last person had just disappeared inside when he caught up with it and launched himself onto the bus, to the surprise of the driver and some passengers at the front. As Harrison paid, he scanned the faces on the lower deck. The young woman with the pushchair was there, but she didn't even blink at him. There was a middle-aged woman reading a book. A young mum with two toddlers who were whining and complaining, and a guy who looked like he was on his way back from working as a security guard. Where was the older couple? They must have gone upstairs.

He was oblivious to the driver's anxiety at the large, red-faced man in front of him, wired with laboured breathing and eyes darting everywhere. Harrison was hot and tired, but he wasn't going to let them get away.

With one final double-check around the ground floor, he bounded up the steps to the top deck.

Empty, except for four teenage girls sat giggling at a phone. They barely acknowledged his presence.

Harrison collapsed onto one of the seats. They'd tricked him. How could he have been so stupid? The sweat beaded on his forehead and his back felt wet with the exertion. Yet again, they'd got away, but why show themselves at all?

He'd been searching for them for years. Now it seemed they'd found him.

16

The walk back to Harrison's motorbike helped him calm down, but he had to stop for a few minutes and gather his thoughts. He was so bloody angry with himself. He'd lost his concentration and self-control. Everything he had trained himself to do had gone in a moment of pure fight-and-flight mode. He was ashamed of himself.

Had the whole thing been a setup? The graffiti to lure him out? Her in the graveyard, him at the gates to draw Harrison away so they could both escape? They must have planned the whole thing. The lift notice, the stick and bags for the old man's disguise. He should have seen it was him. Should have looked properly and not assumed, but the chase had blinded him. The question was, why did they go to all this trouble? The only reason he could see was to taunt him. To show him he wasn't as in control as he thought he was. Well, it had worked. They'd pressed the right buttons, and he'd lost it. He'd let his mother down again.

When Harrison returned to New Scotland Yard, he put his hand in his pocket to pull out his ID to get into the building. Instead, his hand found something else. It was the photograph Sally Fuller had given him yesterday. Harrison looked at the faces captured in the shot. Alex, his sister, and their parents. Smiling. Happy times when they couldn't even contemplate the nightmare they were going through right now. He wouldn't let his own personal crusade get in the way of saving their son's life. His had been ruined many years ago by two evil people. He couldn't let them ruin his chances of helping Alex now.

By the time he'd got down to his basement bolthole, he had calmed down. This had been a huge lesson for him and one he'd learn from. They wouldn't make a fool of him again.

As he approached his office, he didn't need to see her to know that Dr Tanya Jones had come to pay a visit. Her perfume left a trail of scent down the corridor. She seemed to have more on than usual. Perhaps she'd had to work a particularly nasty-smelling scene. He almost turned round to walk the opposite way, but while his mind was wary, his body kept walking. He wanted to see her. Perhaps she'd brighten his day.

As he entered, she was looking at the Ouija board, her pretty face frowning at the bone planchette she held in her hand. He allowed himself to watch her for just a moment.

'That's how I solve all my cases,' he said.

Tanya jumped at his voice and nearly dropped the planchette onto the Ouija board. She quickly regained her composure, but he knew she wasn't sure if he was joking or not.

'If you believe the rumours…' he added.

She smiled, relief on her face, and he couldn't help smile back with his lips and eyes.

'That Ouija board was used by Maggie Osmond who, over the course of her spiritual career, conned her clients out of several hundred thousand pounds,' Harrison said. 'One of them committed suicide as a result.'

He watched as Tanya raised her eyebrows.

'She got six years, but apparently she'd not learnt her lesson and tried to conduct a séance at Holloway Prison. One of the inmates believed herself to be possessed by a demon afterwards. They found Mrs Osmond strangled in the showers a year into her sentence.'

As Tanya put the planchette pointer gently back on the board, she wondered how many hands had held it, their hearts jumping into their mouths as it seemingly moved across the board, spelling out messages from the spirits. Harrison had startled her, but she was glad he'd turned up. When she'd arrived to find him not in, disappointment had been an understatement.

'I was just on my way back from a location visit and thought I'd let you know I'll be emailing you a report on the *Bible* scriptures in the next couple of hours. We're almost done.'

'Good,' Harrison replied. Then, 'Thanks,' as an afterthought.

Tanya nodded, making an effort to look around at the other artefacts and not at him. It wasn't easy.

'What's this?' She pointed to a strange creature that looked like a deformed miniature human. 'Please don't tell me it's real?'

'Well, I guess that depends what you mean by "real"'. Harrison took a couple of steps closer to her and now stood next to her in front of the shelf. That was a mistake. He felt the warmth of her body radiate next to him, and when she turned to speak, her breath was on his neck. It took him a few moments to stop imagining just turning round to her and kissing those pink lips of hers.

'I mean it wasn't an actual living thing, was it? It's grotesque.'

Harrison regained his composure by focussing. 'The story goes that in Cornwall, a family walking on the beach following a storm one day in the late seventeenth century, came across this poor washed-up creature, the Welaman. It was still half alive, and they tried to help it. It told them it had special powers to grant wealth and fertility to those who touched it.'

Tanya raised her eyebrows and reached out gingerly to place her hand on the object.

Harrison smiled but reluctantly moved a step back from her. It seemed as though his presence had made her more nervous. He could feel her discomfort. 'The legend is that the Welaman brought gold to the men and babies to the ladies.'

'Oh!' Tanya exclaimed and withdrew her hand as though it had been burnt. 'I'm not quite up for that yet.'

She looked at Harrison and saw him smiling broadly. She smiled just as broadly back, but wished he hadn't stepped away from her. Tanya had enjoyed his closeness. It was the most she'd ever seen him smile, and it was enough to make her knees go weak and her stomach do a flip. She'd touch the Welaman every day if she could see him smile like that at her. She stopped herself short of imagining having his babies too.

'But the Welaman also came with a warning. It had been washed up and injured in a storm, and every time a storm returned to the coast, his own kind would come looking for him. They didn't like humans. They'd kill any living creature found on the beach as they searched for their friend. He told the family that because they'd been kind to him, and he wanted them to be safe.'

'Okay, so what happened?'

'Good luck indeed came to the family who had found the Welaman, for they grew rich and so folks around that area heeded the warnings and stayed away from the beaches. People would come from miles away to touch the Welaman and receive its blessing.'

'Hmm, I feel a "but" coming on.'

Harrison shrugged and smiled at her again. 'The family grew rich because they were luring ships onto the rocks, wrecking them, and stealing their cargo during storms. They even slaughtered the crew to prevent them from telling people what was going on and left their bodies on the beach to make it look as though the Welaman's kind had been there.'

'That wasn't very nice.'

'No. Eventually, a few of the locals, who were less gullible and not so taken with folklore, watched the beach one stormy night. The family were arrested, put on trial, and found guilty. The women of the family died of disease in jail while the men were hanged.'

'So what exactly is that thing? The so-called Welaman?'

'It played on the Cornish folklore of mermaids and of course the long history of seafaring invasions from the likes of the Romans, Irish, French, and Vikings. It was scientifically examined in the nineteen eighties and found to be a mixture of different birds and animals, put together to create this tiny humanlike form. That's pig's skin covering it and blackened with some kind of tar.'

'Eugh!' said Tanya, screwing up her face and rubbing the hand she'd used to touch the Welaman on her leg. 'Well, I guess I'd better get…'

'Why are you nervous around me?' Harrison asked her.

She turned to face him and saw him studying her. 'Nervous? I… well…' She was flustered now.

'I don't believe in any of this, you know,' he said, gesturing around him at the various witchcraft and cult relics in his office. 'They're just stories made up by people who want to control others.'

'No. I mean yes, but no, I didn't think... I'm not nervous because I think you do this stuff...' Tanya was still flustered and couldn't seem to get her brain to engage under his scrutiny. She was a grown, intelligent woman, and she was behaving like a shy schoolgirl. She needed to get a grip.

Fortunately, Ryan saved her as he arrived back with a new batch of junk food, which he deposited on his overflowing desk.

'Hi, boss. Hi, Dr Jones,' he said cheerily, the prospect of consuming his haul making him beam from ear to ear. He looked at the pair of them with his eyebrows raised and forehead wrinkled, waiting for them to reply and realising he'd just interrupted something.

Dr Jones took the opportunity to escape. 'I'll make sure the results get to you asap,' she told Harrison, then disappeared out the office.

Ryan looked at his boss and smiled. 'She's got the hots for you, that one.'

Harrison looked genuinely surprised. Ryan laughed to himself. For a man who prided himself on his observation skills, spotting that someone was attracted to him clearly wasn't one of those he had mastered.

He watched as his boss went to his desk and took out a photograph before pinning it onto the board by his desk. It contained three people: an evil-looking man in black robes, flanked by two women. One was a young blonde woman who was staring at the man with what could only be described as an adoring look. The other was a plain-looking but hard-faced woman who stared straight at the camera.

'Who's that?' Ryan asked.

'Someone I've been looking for a very long time, only I think he's just found me.' He peered at the hard-faced woman's features. It was her, the old woman from the graveyard. That's why she seemed familiar—just twenty years older.

'What happened with the graffiti?' Ryan asked.

'Graffiti? Oh, just kids.'

Ryan knew Harrison well enough to know that was the end of the conversation. If it was nothing of any use, he wouldn't waste time explaining it.

'Actually, Ryan, would you mind doing some digging for me?'

'That's what I'm here for.' He smiled back. He loved nothing more than doing a bit of digging.

'Nunhead Cemetery. It used to be shut and was quite rundown and neglected, but I have a vague memory of something happening there back in the early to mid-nineties before they properly reopened it. I know fire destroyed the chapel, but that was in the mid-seventies. It's something else. Maybe not even a major thing, but it could be significant for some reason. Also, look further back. I'll send you some GPS coordinates. See if the site has any kind of ancient significance. Not a priority, though. Anything to do with the murder of Darren and finding Alex Fuller takes priority.'

'Got it. Leave it with me,' Ryan replied. He knew not to pry and ask too many questions. Harrison always told him that if he gave him too much information, it could cloud his research, cause him to look more narrowly for something that would reinforce what he suspected rather than open his eyes to possibilities. Something to do with confirmation bias. So he preferred him to have the vaguest of briefs and see what he came up with.

The pair turned their attentions to their screens, and the natural balance of silence settled back in their workspace, broken only by the click of a computer mouse, or the rustling and crunching that emanated from Ryan's corner.

Harrison tried hard not to think about the lingering scent of perfume which seemed to hang like an invisible will-o-wisp in the air around his desk, teasing his nose and leading his imagination to a mirage of an oasis for his heart.

Eventually Ryan stood up again and stretched. The fizzy drinks had gone through him and he needed a toilet break. Harrison had been concentrating on something for about an hour, so before Ryan left, he wandered to his boss's desk to see what had been keeping his interest.

He had up various CCTV camera feeds from the streets around where Alex Fuller had been snatched. There was no camera in the exact vicinity of where he'd disappeared, but they'd pulled every other available camera in the area, hoping to find something.

'I thought they were looking through the CCTV at Lewisham,' Ryan said.

'They are, but you know as well as I do that just because they're looking doesn't mean they'll actually see anything.'

'Right. Well, I'm heading out for five minutes.'

Just as Ryan reached the door, a burst of noise came from behind him. Harrison had thumped the table and sprung from his chair.

'Got him.'

Ryan stopped and waited for it.

'Ryan?'

'Yes, boss?'

'I need you to track down this post van.'

An hour later, Harrison was in DCI Barker's office, pointing to a post office van in a grainy CCTV image on her screen.

'It's not an official van, but it looks like it is,' he said. 'Just one road away from where Darren went missing. That's what the smell in Darren's hair was: spray paint. I tracked the routes of the genuine vans. This one didn't follow any of the set routes. It didn't stop at any postboxes.'

He pulled up another image. This was from the streets around where Alex Fuller had been taken.

'Same van. Same random route. This time he drove around for a bit… I suspect scoping for his next victim. Post office has confirmed it's not one of theirs.'

'Well done, Harrison. Amazing how four officers doing nothing else but trawling through CCTV didn't spot that.'

'They were looking for something unusual. To get away with this, it had to look completely usual. Blend in with everyday life and no one gives you a second glance. That's why the boys seemed to disappear into thin air.'

DCI Barker took a chocolate from the box in her top drawer.

'Chocolate?' she offered Harrison.

He shook his head.

'No, thanks, Sandra. Don't like chocolate,' he replied.

The office door opened, and an exhausted-looking Jack Salter walked in, just as Harrison had turned to leave.

'You're not normal, Harrison Lane,' DCI Barker shouted after him as he exited.

Salter's ears pricked up, and he closed the door behind Harrison conspiratorially. 'What's he done? What's not normal?'

'Him. Do you know, not only does he not drink alcohol

or coffee, but he doesn't like chocolate? How can anyone not like chocolate? I'd have been dead years ago without all three. Want one?'

She offered Jack one, but he had slumped into the chair opposite, all enthusiasm and energy drained. He looked done in. His shirt was creased, his skin pale and drawn.

'You okay, Jack? Do you want to talk about it?'

'I'm struggling to get on top of this case,' he admitted.

'You need to trust him more.'

'What? The man with no vices?'

'I never said he didn't have any vices. Now what's the problem?' Barker asked, her voice softening and losing its joking tone.

'I tracked down the two men our witness saw. Managed to wreck some bloke's marriage. Turns out that car park is a gay pickup spot. I just don't know how he does it. He said it wasn't them.'

'You're a good cop. You just need to focus on the job and stop seeing Harrison as a rival. This isn't a competition. He sees things neither you nor I can see, but you're methodical and intuitive, you know the system. You have a great track record and an excellent career ahead of you. Don't lose sight of that. Together you're a brilliant team.'

'Yeah,' he replied, but his voice told her he wasn't convinced.

'So we're looking for a fake post office van,' she said, changing the topic; it had always worked well as a distraction technique with her kids. 'He had to get it spray painted somewhere. It's a professional job.'

'Yeah, okay. I'll get onto all the spray-paint workshops,' Jack replied, trying to rally himself.

'First thing in the morning. They'll be shut on Sunday. Go home. You look exhausted.'

He got up to leave.

'Jack, it's not a weakness to ask for help or to take a break. We all need it sometimes. Your family has to come first, so if you need some time off, ask me. We'll manage here. I'll shift resources around. Jack?'

'Thanks. I'm fine.'

Sandra Barker wasn't convinced. This job was tough on a good day. With stress at home, she'd seen officers like Jack make some poor choices and lose sight of what they'd joined the service for. She watched him leave before returning her attention to the box of chocolates in her drawer and the computer screen in front of her.

17

Sally Fuller walked into the Lewisham Police Station reception at eight the next morning. Despite the relatively early hour, the place was already full of the various detritus of human life waiting to be seen or still there after the previous night. It was open 24/7, which meant a nonstop flow of traffic. Sally walked straight up to the desk. She'd been crying, and her clothes were dishevelled; she was clearly distraught.

'My name's Sally Fuller. I want to speak to the officer in charge of the search for my son. I want to talk to Detective Chief Inspector Barker or Dr Lane.'

The receptionist, a woman in her fifties, could see she was upset, and as soon as she said her name, she understood why.

'Is the DCI expecting you?' she asked.

Sally shook her head.

'Why don't you come with me into one of the waiting rooms? Then I can see if either of them are in.'

'I don't want to go in a waiting room. I'll stay here as long as it takes,' Sally replied, and went across to the plastic seats, which were fixed down in case someone decided to try to throw them at somebody. The woman at the front desk got straight on the phone.

Sally was so agitated she could barely sit still. She folded and unfolded her legs, then stood and sat down again. Her eyes darted everywhere but saw nothing. The middle-aged man who'd been waiting to discuss a robbery at his garage eyed her warily. He got up on the pretence to look at a poster but sat down on the other side of the room. His imagination had her high on some amphetamine, and he didn't want to be close to her in case she did something like pull a knife on him.

Another occupant of the waiting room was a woman with pulled-back grey-streaked brown hair, who looked like she'd lived a hard life. She was waiting for her son to be released after a night in custody. She watched Sally. Although she had no idea who she was or why she was there, she recognised the anxiety of a distressed mother. It reminded her of the days when hers had been younger and the worrying had only just started. It also reminded her she needed a smoke, so she got up and stepped outside to light up.

'DCI Barker will be down, and Dr Lane is on his way.' The woman behind the front desk had come out and walked over to Sally, worried she might faint or hyperventilate. She had kids of her own; and wouldn't wish what Sally was going through on anyone. She wanted her some place where she could get some privacy.

'The DCI has asked if you could come into one of the interview rooms. She'll join you in a moment,' she told her, hoping that by quoting the DCI, she might persuade Sally to move.

'I'm not moving. You're not shoving me out the way. I

need to know what's going on,' Sally replied, and didn't budge.

The door opened with a blast of outside air. They both looked up, but it was a courier making a delivery. He stared at them, left the package on the desk, and exited.

Sally chewed at her inside cheek and rocked in her chair. The receptionist went back to her desk on the pretence of seeing who the parcel was for, but in reality she went to check where her first aid book was. She'd done the course, but that had been a while ago now, and she was trying to remember exactly how you were supposed to position someone if they'd fainted, so they didn't swallow their tongue and block their airways. She was more than relieved when DCI Barker appeared through one of the internal doors moments later. She'd rushed down as fast as she could.

'Mrs Fuller, how can I help you?' The woman's state was immediately apparent. 'Please, why don't you come somewhere more private? We can talk there.'

'My Alex, he's been gone nearly two days. I want to know why you haven't found him, what you're doing. I want to know where he is.'

'Mrs Fuller, we've been keeping you up to date with the enquiry...'

'You're not telling me everything. I know you're not.'

Sally seemed to have found a strength that her previous agitated state wouldn't have suggested possible. She planted her feet firmly on the floor and stood in front of DCI Barker, eyes wild but her gaze unflinching. Sandra Barker had seen this look before, the look of a mother who'd do anything for her child. The look of a mother who was completely helpless and verging on hysteria.

'Mrs Fuller, please come with me. Let's go sit down, and we can talk through the investigation in private.'

'Why can't you tell me now? You've no idea where he is. You think he's dead! Oh, God, he's dead, isn't he?'

'Mrs Fuller, I can't talk in reception. Does your husband know you've come here? Please let me take you home, and I can give you both a progress report.'

'Progress report... I don't want a report. I want my little boy! I want you to find my son. He's not coming back to us, is he?'

Sally dropped to her knees, sobbing, just as Harrison walked into the reception area. DCI Barker crouched beside her.

'Mrs Fuller, please, let me help you up,' she pleaded. 'You're going to hurt yourself.'

A uniformed police officer had been alerted by the front desk and had also come round to help. The two of them were attempting to take Sally's arms to help her up. She rejected them both, pushed away their hands. Her voice was rising in pitch and volume. She was getting close to the point of hysterical no return, and DCI Barker was considering calling a medic.

Harrison walked up to the group and stood directly in front of Sally. 'Mrs Fuller... Sally, please look at me.' His voice was calm but authoritative.

Sally paused and looked up at him. Her tear-streaked face was pale with anxiety, and her whole body shook with nerves. Her breathing was shallow and fast.

'Give me your hand,' Harrison said, offering his. 'I need you to come with me and help us with the enquiry. Help us find Alex.' DCI Barker and the police constable stopped their attempts to hoist Sally and stepped back as she slowly stretched out her hand and took Harrison's. He didn't take his eyes from hers, his face reassuring.

'Come with me,' he said, and helped her up from the floor.

The woman with the pulled-back hair walked back into the scene with a puff of fresh air and smoke. She stopped in her tracks as she saw a large muscular man in black bike leathers helping the hysterical mother off the floor. He was good looking too. *Lucky bitch*, she thought as she watched him support her out of the reception area and into the depths of the police station.

The receptionist quickly opened the security door to allow them through. 'Interview room one is free,' she told Harrison and the DCI.

'I just want my little boy home, I just want my Alex,' Sally sobbed as Harrison helped her into the room, closely followed by a relieved DCI Barker.

18

D S Jack Salter and a young detective constable, David Oaks, stood in the entrance of Davey & Thomson's spray-painting workshop, a large rundown warehouse split into compartments by plastic curtains and booths. It wasn't the most technologically advanced and modern setup. Jack guessed part of the reason its owner was decidedly shifty and defensive was because the business probably was on the borderline with safety standards, not to mention the dodgy deals he was cutting on the side with less-desirable members of the community. There were four staff working in full overalls and facemasks; any one of them could be their killer or know who he was.

'I'm not interested in anything else but this one case. A post van.' Jack was trying to get across. The tiredness and lack of patience showed in his voice and body language.

The man in front of them stood his ground and blocked their further progress into the building. He was balding but with a neck as thick as his head and tattoos that covered its entirety. Jack imagined him as a regular at the local boxing gym, and he certainly wasn't a bloke he'd pick a fistfight with. He guessed he was either Mr Davey or Mr Thomson, but they were unlikely to find out, as he wasn't giving anything away. As the overpowering smell of spray paint wafted over his head, Jack hoped, at the very least, it might act in a similar way to glue and give his tired brain a chemical pick-me-up. He certainly needed it.

Two of the workers, facemasks on, had drifted over and were taking an unsubtle interest in the proceedings.

'Seriously, mate. I ain't lying. It's nothing to do with us. We ain't done nothing like a post van,' the thick-necked man replied. There was an insincerity in his voice; he clearly wasn't a fan of the police.

For a moment, Jack Salter glassed over in the face of Mr maybe Thomson or Davey. The smell reminded him of walking round boring stately homes and museums with his parents on holiday, sniffing at the intoxicating aroma of the guidebooks. His parents had never realised his real motivation behind wanting to carry them. He still loved that fresh glossy print smell to this day.

'Okay, thanks for your help.' Jack's clipped tone gave away his frustration and sarcasm.

The two detectives turned and walked away from the entrance. They felt several pairs of eyes on their backs as they went.

Jack also felt the young officer beside him bristle at the attitude they'd just come up against. The detective was still fairly new to this work and had a lot to learn. David Oaks stuck out like a sore thumb and hadn't yet learnt the art of being a chameleon. Change your accent and your demeanour to suit the environment. Instead, he spoke to everyone with the same perfect English accent. Jack was Cockney one moment and Queen's English the next. He could draw himself up to be tall and threatening or crumple himself down and meld into the background. It was a skill learnt from watching people closely and trying to get the best from them. DC Oaks was smart, though. He'd learn.

He couldn't contain his annoyance. 'If he isn't lying, I'm Lady Gaga,' said David. 'Word is they take in stolen cars and respray them. He's not going to admit to anything off the books and certainly won't want us sniffing around.'

'Nope. I suspect they're having a quick clean-up right now, just in case we come back. Might need to tap into uniform or the Specials, see if any of them have a better relationship, but somehow, I doubt it. How many more on the list?'

'Another six, then the paint retailers,' Oaks replied. 'But that's going to be like looking for a needle in a haystack. Asking if anyone has bought a red post van colour isn't going to be an easy hit.'

'Bloody hell, six more? Hang on, will you? I've gotta make a call.' Jack stopped about fifty yards from the spray painters and dialled 'home' on his mobile. It rang and rang, but no one picked up; instead, the message-answering service kicked in, and the cheerful voice of his wife telling him no one could answer his call filled his ear. It made him wish for the time when "cheerful" had been her default state. He hadn't seen Marie smile in weeks.

Just as he was about to follow Oaks to the car, a man in paint-covered overalls appeared from down the side of the building. He looked around shiftily and kept back in the shadows.

'I 'eard you was looking for someone who might 'ave sprayed a van, yeah?'

Jack looked up from checking the messages on his mobile. The guy kept looking towards the entrance. He obviously didn't want to be seen. Jack stepped towards him and out of the workshop's direct line of sight. He kept it casual, though. Last thing he wanted was to scare the guy off or alert the others that he was talking to someone.

'Yup. Needle in a haystack. Don't tell me,' he said.

'It's about that kid wot got murdered, innit?' the man continued in his Cockney accent.

'Yeah,' Jack replied, unsure if he had a nosey voyeur on his hands or someone who might know something.

'I got kids, yeah. I'd like to see 'im banged up.'

'So would we, and more important, so would Darren's parents.'

For a moment they both stood there in a mental standoff. Jack could see the man was working through the pros and cons of telling what he knew. He wasn't going to pressurise him too hard. He'd learnt that one a long time ago. Silence and patience can often bring far better results than bombarding someone with questions.

The guy did a quick look around to make sure no one was near enough to hear. 'There woz this geezer, used to work 'ere, yeah. Left 'bout two months back. Right weird he woz, gave me the creeps, yeah. Kept saying religious stuff to us, but he woz good at the spraying.'

'He left?'

'Yeah, see his old man got sick. He lived with 'im. Stopped coming to work all sudden. Yeah, so Mick sacked 'im, like. I 'ad to clear out his locker. Right odd that woz, full of religious stuff and things about the Devil, like he thought he was worried about being possessed or somat. Sick in the 'ead if you ask me.'

Jack's interest levels had perked up with each sentence. 'Got a name for this geezer?' he asked. Salter modified his accent to suit his audience.

'Yup, Cameron Platt. Lives at the Marion Estate flats.'

'Cheers,' Jack replied, writing down the name and details.

'Don't tell 'im I told you, ay? As I said, the bloke gives me the creeps. And don't tell Mick.' He cocked his head back towards the spray-paint workshop. 'He don't want no attention, and he'd throw me out if he knew I told you.'

'No worries,' Jack replied. 'I don't know your name and I won't ask.' His mood and energy levels had suddenly boosted. The guy might be lying, sent to put them off from sniffing around the workshop, but his gut told him not. He came across as genuine, which meant they could have their first strong lead. The criminal community might be tight-lipped about nicked cars, but no one liked a child killer.

19

Harrison couldn't help it. He told himself it was his lunch hour. He wasn't losing any work time. He had returned to Nunhead and was stood looking at the area outside the block of flats where he'd chased the man. Did they live around here? Unlikely. Where did they go if they didn't get on that bus? The graveyard could wait, but if he was going to find out anything about what happened yesterday, he needed to act now. See if anyone knew how that graffiti had appeared on those particular headstones. He'd been involved in enough police investigations to know you needed to investigate quickly before the trail went cold.

He wandered around the streets surrounding the flats. Harrison was looking for teenagers or any bunch of kids who might spend their time hanging around and be easy recruits if you wanted something like that done. He knew just asking straight out wouldn't be easy. He'd worked with disadvantaged teens for years at the Taekwondo club. They took a fair bit of work before they'd trust you, and even then, it was arm's distance until they had your measure.

He also knew there were some nasty individuals out there. Boys and sometimes girls, who'd already been so tainted by the drugs and gang culture that they'd stab or shoot first and ask questions later. He didn't fancy becoming another statistic. He could see Jack Salter's face now when he was called out to investigate his murder. *Didn't see that one coming, did you?* written all over it.

He made his way to the newsagents, which he knew was on the other side of the flats. It was a classic London corner shop located away from the more refined wealthy areas and tourist hot spots. Wire caging covered the windows to prevent robberies. CCTV cameras were everywhere, with signs stating the shop had CCTV plastered in every vantage point as deterrents. It looked like a shop under siege. Harrison peered into the gloom and saw the counter stacked high with shelving. Only a small gap remained for the thin Asian man who was serving to peer at customers. Another protective measure. He suspected the guy had already endured robberies, attempted or successful, and behind one of those shelves was some kind of implement that could be used as a weapon, along with a panic-alarm button. A bank of small screens showed video footage of the shop from every angle. Harrison wondered how much the guy had lost through shoplifting a year and suspected it wouldn't be insubstantial.

Someone like him, a newsagent who sold cigarettes and food, was at the heart of communities like this. He'd know where to find the local posse of teenagers, but would he tell him?

Harrison looked around for something to buy. Something small. He didn't want a lottery scratch card. Why anyone would think they could beat the odds on those things and win anywhere near as much as they were going to spend on them, he'd never understand. It was a totally human trait. A bit like someone who hedged their bets that they were going to go to heaven, paradise, or whatever their idea of nirvana was. The unbeatable psyche of human optimism. Do enough good, scratch enough cards, say enough prayers, and your lucky card will come up. Animals, even our nearest intelligent cousins in orangutans and gorillas, were purely reward and risk-driven by the facts they saw before them. Fight the dominant animal, and I might win some more territory—or they might kill me. Look at the odds: how much bigger is he? Am I strong enough? Is the reward worth trying? Make a decision. Simple. They never said a quick *Hail Mary* before they started fighting, thinking it might help them win, or make a wish on a falling star and expect to get lucky.

Humans were illogical at the best of times, but it made them more interesting.

Harrison picked up a pack of chewing gum. On long days like now, it was good to refresh his mouth now and then.

'Hi.' He smiled warmly at the newsagent. He was about thirty years old, with stubble on his face and bags under his eyes. He obviously kept the shop open all hours and spent very little time on his own care. A wedding ring told of a wife, probably kids as well at home, so no need to attract a mate, but every need to earn money.

'Sixty pence,' the man said.

Harrison wondered if maybe he should have spent a bit more to get him on his side.

'I was wondering if you know of a group of lads around here. Someone saw them yesterday with spray cans.'

As the newsagent held out the card-payment machine,

his eyes darted around the shop. Harrison had chosen his moment well. There was no one else there to hear their conversation.

'I'm with a charity. We work with disadvantaged kids on art projects,' Harrison lied.

The newsagent humphed.

'I just want to speak to them, see if they're interested in the project,' he continued.

'You'll be lucky,' the man replied, taking the card machine back after Harrison had waved his phone at it.

'I'll be lucky to find them or speak to them?' Harrison tried to clarify.

'Oh, you'll find 'em, all right. They hang around near the Benson Estate. But they don't do talking, least not the kind that anyone would appreciate.' He almost snarled the last part of his sentence.

Clearly some of the precautions in his shop were aimed at the Benson Estate lads, and the idea that they were going to benefit from some kind of charity was an anathema to a man who worked as hard as he did for his living.

'Okay, Benson Estate. Cheers and thanks for the warning.' Harrison gave the guy another smile. *Must be tough running a business like this*, he thought. *Stressful*.

The newsagent was right. It didn't take Harrison long to find them once he'd crossed a couple of roads to the Benson Estate. They sat on a low wall, smoking. Occasionally they shouted abuse at passers-by, most of whom looked intimidated or had already crossed the road to avoid them. They were exactly the kind of group he'd ask to spray graffiti on something—for a price. Cocky. Thought themselves untouchable, and had probably already had more run-ins with the police than Harrison had worked on cases, but the difficulties the force had in convicting and sentencing young people had emboldened them. There was also something else they exhibited, something he loathed: they were bullies.

After watching them discreetly for a few minutes, Harrison strolled over.

'Y'all right?' he addressed them.

They tensed and looked at him like he was a piece of filth on their shoes.

There were six of them. All in the basic street gang uniform. Hoodies, trainers that looked more expensive than most teenage kids on a council estate should be able to afford, and sweatpants or jeans. The latter were in some cases so low down their backsides they were nearly falling off. Harrison never could understand that fashion statement.

It was obvious what the pecking order was. There were four black kids and two whites. Probably all roughly the same age—about sixteen, maybe seventeen—but one of them sported full facial hair. He'd clearly matured earlier and was top dog. His sidekick was another black lad. He watched his 'leader' keenly, taking every cue like an out-of-sync echo. Number three was a white boy. He looked like the one with the least brain cells, but was the biggest. The muscle and the kind of kid who spelt 'babies' as 'babys'. Four and five were wannabe leaders, but probably destined to always to be followers, while six didn't even have aspirations. Harrison worked all this out within a few minutes by just watching how they interacted with one another. It was the same principle David Attenborough used when looking at an animal pack.

'I'm not police,' he tried to reassure them.

'Wot? So you some paedo after a piece of my arse?' That came from number two, who looked to number one to see if he'd found it funny. The entire group sniggered and sneered.

They carried on assessing him. He was no wimp who'd be easily overpowered, but with it being six against one, they felt confident enough. Number one stood up and strutted forward. He'd clearly decided that instant aggression was the best way to show this stranger just how hard he was and to show off in front of his gang.

'Yeah, what you want, man? Why'd you bring yourself into my yard?'

'I don't want to cause any trouble. Just wanted to see if you knew whose graffiti handiwork it was in the cemetery. I'll pay for info. Not going to report anyone—only want to talk to them about who it was that paid them. No names needed, just a description.'

'That ain't none of your business,' the strutting adolescent replied.

'Actually, it is my business,' Harrison countered. He was still being polite, not rising to the aggressive levels being displayed to him.

'Why don't you just fuck off before I cut you?' the boy said, turning to smirk at the group of lads lounging on the wall behind him. Two of the others stood up intimidatingly, taking their cue. They swaggered a few steps towards him, sneering with confidence.

'That's not polite,' Harrison replied, completely unfazed.

'Not polite!' the boy tried to copy Harrison's accent and laughed.

'I haven't been disrespectful to you, so why are you being rude to me?' Harrison persisted.

'Yo, this wallad gem thinks he's teachin' me manners,' the boy shouted over his shoulder to his gang. He pulled a knife from out of the back of his trousers and walked threateningly towards Harrison.

Although Harrison didn't think the boy was serious about stabbing him, he'd had enough of his abuse. He had a pathological dislike of bullies and would be happy to teach this one a few lessons. The lad gave him his excuse when he lunged at him with the blade, a little perturbed by Harrison's lack of fear and the fact he hadn't moved a centimetre in the face of his aggression.

Without batting an eyelid, Harrison grabbed him, had the knife out of his hand, and both his arms behind his back in seconds. All without seeming to exert any effort or thought.

'Now that really isn't polite,' he told him. The lad tried to wriggle like a caught fish, kicking out with his legs. Harrison took them both out and sat him on the floor, still holding his arms up behind his back. He wouldn't hurt him in this position, but he could use his weight to keep the boy still and protect himself if he needed to.

A string of expletives came from the wriggling youth on the ground, and the other lads walked towards Harrison threateningly.

'So,' Harrison said, addressing them all, 'we can do this my way, or we can do it yours. One will mean I break both his arms…'

Harrison took one of the boy's arms and held it out straight, lifting his knee to show how easy it would be to snap it back. The boy was no match for his strength. It looked like he wasn't even trying to resist, but the exertion on his face told a different story. Then Harrison placed one foot lightly on the front of the boy's knee to show his intention.

'…and I could also sort his legs out, before I deal with the rest of you. Or you can just tell me who did the graffiti and why.' Harrison was bluffing, but they didn't know that. He wouldn't have broken any of the boy's limbs, although a part of him felt the urge; they were after all just kids, even if they weren't very nice ones. He'd got himself out of tougher situations than this one and while the lads were clearly street wise, they didn't have his training and even number three was no match for his strength.

'Get off me, man,' the boy whined. He was exhausted, overwhelmed by the power and speed of the man who held him. He stopped struggling.

For a few moments the rest of the gang thought about the proposition. Without their leader, the bravado had turned to confusion. None of them seemed prepared to step up and make a decision. Instead, one by one, they made the right choice and backed away. Seeing they were beat, their number one gave Harrison what he wanted.

'It was some old woman. Told us what she wanted, paid us. Dunno why. Didn't ask.'

'Okay, thank you. Now that wasn't so hard, was it? One last question: you ever seen her before?'

'No, man.'

The boy could have been lying, but from where Harrison was, poised ready to snap his arm, he didn't think so.

Harrison pushed the lad away from him and kicked the large knife that still lay on the pavement down a drain. The lad picked himself up and dusted down his clothes. The street muck was easy to get rid of, but he couldn't wipe off the look of humiliation that was all over his face.

Having got what he came there for, Harrison turned his back on the gang and started to walk away. Lunch break was over.

For a few moments the teens considered jumping him from behind, but then their survival instincts kicked in, and instead they just watched him walk away, stunned. Harrison had confirmed what he'd suspected. The couple had baited him, and he'd come, like his mother had all those years ago. But what did they want from him? Whatever it was, he'd be ready next time.

20

D S Salter and DC Oaks walked towards the estate
manager's office at the base of one of the Marion
Estate flats. It was one of the older estates, built in concrete
in the late 1960s, to replace the rows of bombed-out
houses from the Second World War, and meet the
desperate need for affordable housing. They'd called them
'streets in the sky' as the tower blocks rose above the city.
For many, that anticipation had turned into an isolated
living experience, a social experiment that failed. Jack
looked up. There were about twelve storeys, and the area
around the estate, which was initially promised as a green
oasis for the residents, had long since been built on as the
local council tried to meet growing demand and rising
costs. They'd passed a patch of grass, worn and tired, a
small concession to nature. Large graffitied initials were
sprayed all along the wall which ran beside it. Jack had
read a newspaper article recently that said a lot of these,
what he considered ugly tower structures, had been made
listed buildings. Other blocks being demolished or
refurbished, and their residents decanted into newer social

housing. He wondered what kind of living experience
Marion Estate was for its families.

They turned a corner, and in front of them was a huge
colourful mural, painted on the end of the block. A
transcendental multicoloured face, smiling down on those
below in an attempt to encourage smiles in return.
Underneath it, there was the usual mix of multiracial kids
playing on battered bikes and skateboards along the paved
area outside the block.

One kid shouted, 'Watch out! The filth are about!' and
his companion joined in. 'It weren't us, rozzers. 'onest,'.
The boys were about ten years old, going on sixteen. They
had an innate ability to spot a police officer in their midst,
Jack wondered if it was in the genes or part of their
upbringing. Estates like this one were fertile recruitment
grounds for the drugs gangs who needed a constant supply
of young couriers to keep their county-lines business
networks running. The fact their bikes were both battered
and old gave Jack some reassurance that these two had so
far managed to avoid the temptation. He hoped for their
sakes it stayed that way.

Jack was on his mobile again, but whoever he was
calling didn't pick up, so he pocketed it. The kids laughed
and scarpered quickly, thinking they'd said something
daring, pedalling their bikes as fast as their scrawny legs
would go. He saw them turn round to check they weren't
being followed. They were still just kids, after all.

The estate manager's office door was open. He came
out before they'd reached it, alerted by the shouts from the
kids. He was one of those nondescript types of men, a Mr
Average who'd blend into a crowd and bore a resemblance
to countless other Mr Averages. Average height, average
build, brown hair. The only distinctive feature on his face
was a large scar that stretched from the corner of his right

eye all the way down to his mouth. *However that had been caused, he'd been incredibly lucky not to have lost his eye in the process*, thought Jack.

'About time you came. I phoned it in hours ago,' said Mr Average.

'Phoned what in?' DC Oaks asked. The pair of them hadn't even uttered a word.

'The smell.'

'Smell?' DS Salter caught up with the conversation.

'Yeah, phoned it in first thing,' he replied, and looked at them both like they were speaking a foreign language.

'No, mate. We're not here about a smell. We're looking for a Cameron Platt.'

'Yeah, that's it. It's his flat I'm talkin' about. I ain't goin' in there, mind. Smelt that stench before, and it ain't gonna be pretty. Don't want no nightmares. Been doing this job fifteen years, and I can still remember my first one.'

The hairs on the back of Jack's neck instantly rose. There was no confusion over exactly what the estate manager was intimating. Question was, who was inside that flat?

'Show us the way,' he said, and checked his jacket pocket for a pair of gloves. He'd been faltering. The long hours and lack of a decent lunch had dragged down his energy levels, but now the adrenaline fired up again.

The flat was one of eight on the second floor, positioned at the end. The smell filled the entire corridor, and someone had obviously tried to clear the air by propping open the door. It might have helped, but it didn't solve the problem.

Jack double-checked with the manager. 'So you've not been in?'

'Nope. A couple of the neighbours mentioned it a day

or so ago. I came up this morning to check. Thought it was going to just be the drains, but that ain't no drain.'

The man knew his smells, thought Salter, but then again, once you'd smelt rotting flesh, you didn't forget it. He pitied the poor neighbours who must have been getting fed up with their lazy estate manager for not doing anything about their complaint.

'Who lives in the flat exactly?' Salter asked.

'It's rented by John Platt, but his son Cameron lives with him too. I ain't seen either of them for a while.'

Jack thought it would be difficult for anyone—even someone who was deranged—to live with that stench and its primary cause, but you never knew.

The manager headed toward the flat door, key poised, ready to insert.

'Hang on. This might well be a crime scene,' Salter said in a loud whisper. The man's eyes widened, and he looked from Salter to Oaks and back again, then thrust the key at him.

'I need you to step back and away, please,' Jack said. There was no hesitation. The estate manager scuttled straight back to the safety of the fresh air at the other end of the corridor.

Jack got on the radio and alerted the team back at the incident room of what they'd heard and found. Then he left his radio on and open. He was going to have to go in there, and he had no idea what he was going to find.

'We need to do this quick and cleanly,' Jack told Oaks. 'The boy could be in there, so I'm going to have to check that there's no life inside. I'll go in first, you stay outside to avoid further contamination of the scene, unless I call for assistance.'

Oaks nodded. His heart was pumping hard, and his stomach churned with the bile-creating odour that filled his nostrils outside flat number sixteen. He'd thought they'd drawn the short straw plodding round all the spray-painting workshops; he'd had no idea they might end up finding the nest of their key suspect, a nest that clearly contained a deceased individual, or more. He was, however, quite glad he didn't have to go inside.

Jack's heart was also beating fast. The adrenaline rushed through his system, ready for whatever was next. The moments before he entered a property like this were the closest he got to the Christmas Eve feeling he'd had as a child. That mixture of excitement, anticipation, hope, and a little fear. The balance between those elements wasn't exactly the same. In this instance, fear played a larger role than when he'd been a child, but the hope that they might find Alex alive, or at least take a big step towards that goal, was as important to him as an adult as Father Christmas when he'd been little.

He couldn't put crime-scene covers on his feet because if Cameron Platt was in there with the boy, he'd need to restrain him. Slipping around on plastic overshoes wasn't a good move. He double-checked that his body cam was on and recording. The first look at the scene was critical for forensics. He motioned to Oaks to put his gloves on too. Jack would slip the key in the lock, and Oaks could open the door with his glove; that way he'd dive straight in, unencumbered. If there was even the tiniest chance a young boy was alive behind that door, he had to check it out.

Jack spoke to his body camera.

'It's Monday, the seventeenth of October at fourteen twenty-one. We have reason to believe there's a deceased individual in flat sixteen, Marion Estate. We were attending the premises while investigating a tip-off during

Operation Genesis. I'm now entering the flat to ensure there are no individuals in need of medical attention.'

Oaks pushed the door open on cue, and Jack went to dive straight in.

As it was, it was the blowflies that dived first. The instant the door was opened, a small swarm made a dash for the light, nearly making Jack lose his balance as they flew straight into his face. But it wasn't just the flies they'd released. The noxious stench billowed out with them, and Jack heard Oaks gag behind him. He had a split second of feeling sorry for the young officer before he too gagged as it hit the back of his throat. Jack struggled, but he regained his composure and wasted no time stepping straight into the flat. He couldn't worry about Oaks; he'd be okay. Jack had seconds to gain his bearings, just in case Cameron Platt was in there and been alerted to their presence.

It was dark inside, and his eyes struggled to adjust. Directly in front was a room with yellow curtains drawn across the windows, giving a dull golden hue to the scene. There was also a shape in the large armchair facing him. It made his heart jump into his throat and his breathing stop. For a few seconds he thought it was a man staring at him before he realised that what he had mistaken for staring eyes were in fact the empty sockets of a well-rotted corpse. He still couldn't see the face in detail because the little light that escaped through the curtains had turned the bulk of the chair and body into shadowed outlines. Right now, the body wasn't his concern anyway, and if he was honest, he didn't care to look at it in too much detail, anyway.

As he stepped forward, there was a crunching underfoot. Dead blowflies. That meant the body had been rotting for weeks.

Gut instinct told him there was nothing alive in the flat besides the flies and their maggots. He'd felt this feeling before when entering properties where he was the only person alive. It was a stillness that embalmed the air in a room with the weight of death. Not something he'd ever try to explain to anyone, a bit too woo-woo for his liking, but he felt it. Nevertheless, he had to be absolutely sure. Check every room in case a boy was being held captive here.

The smell was overwhelming. Sickly sweet, it clawed at Jack's nose and throat. He could taste it on the back of his tongue, and his stomach bile burnt as it battled to stay inside. He could almost feel it sink into his hair and clothes, a heavy weight of stench.

He progressed carefully, but also as fast as he could, desperate to get out of there. All the time he tried to relay his progress so Oaks and the rest of the team were kept informed—but it wasn't easy.

'A deceased male in the sitting room with plenty of evidence of blowfly activity and advanced putrefaction.'

His voice came out breathless and broken, the smell getting to his vocal cords and settling in his lungs. He was trying to take the minimum breaths possible to avoid sucking in the putrid air.

To the left of the corpse was a door that led into a bedroom. Jack walked in. He pushed the door with a gloved fingertip so as not to contaminate prints. A bed. A wardrobe. A chest of drawers.

He looked inside the wardrobe and peered under the bed.

Clear.

Back past the corpse to the other door. Same routine. Same setup. A bed. A wardrobe. A chest of drawers.

Clear.

Back out. The open-plan galley kitchen, nowhere to hide, but he checked the cupboards, anyway.

The bathroom. Also clear.

Jack sucked in a quick breath of air. 'Alex?' he called out into the empty flat. It was definitely more of a forlorn shout than a hopeful one. His ears strained to hear the slightest noise. A muffled cry. The sound of fabric rubbing against a hard material. Any sign of life. But there was nothing except the buzzing of the flies.

Jack walked straight back out through the front door, trying to follow the exact path he'd used to enter. Then he closed it. Shut the door on the stench, the flies, and the ghastly vision of the rotting corpse behind him. A scene he'd carefully averted his eyes from. It was a vision he didn't want in detail in his head, because it was one that even a cursory glance could tell him would stay in his memory forever.

'Call Barker and get SOCO down here now,' he told Oaks, his voice cracked and breathy with the effort of trying to hold his breath inside the flat. Oaks was wiping his mouth. He'd clearly been sick while Jack had been inside the flat, but he didn't draw attention to it.

'You're right,' Jack addressed the estate manager, who was peering at him from the end of the corridor. 'It's not drains.'

As he watched the attractive forensics crime-scene manager, Dr Tanya Jones, get suited up ready to enter the flat, DS Salter felt almost guilty. 'It's not pleasant in there,' he told her.

She smiled at him, but only out of politeness. 'It's okay. It's my job,' she replied, and he immediately felt chaste, as though he'd insulted her intelligence and experience. Of course it was her job; she must be used to stuff like this. How sexist had that comment sounded? He made a mental note not to say anything like that again to her. But even so, what she was going to find in there wasn't your average deceased body. He'd have said the same thing, even if she'd have been a bloke. Inside the flat was the stuff of nightmares.

The SOCO team prepared to open the door. They had nets for the flies, which could still be heard buzzing around the flat, and would dive into the corridor again within seconds. Some of them would be euthanised and kept as vital entomological evidence, along with the scooped-up carcasses of their dead cousins on the floor. If they could see how many fly life cycles were present in the flat, it would help date the death.

As the door to the flat was pushed open, dozens of them rushed at freedom and light again and flew straight into the nets, although quite a few dodged their prospective captors and ended up buzzing at Jack and the rest of the team in the corridor. He swatted them away. The thought of one landing on him after what it had just been sitting on and eating turned his stomach.

Tanya Jones wore full-face protection, including an anti-odour mask, and was completely suited. She was still a little annoyed at DS Salter's comment, like she was some fragile female he had to protect. She wasn't sure why it annoyed her so much, but she thought it was probably because it was him who'd said it, with his overall machismo attitude. If DCI Barker or Dr Lane had made the same comment, she'd have just felt like they were keeping an eye out for her. Lots of police officers struggled with the smell; it was because they were literally in and out after about five minutes. Her team had to work with it sometimes for hours on end. They got used to it, although there was no doubt it was much more pleasant to wear an anti-odour mask. Nobody would breathe that stench by choice.

The presence of so many flies was indicative of what she might find inside. As she stepped into the hallway, her foot crunched on the carcasses of their dead predecessors. Just outside the door of the flat, Jack gave an internal shudder at the sound of her footsteps and the memory of what he'd seen.

'The victim has been dead for weeks,' she called out, 'We've not only got adult flies, but dead adult flies.' As Tanya proceeded, a photographer walked with her, taking images of the scene before them. Another member of her team was already scooping up fly carcasses so they could determine how many generations had lived and died.

'Going to be a long shot, I know, but we need to confirm if it's Cameron Platt or his father asap,' Jack called to her from outside. He saw the flashes from the camera lighting up the doorway. Anytime now, Tanya and the photographer would come across the corpse, the image of which still sat in his mind's eye. At least his view had been in the semi-darkness. She would see it in full flash-lit glory.

Tanya knew DS Salter had already made sure the flat was safe, and there was no one alive—apart from the buzzing insects. They raced around her, confused by the sudden flashes and the entry of light into their dark, enclosed prison. Nevertheless, there was a definite cold chill in her spine. She got that sometimes, not because of the presence of death, that was a mechanical process which held no surprises to her. It was the spirit of evil which permeated into the fabric of the flat and made her shudder.

She could see where Jack had walked up the short corridor into the flat, squashed flies showed the trail of his feet. She also knew the body was directly in front of her in the sitting room. He'd described the layout, and as she and her team slowly progressed, preserving evidence, covering the floor with protective plates as a walkway, she steadily took step after step towards it.

Tanya had seen a multitude of deceased humans in her career, some brutally murdered or having suffered horrific injuries in accidents. She'd attended the results of beheadings and train suicides, drownings, and fires. She'd seen the mortal remains of individuals in every stage of decay, from early rigor mortis to almost skeletal. What she saw in front of her now caused even her to let out a quiet gasp of shock, which sent waves down to her stomach and back up again.

In front of her was a black, rotted corpse in an armchair. Its stomach ruptured from decomposition and covered with a layer of wriggling creamy white flesh. She hadn't needed to step any closer to know that this flesh wasn't human; it was fly larvae eating away at whatever was left of the soft tissues. The ghastliest part of this scene, though, wasn't the natural process of decay, but the fact that on top of the now lopsided head was a pair of red plastic devil's horns, the kind you get at a joke shop at Halloween. Underneath the hollowed-out sockets, which had once contained the man's eyes, the jaw was fully extended and what looked like a copy of the *Bible* had been shoved into his mouth. It looked horrific. It looked as though evil had been here.

'Have you seen this?' one of her team asked, breaking the spell the corpse had placed on her. She looked to the right, where her colleague was shining his torch onto the walls of the flat. The beam from the torch slowly illuminated what had once been wallpapered walls but which now were covered from floor to ceiling with black writing. Someone had written on every inch with some crazed, but neat graffiti. 'Looks like passages from the *Bible*,' he added.

'Give us a couple of hours to get some initial evidence and lock the place down. Then we'll get you back in here,' Tanya called out to the detectives outside. Her mind went to Harrison Lane. Perhaps it was her coping mechanism, but the horror of the flat receded slightly with the knowledge that he would have to be called in here soon to review what they'd found. It was clearly related to how the boy had been discovered. Question was, who was the corpse?

As Jack stood outside flat sixteen, he thought he wasn't in any hurry to go back in there. SOCO could take as long as they wanted. DC Oaks had already stepped outside for some air again, and after getting his shoes checked over by forensics—so they could eliminate his footprints from the evidence—he went out to join him. He'd reached the fresh air outside just as DCI Barker arrived.

'What we got?' she said seriously. One look at both of her men had already told her whatever it was, it wasn't pleasant.

Jack pulled himself together, took a big breath of fresh air, and pulled out his notebook. 'Spray-paint workshop colleague of a Cameron Platt told us he was weird, kept quoting *Bible* stuff at them, and stopped coming to work about two months back after his dad got sick. When they emptied his locker, it seemed he had an obsession with religion and being possessed by the Devil. We get here and the estate manager's apparently put in a call to say he suspected a dead body in one of his flats due to the smell. Turned out to be the very same address we were given.'

'So this Cameron Platt, you're thinking he might be our man? Or is he the corpse?'

'I think the body is Platt Senior. Neighbours say he was a big man, but Cameron was shorter and slightly built. The corpse was a big guy. They also reported seeing

Cameron a few times over the last couple of months, but no sightings of the father. He was sick, could be natural causes or could be homicide. Too coincidental that the flat is covered in *Bible* quotes all over the walls and Cameron was apparently a good paint sprayer. There's a pair of Devil's horns on the body and a copy of the *Bible* wedged into the mouth. I think Cameron's our man, but he isn't here. No one has seen or heard anyone in that flat for a few weeks.'

'So this might be the trigger that Harrison mentioned, the death of the father,' Barker said. 'Okay, let's throw everything we have at this. We need all known associates, family, friends. He's got to have gone somewhere and not too far away with those boys. Where the hell is he?'

21

S ally Fuller was on a laptop computer at the kitchen table. Her right leg jiggled up and down as her eyes flicked across the screen and her finger scrolled the mouse through her Facebook feed. She searched for news. Mentions. Gossip. Anything.

Around her, the kitchen was full of dirty mugs and plates. She heard Edward's voice in the other room. A murmur of one-way conversation. He was on the phone again. She hadn't tuned into him; his voice was just background hum. Her focus was only on the screen in front of her. Edward had fielded all the calls from concerned friends and relatives because she'd neither the inclination nor time to talk to them. She only cared about one person right now: Alex. Her baby was out there, and she needed to help him.

Sally flicked between Twitter, news sites, and Facebook, where she'd put an appeal for information. Her mobile sat on the table next to her and now and then she checked that too, even though it hadn't made a sound. She hunted through Facebook for local mothers and community groups, requesting to join then posting her plaintive message.

Hi, my name is Sally Fuller, and my seven-year-old boy, Alex, has been taken from us. The police think it's the same man who recently murdered Darren Phillips. Alex was snatched from Fenton High Road at 11 a.m. on Saturday.

Please, please, if you know anyone who might have anything to do with this, if you saw or heard anything, I beg you to get in touch with me or the police.

Our little boy needs us. His little sister misses him. We love him and desperately want him home.

The Facebook alerts racked up in the hundreds, but it was all the same replies and messages,

So sorry. I can't imagine what you're going through.

I hope you find him, it's my worst nightmare.

Some of them weren't so kind. No matter how upset and vulnerable you were, it seemed the internet trolls still picked on you.

Why weren't you watching him? He's seven!!

London gets worse by the day. It's all them immigrants coming in.

One of the local community boards turned into a full-scale row, with several women arguing. It had become a racist slanging match. Amazing how a social group designed to bring people together could encourage such vitriol and spite.

Sally skimmed through all that noise. What would in normal times have had her angry and sad didn't even register.

'Mummy?'

It was Sophie. Her mother had brought her back an hour ago because she'd been pining for them all. What Sally didn't know was that her mother and Edward had discussed it. They hoped it might calm Sally down. Give her the chance to focus on her other child and take her mind off Alex. So far that tactic hadn't worked.

'Mummy?'

Sophie walked up to her mother at the table. She looked pale, her skin almost translucent, as though the sadness had sucked the colour from her. Her favourite doll was with her, and she trailed it by the arm behind her.

'Sophie,' Sally exclaimed as though she'd not seen her until that moment.

'When's Alex coming home?' the little girl asked, her chin crinkling into an impending flood of tears.

Sally couldn't answer. She didn't know what to say, and even if she did, her throat was so tight and constricted, battling down her tsunami of tears, that her words couldn't make it to her mouth.

'Mummy?' Sophie asked again.

Sally reached out and touched her daughter's cheek. She gulped back the tears.

'Soon, honey,' she replied.

'I miss him,' Sophie said.

Sally had no reply.

'Are you hungry?' It was all she could think of to say.

Sophie shook her head.

Another message flashed up on the screen, and Sally's eyes went to it.

Sophie stood there for a few more moments watching her mother. Her little shoulders had sagged; she was as lifeless as the doll she carried.

She stood by the table for a while longer, but Sally was engrossed in whatever it was she'd seen on her laptop. Sophie silently turned and wandered out of the room.

At some point, Sally looked up and saw she had gone. Guilt flooded through her again, but Sophie was safe. She was here. They had to prioritise Alex.

In the next room, Edward finished the phone call, and there was the sound of him talking to Sophie before a cartoon voice dominated the background. He'd put the TV on, and Sophie was now curled up on the sofa, watching a pink-haired cartoon girl with a mouse, cat, dog, and a walking hunk of cheese. When a boy joined them, Edward hoped that wouldn't remind her of Alex, but there was no reaction. She'd zoned out. He figured she was probably exhausted, like they all were.

He'd just come off the phone with his sister. Having to explain the series of events to her then deal with his own and her emotional response had been draining. His throat was dry; he needed a drink.

Edward went to the kitchen where he found his wife hunched over her keyboard. He saw the tension in her rigid body, shoulders up by her ears. He was concerned about her. She'd become obsessive, worried the police weren't doing enough to find their son.

He walked up behind her, but she didn't even acknowledge his presence. She was looking at Twitter, typing in hashtags and keywords: #kidnapping #crime #murder #missingboy. Edward gently put his hands on Sally's shoulders and attempted to rub them. She shrugged him off.

'Sweetheart, give that a rest for a bit. They're looking for him,' he said to her.

'They haven't found him yet, though, have they? Like they didn't find Darren until it was too late. I can't sit and do nothing.'

'You'll wear yourself out. We have to stay strong.'

'Strong? What for? We have to find him. That's all. No matter what.' She looked at him as though he were a total stranger.

Edward sighed and waited a few moments longer, not

knowing what more to say. She'd transformed into an android-like replica of his wife. His Sally—the funny, loving, vivacious woman—had gone. Now there was a wax facsimile of her, without the colour and warmth of his wife. This Sally was driven by a cold, determined force that made her operate on nerves alone. She hadn't brushed her hair or attempted to put on any make-up, but most importantly, her eyes didn't look at him or Sophie. She didn't seem to even see them.

He understood. Alex was his son too. But they were at different ends of the spectrum. It was as though all the energy of their fears and loss were channelled into Sally. He felt as though his guts had been ripped out. Perhaps it was the guilt. It had already hollowed him out with its accusations. Why hadn't he protected his son? How could he have let another man snatch him? He was there. Alex had been yards away from him, and he'd done nothing to save him.

'Sally, take a break. Go sit with Sophie for a bit. She needs you too,' he tried again.

She turned and looked at him properly this time, her eyes pools of despair.

'I have to do something. I have to believe he's out there safe and he's coming home. If I stop, all I see is him crying. Frightened. Calling out for us. Asking why we don't come.'

She didn't wait for his response; she just turned back to the laptop and carried on her endless scrolling.

Edward made them both a cup of tea. He put Sally's on the kitchen table and poured Sophie a glass of milk. In his despair, that was all he could manage.

22

Harrison was deep in thought as he parked his bike in the Lewisham Police car park. He was frustrated. There were things he knew he'd forgotten, things that had happened before his mother's death, but he'd been too young or he'd blanked them out. He had pieces, but it was like trying to finish a jigsaw puzzle so you could work out what the picture should be—only too many pieces were missing.

What angered him the most, though, was the fact that his last memory of her was of her hanging dead from a tree. It was like some magnetic force in his mind. All the other memories that surfaced regularly were negative ones relating to her death. The times they'd spent having fun, swimming in the sea, walking in the fields, cuddling up on the sofa or in bed. All those memories were gone, barricaded in, or had been shoved out by his overriding obsession to find her killer.

Harrison's phone buzzed in his jacket pocket. It was DCI Barker saying they'd had a breakthrough. They'd found where the suspect lived, along with his deceased father. She wanted him in the incident room in fifteen minutes. Harrison hoped it really was a breakthrough, and they were close to catching the killer and getting Alex back to his family.

He checked to see what other emails he'd had. Tanya had sent the *Bible* texts they'd found in Darren's mouth. Harrison was eager to see them, so he stood in the car park for a few minutes, scrolling through the report.

The images of the actual paper weren't easy to read. Some of the ink had been smudged, and the writing was tiny and juvenile, but forensics had typed it out for legibility. As Harrison looked at the writing, his heart and mind returned to Louise Phillips and the boy who lay cold in a mortuary body bag.

It had been a depressing morning. He hated confrontations like he'd just had with the lads in Nunhead. It was soul destroying seeing young men whose mentality in life was violence and using it to take what they wanted. That's why he found teaching Taekwondo so rewarding. The ethos of martial arts was one of self-control and using your mind, not your fists. Even so, they'd lost one of their lads a year back; he'd been stabbed in a gang fight. Such a waste.

Harrison needed an antidote for the ugliness of the morning, so he decided to go see Tanya to run through the report. He told himself it was purely a distraction, even though he wasn't a man who usually did distractions.

He found her in the lab working. Her hair was pulled back by one of those elastic band things women wear to make ponytails, and she had on a pale-blue lab coat that was surprisingly complimentary to her figure and her flawless skin.

Harrison wasn't a man who could creep into a room,

not that he was noisy, just that there was a presence about him. Tanya had been concentrating on a specimen under a microscope, but she knew he'd walked in before she'd even looked up.

Perhaps it was his tall, muscular physique, which took up more space in the room than the average person. Or maybe it was something else, something she couldn't describe as a scientist. An aura, an atmosphere he carried.

Apart from his looks, he was different from any other man she'd ever met. There was an intensity about him that in another person would be intimidating, but because it was paired with an understated gentleness, it took on a protective quality.

She was glad she'd just been to the toilet, ready for the briefing in the incident room, and had spotted a smear of soot that had been on her face from where she'd been examining something from an arson case earlier. When she looked up and greeted him, she could do so with confidence, knowing her make-up was refreshed.

'Dr Jones,' Harrison greeted her.

'Oh, Tanya, please,' she replied. There was a little more confidence in her reply than usual, which surprised her. Perhaps she was getting used to his enigmatic presence.

At that moment, Harrison realised he didn't really have any reason to come see her. It almost threw him.

'I got your email with the sheets,' he said.

'Do you want to have a look at them?' she asked. 'I think they should be read along with some of the writing on the wall of the flat.'

He felt grateful she'd given him a way out, but he must have looked quizzical about the flat because she qualified it.

'I've just come back from the Platt flat. Not pleasant,'

she explained. 'Left the rest of the team there, but the walls were covered in *Bible* graffiti. Almost certainly our man.'

Tanya walked over to a laptop on a bench, took off her gloves, and typed in her password. Immediately a gallery of photographs came on the screen: images of a small, dingy flat with black writing all over the walls.

'You were right about the trigger,' she said. 'The father died, which seems to have coincided with our suspect going off the rails. DS Salter is on his way back. He's got more information, but you should read some of the writing before we go up to the meeting.'

Despite having to stand right next to her, Harrison pushed away his thoughts of Tanya and focussed on the images in front of him.

Do you not know that the unrighteous will not inherit the kingdom of God? Do not be deceived: neither the sexually immoral, nor idolaters, nor adulterers, nor men who practice homosexuality, nor thieves, nor the greedy, nor drunkards, nor revilers, nor swindlers will inherit the kingdom of God.

For all who are led by the Spirit of God are sons of God.

It went on and on, over every single wall of the sitting room. Harrison felt the warmth of Tanya's body next to him and her breath on his cheek. He stepped back and away quickly. He was losing his focus; he had to remain professional.

'Thank you,' he told her. 'This confirms what I'd thought, along with the pages that were found with Darren.'

Tanya looked up at him and nodded. Right now, he could say anything he wanted; she'd still nod at him. He smelt of fresh air and leather with an undertone of sandalwood, a treat for her nose after the stench she'd endured at the Platt flat.

'We'd better get upstairs,' he said.

She wondered if he ever chilled out. She'd certainly love to try to get him to.

23

R yan was in his default position, sitting in his chair surrounded by computer screens and snacks. He was engrossed in something. His fingers moved across the keyboard faster than his body could ever react. His glasses reflected the flickering light of the screens.

From the corridor came the sound of footsteps, and then the door was flung open. DS Salter rudely disturbed Ryan's concentration as he burst into the office. He was animated, his eyes alive.

'Where is he?' Jack asked Ryan.

Ryan raised his eyebrows at the abruptness of the question.

'Out.'

'Out where?'

'Dunno. He didn't say.'

'We're in the middle of a murder enquiry. What's his mobile number?'

'I can give it to you, but he might be on his bike.'

'Bloody hell.' Salter made no attempt to hide his exasperation.

Ryan watched him, could almost see the turmoil boiling in Salter's head as he tried to work out what to do next. He turned as if to walk out then changed his mind and walked over to Ryan. He found the only tiny bit of clear space on his desk and sat down, perched on the edge.

Ryan stopped what he was doing and looked pointedly at him, decidedly unhappy that his personal space was being invaded.

'So what's he like to work for?'

'Fine.'

'Fine? Come on. The guy's strange.'

'That guy saved my life. If it weren't for him, I'd have been space dust years ago. He's just quieter than most.'

'Quieter… that's one way of putting it,' Jack humphed.

'He's a good bloke,' Ryan qualified again, and looked directly into Salter's blue eyes. Despite being bloodshot and tired, they stared back at him, but he didn't budge.

'Fine.' Realising he was getting nowhere, Salter sprang off the desk and headed towards the door.

'When he decides to show up, tell him the boss wanted him in her office, and I doubt she's going to be happy with him for being AWOL. I'm not covering his arse.'

'Okey dokey,' Ryan said with as much disrespect as he dared.

Salter turned and glared at him as he walked out.

'This is what happens when civilians do police work,' he spat back.

Ryan sighed. Time to take a chill pill and cool your beans, DS Salter. When he was sure he'd gone, he picked up his mobile and texted Harrison. '*Salter's on the warpath looking for you. The DCI wants you in her office now.*'

He smiled when he put the phone down then went back to his computer screen. Harrison always kept his phone on, day and night, and Ryan had a tracking app on it. He always knew exactly where his boss was, but he wasn't going to tell Jack Salter that.

HARRISON AND TANYA arrived at DCI Barker's office just before Jack Salter returned to the incident room. They'd already taken their seats at the table when he walked in, and Harrison had no idea why he received the glare he got from the DS.

'You up with the latest, Harrison?' DCI Barker asked as he came into her office. She was halfway through a pack of Maltesers.

'I've read the initial report, yes,' he confirmed.

Jack shot him another disdainful look.

'Okay, let's see where we are with this.' DCI Barker waved Sergeant Steve Evans in. He joined them at the table, along with two other detectives. Everyone else was out. 'So, first, well done, Jack, for coming up trumps and finding who our man is. There's no doubt in my mind that Cameron Platt is who we're looking for. The issue we have is where the hell he is.' She looked around the table at her team, knowing she was stating the obvious. 'Jack, you've been collating the latest intel. What do we know about the Platts?'

'Platt Senior paid one visit to the doctor where cancer was confirmed,' DS Salter said. 'It was advanced, and he refused treatment, said God would take care of him. That was around six months ago. Doc reckons he'd only had around three to four months to live untreated. Looks like that was quite accurate, as it seems the smell had been evident for some weeks. 'Neighbours say they complained several times, but the manager, like a lot of them, was wary of Platt Senior and thought the smell would just go away. But once he'd got a complaint of a stain coming on the ceiling into the downstairs flat, he finally plucked up the courage to investigate. He realised it was more than a blocked drain and called it in, but we were already on the way there after speaking to a colleague of Cameron's at the spray-paint shop.'

'So what kind of people are they?' She looked around the table.

'Neighbours said they kept themselves to themselves,' Sergeant Evans said. 'After the dad gave up work, they rarely saw him around. Seems he stayed in the flat most of the time, unless it was to go outside and shout at them to be quiet. Jabba they called him, like the big fat one from *Star Wars*. The son is the opposite. Small bloke, thin. He did all the shopping, and although he wasn't friendly, neighbours had seen him around the place up until a few weeks ago. We're still on the door to doors, so I'm hoping we might get more information.'

'Relatives? Friends?'

'None of the neighbours ever saw any visitors. The mother disappeared decades ago.'

'You're trying to track her down, I assume?'

'Yes, ma'am.'

'Great. So likely natural causes for death with Platt Senior.' DCI Barker nodded. 'And Cameron Platt?'

'No previous, but we've got the DNA back from the Darren scene, so that'll be cross-referenced with the flat. There are no mobile phones registered to him or his father. We're chasing bank records now. No vehicles registered to him, but that doesn't mean the van isn't his. He has no known friends, or close family. The guy was a complete loner with no links to anywhere else in the country or round here. We've drawn a blank so far on where he could have gone.'

Barker looked at Harrison and raised her eyebrows to cue him.

'From what we have so far, the Platts were very religious,' said Harrison. 'That's pretty obvious from all the *Bible* quotes on the walls, but the *Bible* shoved into the father's mouth along with the Devil's horns are more interesting. We need to ask the neighbours about his childhood. I suspect the father was harsh, perhaps abusive, emotionally rather than sexually. His death has triggered something in Cameron, which isn't unusual in relationships where an overbearing person suddenly dies. Why take the boys? I'm not sure yet. I think it's their relationship—his and his dad's—that's key. We need to look into the father as well as Cameron.'

Barker nodded. 'So we know who he is but we're no closer to finding him. A ghost! I'm going to use the press, put out a call for information. They'll need food. Can you both work together on interviewing everyone who knew him? We need a list of potential sites to search by this afternoon. We have to turn this neighbourhood upside down until we find them. He's had Alex for forty-eight hours now. We're running out of time.'

'I'll get on it now.' Harrison got up to leave.

'Thanks for your help earlier with Mrs Fuller,' DCI Barker said before he left.

'She all right?'

'As good as she's going to be until we bring her boy home.'

Harrison gritted his teeth and left along with Tanya and the other three officers. DS Salter hung back.

'Everything all right, Jack?' DCI Barker asked.

'Not really. I can't get hold of Marie. She's not picking up at home or on her mobile.'

Barker frowned. 'I need your full focus on the job.

There's a boy's life at risk. If you need time off, I'll have to pull someone else in.'

'No, I know, I'll sort it, Sandra. I mean it. Just need an hour to make sure they're okay.'

'Be quick and get it sorted. You can't go on like this. Get some help for her.'

Jack left her office, head hung. She was right, he knew he couldn't go on like this. His stomach was a tight-fisted knot of anxiety. He wasn't eating, wasn't sleeping, and wasn't focussing on his job. Something had to change.

24

D S Salter drove home as fast as he could, legally or not. He'd tried Marie again, but there was still no answer. His anxiety levels were through the roof. He'd seen it before, walked in on scenes where mothers had been suffering from post-natal depression—invariably younger women and very young children; it was heartbreaking stuff you never forgot. He'd tried to talk himself down on the journey home. Kept telling himself his paranoia was because he was a police officer and he'd been exposed to some of the worst sides of life. He felt as though he were betraying Marie whenever those bad thoughts came into his head, but he couldn't lose them. He had to get home and see for himself.

When he reached the house, he pulled up on the garage ramp and peered at the front. Their bedroom was at the back, so he couldn't see if the curtains were closed. He knew he'd opened the ones in the sitting room before he'd left for work that morning, but had Marie got up since?

Jack strained to hear something as he rushed towards

the front door. There were no sounds other than the bin men banging and clanging a couple of streets away. The house gave away nothing.

He plunged the key into the lock and let himself in.

Silence.

Immediately he went into investigation mode. He clocked that the baby's pushchair sat folded in the hallway and Daniel's coat was hung up next to Marie's. They hadn't gone out. So why was Marie not answering any of his calls? He'd tried the house and her mobile. Panic rose from the pit of his stomach.

'Marie? Marie?' he called out.

He burst into the sitting room. Empty. He spotted a crumpled nursing cloth from where Marie had fed their son and a cold empty cup that had once contained her tea.

The kitchen. Empty again. The silence hurt his ears, its presence foreboding. Surfaces that had been messy and full of dirty dishes yesterday were cleaned and empty. It shouldn't have, but that made him worry more. He'd seen homes like this. Organised. Cleaned. Prepared and ready.

He sprinted up the stairs, two at a time.

First room at the top was Daniel's. Empty.

Their bedroom door was closed.

He hesitated, fear strafing his spine and sending hot metal into his heart.

Jack breathed deeply then held his breath.

He opened the door.

On the bed was Marie and next to her their baby.

They were both still. Eyes closed.

His eyes caught sight of the bottle of sleeping pills on the bedside table. He'd forgotten to move them. So tired and preoccupied last night.

'Marie? Marie?' he called to her.

They didn't move.

He rushed across to the bed and shook Marie first. She groaned. Then he picked up their son.

'Marie, what have you done?'

Marie came to with shock, just as the baby kicked off, crying after being so rudely awoken.

'What are you doing, Jack? Why are you waking him?' Panic was written all over her face. Her heart was beating so fast and hard that her skin had paled. The blood drained from it. 'You frightened me. I'd just managed to get him to sleep.'

Jack's heart was also racing, his breathing shallow and rapid. For a moment he thought he might pass out. He slumped down onto the bed, cradling his son to him. Relief first, then shock that he had reacted like that. What was wrong with him? He was so tired. So stressed.

'I thought you were…' He felt ashamed to even say the words, as though he'd betrayed his wife.

'Thought we were what? Why are you even home at this time?'

'I'm sorry,' he whispered, and bent his head so his lips touched Daniel's soft hair. He kissed him and breathed in the smell of him.

'Oh, my God, did you think we… I'd…?'

'You didn't answer the phone. I called the house phone and your mobile.'

'We were in the garden and went for a walk. I thought some fresh air might make him tired. It did.'

Jack comforted his crying son, his own eyes welling up as he rocked him back and forth. He couldn't carry on like this. He was going to lose his job. Hell, he was going to lose his mind if they didn't sort this out. He kissed his son's forehead again and looked at his wife.

'I'm worried about you, Marie. You won't talk to me. I can't focus on work because all I think about is you and

Daniel and whether you're both okay. I feel guilty being at work, but I can't be here all the time.'

He tried to look into Marie's eyes, but she turned away and rose from the bed. Her shoulders were hunched. She turned her back to him and went to stand at the window. Jack strained to see her face reflected in the glass, but the pale light and her pale complexion merged so there was nothing but a ghostly outline of her figure. Marie's black hair hung limp and lifeless. She'd not bothered with her appearance since before the birth. Jack didn't care if she wore make-up or if she brushed her hair or put ribbons in it. He just wanted her back, the woman he'd fallen in love with. The woman on the inside. She seemed to have been subsumed by someone else. Where had she gone?

He waited. He'd had enough experience interviewing people who were distressed to know you couldn't force them to speak. Jack wanted her to want to talk to him.

Finally, she did. 'I'm scared, Jack. It's not meant to be like this.' Her voice was thin and strained. He could hear the tears in her eyes. 'I'm a bad mother. There's something wrong with me. I don't think I can do it.'

'Of course you can,' he countered. 'You just need time and some help.'

Marie spun round, panicked. 'Help? No, you can't tell anyone. Promise me. Please. My mother brought up four of us, your mother three, and our friends have babies without any problems. They'll all think I'm useless.'

Jack's face dropped, and tears threatened to spill onto Daniel's forehead. Their son had calmed down now, so he reached out for the rubber soother toy and lay him in the middle of the bed where he could kick his legs and gurgle at the ceiling.

Then he went over to the other person he loved more than anyone else in the world.

He touched her shoulder to turn her around. 'Sweetheart, you aren't well—that's all. There are other women who feel like this. You know that. It's not your fault.'

'But you think I'm a bad mother too. You thought I'd harm our son.'

'I don't think you're a bad mother, Marie. I don't.'

'I am. I am a bad mother, but I still love him. I just don't *like* him, and I don't know how to be his mum.'

She turned to him at last, tears pouring down her face. It broke his heart to see her like this. He wanted to look away from her pain; it was so raw, but at least she was showing some emotion. What he couldn't take was when she was like she'd been last night, silent and unresponsive.

'Why me, Jack?' She looked up into his face, pleading. 'Why can't I be like Trudy or Milly? Her baby, Evan, was ill for weeks, and she just dealt with it.'

'You can't blame yourself. It'll get better. Do you feel you've made any progress at all?'

They both looked over to the bed, and the little boy who wriggled, oblivious to his parents' anguish.

'Maybe a little.'

'It was a long and traumatic birth, Marie. It must have had an impact on you. You need to give yourself a break. Please let me call your mum.'

Marie grabbed him and held the tops of his arms with her hands.

'Promise me, promise me you won't. That you won't tell anyone.'

Jack's mind went to DCI Barker, and a sliver of guilt wriggled through him.

'Jack?'

He didn't know how to respond. He wanted her to get help, wanted this anxiety to end so they could get on with their lives. He wanted his wife and child to bond and be happy. Should he force her and be tough? Or would that do more damage? She stared at his face, searching for his response.

He didn't have time to try to voice his feelings because his mobile rang.

'I'd better see who that is. It might be work. Might be important,' he said, and then felt guilty, as though what they were doing right then wasn't important. It was. It was everything to him, but he also had a responsibility to another family. He took the phone from his pocket.

It was DC Oaks.

'David?' Jack said and watched as Marie walked away from him and back to the bed, where Daniel had just started to grumble after becoming bored with kicking at the air. Jack tried to concentrate on what DC Oaks was saying, but he was watching Marie intently. She sat on the bed and looked at their son. He could see she was trying to fall in love with him. Willing it with every fibre of her being.

He hadn't heard a word that David had said to him, but he got the punch line.

'There's a lock-up Cameron Platt uses. Someone's come forward from the media appeal and tipped us off. They're pulling a Tactical team together now.'

25

Harrison was looking at the photographs taken at the Marion Estate flat, trying to decipher what the *Bible* graffiti meant. He sat putting together a full profile of Cameron Platt. What drove him? What were his motivations and their history? All in a desperate attempt to work out where he might have gone.

His mobile rang. It was a detective inspector from one of the other MITs who'd found herself with an unusual crime scene. The body of a young Brazilian woman had been discovered in a house, and another girl with her was hysterical and trying to harm herself. She was behaving as though she was possessed. The family who owned the house were away for a long weekend, and it had been the dog sitter who'd come across the girls. The SIO had requested that he come view the scene. It was an urgent operational query, and as he needed a change of thought process, he agreed.

When Harrison arrived at the address in Dulwich, he found it to be an immaculate town house in a wealthy street that boasted a couple of celebrities as its residents.

The SIO was pacing the pavement, talking on her mobile. As soon as she saw Harrison pull up, she ended her call.

'Dr Lane, DI Dipika Chowdhury.' She extended her hand to him. She was a petite woman with long black hair scraped back from her face and tied up. It accentuated her delicate bone structure and large brown eyes. Today those eyes looked worried, and they took in Harrison with relief.

'I'm so glad you could make it at such short notice,' she said. 'We need a quick steer on this one. We have one deceased female, and another who's currently sedated at the hospital, but screaming that she's been possessed and is going to die. The medics and I need to know what we're dealing with here. The family is away for a few days and not due back until tomorrow. They're Brazilian nationals, and the man's well connected. I don't want to contact them until I have an idea if they're a flight risk. The girls were discovered by the dog walker, who heard noises coming from upstairs and went to investigate.'

'Okay, has forensics finished?'

'They're still in there, but we can go in. Shall we?' DI Chowdhury motioned for Harrison to enter the house.

'If you don't mind, I'd rather go in alone. I find it's easier to assess the situation.'

DI Chowdhury looked a little taken aback but nodded. 'Of course.' She'd heard that Dr Lane had a slightly different approach. 'I'll make sure everyone gives you the space you need.'

'Thank you,' he said, then turned to look at the house.

She watched him, nothing like what she had expected with his credentials. He was handsome too. Strong. She might have only just met him, but she could see he didn't give much away. He had eyes like traction beams, though. When he looked at her, she couldn't look away. If she didn't have Mr Chowdhury at home, she'd be sorely

tempted to see what Dr Harrison Lane got up to out of
work. She watched him put on a forensic suit and
overshoes and log in with the crime-scene manager before
standing in the doorway for a few moments and heading
inside.

The hallway was like that of any other wealthy house
you might enter. Immaculate with a mahogany table and
mirror. Harrison scanned the walls and floors, opening the
drawers of the table, which were empty. The hallway led to
a neat, understated dining room on the left, set up for
formal dinner parties and clearly decked out to impress. To
the right of the hall, a sitting room with leather sofas and
plush carpets. To Harrison it smacked of show-house,
neat, uncharacteristic decor. There were a couple of
photographs of the family—two small children and the
parents—but it was a sterile environment. Was this a family
trying to distance itself from its Brazilian roots, or were
they trying to cover something up? He saw no evidence of
Catholic or Christian beliefs. No evidence of any religion.

He progressed into the kitchen, careful to only step on
the areas marked out by forensics. In here it was obvious
where the children spent most of their time. A small square
table was set up in one corner; it contained paintbrushes
and paper, along with a stack of storybooks. Next to the
table were a couple of boxes with colourful toys. There was
also another table, which looked like where the family ate.
Salt and pepper and chilli sauce sat in the middle. The
kitchen was immaculate as well. Two empty dog beds were
by the Aga, and all the surfaces were spotless and empty.

Harrison scanned the entire room. Kids' drawings were
stuck neatly to the walls like an art gallery, and a couple of
other creations, obviously from the children, were on the
big American style fridge in the corner. Anyone coming
into this house would think they were the perfect family. If

the dog walker had to come into the house, that's exactly what she would have thought—until she went upstairs.

Harrison headed back to the hall. This was a three-storey town house, and the next level contained the master bedroom; two other bedrooms, which were clearly where the children slept; and a family bathroom. All rooms also had en suites with showers. Harrison looked around quickly. This floor was exactly the same as the ground floor. Show-home tidy. He didn't waste much time. It was the upper floor, contained by a lockable door, where he knew he'd find the real answers.

Smell was the first sense that alerted him. He smelled death, relatively fresh, not overbearing yet, but it was definitely in the air. But there was another odour. He had an idea what it was but needed more evidence. As he arrived on the top floor, the tone of the house changed completely. The walls in the upper corridor were covered in grotesque masks and imagery depicting spirits taking possession of the living, faces painted as skulls, and wooden effigies. Harrison noted the bulbs in the ceiling lamps had all been removed, which meant whoever came up here would have to pass these wall hangings in semi-darkness.

The first room he came to was a small bathroom, certainly not like the luxury en suites he'd seen downstairs, but instead a cracked basin and ancient bath with no shower. Two thin towels hung from nails in the wall, and there were no mirrors.

He went farther down the corridor and into a room that had a dormer for natural light—at least it should do if the large board covering placed across it was taken down. In the middle of the room, at the back, was a small wooden shrine. On the top were rows of candles bookended by two human skulls. Two black dolls sat on either side of the lower ledge on which a beheaded pigeon lay; plaster statues surrounded them. One of them Harrison recognised as the Orixa Omolu or Omulu, a long-haired god feared and revered in the African-Brazilian religions such as Macumba.

Feathers lay scattered on the floor, evidence of previous sacrifices, and coloured candles skirted the edges of the room. Even more concerning, on the floor two flogging whips lay like snakes among the feathers, and on either side large metal rings were attached to the walls.

Harrison took all this in. He also noticed the slight stain around the air grille at the top of the rear wall behind the shrine. When he looked behind him, towards the door, there was a round hole high up in the wall opposite.

There was one more room to visit on this level. It too had a lock on the outside and was the source of the smells that had hit him the moment he'd arrived on the floor. The forensics team had pulled back from the room when they'd seen him come up, so it was empty—at least of the living.

The first smell emanated from the dead girl lying on a bed against the far wall, and another smell came from the rotting goat's head placed on a table underneath what would have been the window, had it not also been boarded up. The other bed was empty, but Harrison saw smears of blood on the pillowcase and some white, chalk-like marks on the blanket. There was a bucket in the far corner with a lid, which he assumed to be the toilet. Next to the goat's head was a large empty jug, and Harrison located two empty glasses by the girls' beds.

He approached the dead girl. She could have only been around nineteen or twenty. She looked thin and undernourished, her skin the colour of fear. Her clothes were worn, and around her neck was a protective talisman. She was curled up, fetal-like, and the look on her face wasn't one of peace. Harrison silently muttered an expletive at the people who had done this. Her neck showed signs of abrasion, as did her left ankle.

He sighed, mindful that their priority had to be the young girl still alive, and crossed the room to sniff at the jug on the table. Straight away he detected what he'd been expecting: a musty fishy smell that hit him at the back of his throat.

Harrison had two more things to check.

In the hallway, he found the muddle of forensics officers waiting for him to finish. 'Have you been into the loft area yet?' he asked them.

'Not yet. It's not been highlighted as a site of interest. We were processing in there first,' an older man replied.

'Is it okay if I stick my head up there? I suspect there's easy access.'

The man shrugged. 'That's fine. You're covered over. What are you expecting to find?'

'Some magic tricks,' Harrison replied.

He pulled the rope for the loft hatch, and as he'd expected, a set of steps unfolded and a light automatically sprang on up above them. Harrison climbed up just far enough to peer into the attic and confirm his theory. The room was used for storage, so there were some boxes on one side, but at the far end, he saw a machine with what looked like a gas canister next to it. He retreated back down.

'You'll want to secure up there as well. It will be critical evidence.'

He didn't wait for the forensics team to question him further, but instead headed straight back downstairs again. DI Chowdhury stood in the hallway, and her face lit up as he came down. It turned into a look of perplexed inquisitiveness when he walked straight past her into the kitchen.

She followed him and watched as he peered out of the kitchen window into the garden. Harrison crossed to the back door. It was locked.

'Is there a key for this?' he asked her.

'It's in the top drawer, just to your right.' DI Chowdhury pointed to a small drawer. Harrison opened it, grabbed the key, and unlocked the door.

She watched from the doorway as he took off his overshoes then headed to the small greenhouse a few metres along on the right-hand side of the neat lawn area.

Harrison peered inside. It was heated, as he'd suspected, and it didn't take him long before he spotted it. A small treelike shrub with delicate fronded leaves.

He spun round to face DI Chowdhury, who had come up behind him, making her jump. 'Okay,' he said. 'You have two victims of modern slavery. The family lives what appears to be a normal, respectable life downstairs, but they keep the two girls captive through fear. This kind of cult-like slavery has grown more prevalent in Brazil.'

DI Chowdhury quickly pulled her notebook from her pocket and busily scribbled down what Harrison said.

'It's some kind of Macumba or Jurema cult variation. Centuries ago these religions were brought to Brazil from Africa with the slaves. In a nutshell, they involve invoking spirits and holding ceremonies where people make offerings and can be possessed by their saints. I suspect the young girl in the hospital had incisions on her head and white spots painted on her body?'

'Yes,' DI Chowdhury said in surprise.

'She was drugged. There's a small shrub in the greenhouse, the mimosa hostilis. Its root bark contains the hallucinogenic drug DMT. I think these girls were given the drink then chained or tied in the room with the shrine. In the attic is a smoke machine, and there's a hole in the wall that can be accessed from the corridor. You'll find some kind of projector somewhere. Or maybe it could even have been done with a mobile phone. They would have projected images onto the smoke and terrified the girls into believing spirits were possessing them. That way neither girl would dare to try to escape or give the game away, even though there were people, like the dog walker, visiting the house.'

'My God, there's a new one every day.' DI Chowdhury shook her head sadly.

'The deceased probably died of a heart attack. The family was obviously worried about leaving them alone all weekend, so they might have ramped up the scare tactics and gone a little too far.'

'That all makes sense. I'll pass on the information to the hospital. That poor girl is going to need psychiatric help as well as medical care. Thank you.' She smiled up at Harrison.

'No problem,' he said and smiled back.

For a few moments, DI Chowdhury forgot she needed to make some arrests.

26

When Harrison left the Dulwich house, he'd every intention of returning to the office, but he saw a road sign that said, NUNHEAD: TWO MILES and found himself pointing his bike in that direction. This connection to the cemetery distracted him. He had so many questions, and it frustrated him that he seemed unable to find any answers.

As he rode up Oakdale Road, he spotted The Nunhead Gardener Shop. Spontaneously, he pulled up and went inside. He knew what he needed. A decent pair of pruning secateurs. He fancied a spot of voluntary gardening.

Within minutes he was back, striding through the cemetery towards the spot where he'd seen the graffiti. It crossed his mind that someone might be there cleaning the tombstones, thus scuppering his plan, but when he arrived, the place was deserted. The volunteers had made a start on the stones, with most of them cleaned up. Just a few areas remained where some black spray paint was still visible.

Harrison felt as though he were about to commit vandalism, but he gave himself a mental talking-to and reasoned with himself. He would be doing them a favour, cutting down some of the brambles and other weeds that had encroached on the graves. He carefully stepped past the tombstones and pushed his way into the undergrowth as far as he could before he needed to start chopping.

He peered through under the canopy of the big tree. It shouldn't take too long to get in, he thought; he could push through part of the way with his bike leathers protecting his arms and legs. He started cutting, holding on to the brambles he'd cut with the blades to pull them out of his way and chopping back other bushes to clear a path through. As he cut, the smell of plant sap triggered a memory. Not a recent one. Not one from here. A memory from before his mother's death. Those memories were so rare that he stopped for a moment and allowed his mind to savour it.

He was with Joe, his stepfather, crouched low to the dusty desert ground in Arizona. Joe had begun to teach him signs, the things you look for when tracking. He'd broken some stems of plants and was getting Harrison to smell them, to recognise how you could tell someone had walked past because of the aroma of a crushed plant. The baking Arizona sun beat down on his head and neck. Joe was explaining that signs aren't just visual like footprints, but also the scents that are carried on the wind or emanate from broken vegetation. This was before Harrison had ever tracked anything. When it had all seemed so bewildering, when the marks in the dust were just marks—not a secret code that showed what kind of animal or man had just walked past. Joe knew it was hard, and he'd been patient. Tracking wasn't like learning his times tables. It's a discipline, a state of mind. Joe was encouraging Harrison to trust the signs and the facts, not to guess at what he would expect to have happened. Our brains look for patterns from experience, it's a necessary trait, helping us interpret our world and the huge number of stimulants and input that we encounter and have to process. A good tracker knows to follow the signs and piece them together based on what he is looking at, not what he expects to see.

Harrison used to look forward to his lessons with Joe in the desert. Ironic that it had taken his mother's death for those teachings to finally click into place and start being used.

The memory was brief but pleasant. It brought a smile to Harrison's lips, and he thought about how he'd not spoken to Joe in a few weeks. He'd have to call him soon. Theirs was the only relationship Harrison had from his childhood. The one man he's always trusted with his life.

For now, there were darker thoughts he needed to follow. His memory of Joe had been a sweetener, a little taste of joy and safety. As he cut through more brambles and got closer to the clearing, Harrison felt a growing dread.

The dread had nothing to do with the tree, which cast its protective arms over the clearing. Something had happened here. Something bad, and he'd been there, witnessed it. Why couldn't he remember it? Harrison peeled back the last of the brambles and stepped into the clearing. It was about ten feet in diameter and probably had been much bigger when he'd been a young child. Leaves covered the ground, fallen one year after another on top of each other. A thick mulch of life that had lived and been shed ever since that night.

He stood for a few moments and tried to think back. Nothing came. Had he wasted his time? Come here on a wild goose chase, just like the Mannings had hoped he would? He listened to the birdsong around him. There'd been no birds back then. They'd arrived at dusk, which had turned into a black night. That much he remembered. The rest?

Harrison walked around the clearing. He knew he was asking a lot of his memory. Not only had he been very young, but it also was a memory hidden behind the trauma of his mother's death. At times it felt like he was standing trying to see over a mile-high wall. There was no way over, no way around, but he could just make out the tantalising sounds of what lay beyond.

He was just about to give up, to struggle back through the gap he'd created, when his foot hit something solid.

He hadn't noticed it before because the carpet of leaves was so thick, and it lay hidden beneath them. The jolt as his foot hit the solid object jarred his body and sent a shockwave to his brain. It was like the long fuse on a bomb. He almost felt the flame travel up from his foot to his head and then *bang*. There it was.

He knew what lay beneath those leaves. He didn't even need to clear them away. It was a flat stone. He saw it, laid bare in the middle of the clearing and illuminated by candles. They were all standing around, his mother in long black robes he had tried hard to hide in. She held his hand so tightly that it hurt. He was scared. Scared by the chanting of the others around him and scared by the shaking of his mother's hand. He knew she was petrified. Even her voice shivered with the fear in her heart.

That flashback appeared in his mind's eye for a split second. He couldn't see faces or details. If he hadn't been here, he might not have even realised where it was. But he knew it had been real. He knew he'd stood here with his mother, afraid of what was about to happen.

Harrison tried to pull more from his mind, but the wall went up again.

He knelt and brushed the leaves away from the stone.

It was flat grey granite. Was it a grave marker? Perhaps that could give him a clue.

He scrabbled around on the clearing floor, tossing the leaves around him, searching for meaning in the bland grey stone. There was nothing. No inscription. No indication of why the stone was there.

Raising himself from the ground, Harrison sighed. He'd confirmed it, but he hadn't explained it. The Mannings had brought him here for a reason. They were definitely there that night. He couldn't see their faces, but he knew. Why were they drawing him back now?

He took one last look around and turned to leave. That's when he saw her. It was almost like a ghost in the clearing, but it was in his mind. A split-second flash of film reel. A woman lying on the stone, blood pumping from her body and spilling over it. The memory kicked him in the stomach, almost made him bend double with its force. This flash of evil was hidden in his mind, but it had shown itself. His self-preservation mode had tried to forget it. To keep it locked away. Now it was out.

Drained, Harrison left a few minutes later. That night was before they'd gone to live with the Tohono O'odham people and Joe in America. He'd always felt as though his mother was escaping something by leaving the UK. Had this been it? For him, though, the biggest question had always been why she went back. Why did she return them both to the centre of her darkness and danger and live with the Mannings? He knew there was only one way to find that out, and that was to track them down and make them tell him.

27

DCI Barker looked at the images on the small screen in front of her. It was of a block of twelve garages, or lock-ups, as they call them now. In her dad's day, when he'd rented one like those, they'd been mostly full of people's prized vehicles and occasionally the odd stash of stolen goods. Nowadays she failed to be surprised by what was found in them. Anything from a mini counterfeiting factory for fashion goods being sold on eBay to a home for migrants and asylum seekers. Like every square inch in London, these were prime real estate, and some had even been turned into illegal housing. Unsafe electrical extension cables ran down gardens to the backs of garages. Last year they'd gone to one that had a family of six living in it. No sanitary facilities, just a bucket. That wasn't a life. Certainly not the life they'd hoped for when they'd escaped the bombing in Syria. Those days on the job made her sad. Others made her angry.

Today she was anxious.

Chief Inspector Graham McDermid was making the final preparations for the operation. He was the Territorial

Support Group commander who was leading the raid on Cameron's lock-up. He hadn't been overly pleased to see DCI Barker arrive in the middle of his operation, but she'd promised to keep out of the way while he and his team did their job. Her boss, Detective Superintendent Robert Jackson, had made the call that the firearms squad wasn't needed. There had been nothing so far to indicate that Cameron Platt had any weapons. Even Darren's death had been nonviolent, so they'd gone with the Territorial Support Group, well used to gaining entry quickly and efficiently during drug raids. They had Tasers on them, as well as the standard issue PAVA spray every officer carried for protection.

If Platt was holed up in garage number five, with young Alex Fuller, then what they needed was the element of surprise. They couldn't give Platt the opportunity to grab the boy and threaten him or kill him. The other option was Alex was in there alone. Question was: in what state? Dead or alive?

Sandra Barker wasn't a religious woman, but it was at times like this that she wished she were. She knew lots of coppers who had some kind of ritual they did before going in on a big job. For her, it was about state of mind. She'd once read a book called *The Secret*, which basically said it's all down to the law of attraction and if you visualise and believe in something enough, you'll get it. If you asked her in the pub if she believed all that, she'd give an 'as if' look and brush it off as nonsense. When faced with life-or-death situations, however, she privately grasped at it. Willing for that garage door to open and reveal a little boy sitting alive and well and waiting to be rescued. Some days she even added in a secret little prayer. Today was one of those days.

CI McDermid had established a perimeter of lookouts

and secured the area, ensuring they weren't caught on the hop if Cameron decided to drive up or walk to his storage unit. Once the operation was about to begin, they'd be boosted by uniformed officers to ensure the public didn't get tangled up and that no one got away.

Two TS guys had done the reccy, scoping out the area and looking at access points, including the lock-up's security, and bringing back the information so a plan could be drawn up. Images of their walk around had been sent to the TV screens in front of CI McDermid and DCI Barker via their body cams.

The garages were all front entrance only. A small alley ran behind them, giving access to the back gardens of the houses behind but no points of entry into the garages themselves. Two young guys were working on a motorbike in unit three, which was two doors down from Platt's unit. Their banter and the sound of the grinders and sanders they were using would be good sound cover. They were going to have to drill the lock to get into Platt's garage, which would mean precious seconds of time when he could hurt the boy. At least with some other noise, they'd gain a few of those back by the time he realised it was his door that was under attack. They couldn't contact the owner of the garage for a spare key, in case he tipped Platt off. Besides, it turned out he was someone well known to them, after more than a few visits to their custody suite; and he was currently residing in Spain. The likelihood of him wanting to assist the police, was slim to say the least.

On the right side of Platt's garage, unit six was empty, its door open and damaged. CI McDermid had considered stationing someone in there and just watching and listening, seeing if Platt ventured out, but it was too risky. If he heard they'd found his flat, he'd know it could be just a matter of time before they came looking for him here.

Alex Fuller could be in there dying right now. They had to act.

Jack Salter caught up with DCI Barker as the team was making its final preparations. Two officers were in position to speak to the young men in lock-up three, and they were to be escorted away from the area and put under watch in a patrol car, just in case they decided to use their mobiles and tell someone. Six officers were making final preparations to their equipment and getting back into the van, which would take them to the entrance of the lock-up area. Joining them was a specialist at gaining entrance to properties. Sergeant Thompson had a flawless reputation in the Met; he'd never failed to open a door in seconds, and he carried the specialist drilling equipment he'd use on the lock.

'All okay?' Sandra asked Jack as he took his place next to her.

He knew she wasn't talking about the enquiry, but with other officers in close proximity she wouldn't voice the exact nature of her question.

'They're fine. Thank you, ma'am,' he replied. She was right; he was going to have to deal with this somehow and soon.

Meanwhile, they both had their eyes glued to the screen, and their ears followed the whispers of the officers as they one-by-one confirmed they were in position and ready to go.

First priority was to remove the two young men from any danger. The officers moved swiftly; two of them took the equipment off them so there was barely a hiccup in the noise, while two others led the shocked men away to safety.

At their unit, the two police officers continued the grinding and sanding noises and spread themselves out a bit farther to be closer to their target. If Platt could see out through his garage door, he wouldn't be able to spot them due to the angle. Having the unit next door empty was helpful; it had given them the chance to work out the size of the units and visibility. They knew just how close they could be before they potentially came into the line of view.

The radios went silent but stayed open for emergencies. It was all sign language now. A well-practiced set of hand movements and facial expressions everyone in the team understood. Watching their colleagues' every move and following the team leader was essential. They all knew it could mean the difference between the success of an operation or its failure—or even the death of one of them. They were ready for anything, adrenaline was pumping. Every single one of them hoped that behind the door of garage number five, they'd find a little boy unharmed.

Silently they approached the garage, careful not to step on anything that might give away their presence. Three came from the left and three from the right. A pincer movement that would ensure the whole garage was covered the second the door was open.

The two officers at unit three stepped up the sanding and grinding noise. As Barker and Salter followed the action, they watched Sergeant Thompson shoot out from the blind side of unit five with his large lock drill. He had it in position and the lock was demobilised within seconds.

It all happened really fast after that.

Warnings shouted. All six officers converged in a coordinated movement, Tasers ready as the garage door was flung up.

On the screens in front of Barker and Salter, they saw beams of white from the searchlights as the officers scoured the dark lock-up for any sign of Alex.

Left. There were some mounds on the floor. They strained to see, but it was just carrier bags of rubbish.

Right. Was that a weapon on the ground? The light shone on it and picked up the detail of a spray-paint gun.

Upwards. Nothing.

Back. More rubbish. An empty milk carton and an old copy of a tabloid.

They systematically scanned the whole of the interior. It was empty.

'Clear,' came the message from the team leader.

The TV screens showed nothing but red spray paint on the walls and floor, and the rubbish.

It was all Barker could do to not let out a groan. Realising she'd been holding her breath, she allowed a sigh to escape. Beside her, Salter muttered an expletive.

'Get forensics in there now. We need to know if Alex or Darren have been in that lock-up, or if Platt has been holding them somewhere else. And find out what date is on the newspaper and the milk carton. That might at least give us a timeframe.'

DCI Barker turned away and cursed *The Secret* and her own stupidity for believing a prayer might be answered. Her hopes of reuniting a little boy with his family were dashed. She had to get back to the station and get everyone together to try to figure out what they needed to do next.

28

H arrison was in his office. He'd just finished writing a brief report on the Dulwich house case. The Brazilian couple were under arrest, and the Crown Prosecution wanted as much information as possible ahead of charging. There was also something else that had been niggling him since he'd left the scene. It was one of those hunches that he was never quite sure came from experience or from what he'd observed in the photographs of the family and the situation. He suggested to DI Chowdhury that she get both the children DNA tested and cross-referenced with the dead woman.

He knew the raid on Cameron Platt's lock-up had garnered nothing that they didn't already know. Harrison heard the pain in Sandra's voice as she told him on the phone and requested he come over for a team briefing in the next hour. He knew she was feeling it, but it was nothing compared to what the Fullers must be going through. He needed to get under Cameron's skin, walk in his footsteps, and see the life and environment in which he lived. The forensics team was still in the flat and removing John Platt's body wouldn't be a quick process. He had to wait awhile.

Harrison went to pick up his jacket to head to Lewisham. Just as he was about to leave, an email pinged into his inbox.

It made him stop and click to read. He'd been waiting for this one.

Afternoon, Dr Lane,

I can confirm that Mr Desmond Manning had been resident in this county at 22 Ridgeway Drive, Cardiff, CF10 1ZP, but unfortunately, he moved in 2001, and we don't have a forwarding address. I suspect he might be living under a false name. There are several debt orders against him and his wife Freda. We did have occasion to arrest him after a disturbance at the property involving a neighbour (photograph attached), but no conviction was attained, as the alleged victim dropped their complaint.

Best wishes,

Sergeant Adam Evans

Harrison thumped his desk in frustration before scrolling down the page to look at the photograph. It was the same man from the photograph now on his pin board, only he wasn't in black robes, just an ordinary T-shirt. Despite the situation and his clothing, and his grey hair and sagging skin, his dark eyes still bore into the camera lens with an intensity and confidence that spoke only of evil.

Harrison clenched his jaw and closed his eyes to calm the rage building in him. If he could only get his hands on that man.

'Y'all right, boss?' Ryan waddled into the office, a steaming hot chocolate in his hand.

Harrison didn't answer immediately.

'Boss?'

'Fine. Thanks, Ryan,' Harrison replied. He shut down his computer, grabbed his jacket from the back of his chair, and crashed out of the office.

'Okay. One of those moods then,' Ryan said to himself as he sat down. His eye caught the photograph on the pin board Harrison had been looking at. He went over to take a closer look.

He knew his boss's history, the tragedy that drove him. He also knew just how many people had benefitted from that drive, himself included. If something had pissed him off, tomorrow he'd be back stronger and more determined. Ryan had tried so many times to emulate him, find the concentration and ability to see what he saw—be the person he was—but he never could get close. Dr Harrison Lane was one of a kind, and it didn't matter if sometimes he was moody; he knew it wasn't personal, and Ryan would do whatever he could to help him.

When Harrison arrived at Lewisham, the incident room was packed. DCI Barker had called everyone in for a brainstorm and to assess what they'd found and, crucially, missed. There was a definite feeling of disappointment following the empty lock-up. A heaviness in the air, but they weren't beat yet.

DCI Barker walked out her office and clapped her hands for quiet. The room fell instantly silent. She had everyone's respect.

'Forensics just confirmed a match between the fingerprints found at Cameron Platt's flat and the partials on the torch with Darren Phillips. I don't need to tell you how critical this is. It's been fifty-two hours since Alex went missing; we could be running out of time. All resources need to focus on Platt and where he might be now.'

DCI Barker looked around at everyone's faces, which were all turned towards her. A few heads hung down, dejected. She knew they were all working flat out. If any of them had managed more than a handful of hours' sleep for the last two nights, they were very lucky. They all knew the first forty-eight hours of the case were the most critical. That golden window when you were most likely to catch your culprit before the trail went cold. She had to rally them, keep them giving their all for Alex, as well as Darren Phillips's family.

'We've made progress,' she said. 'We now know who the killer is, who has Alex. We've just got to find him.' She breathed for a moment and let the words sink in before she went on. 'I want every one of you to share the latest information, no matter how tiny, no matter how much you think it's insignificant, with all of us. One or two things you've heard or found out about Cameron Platt that you think are important. With the collective experience in this room, we need to pull together, and rather than just read words on a screen, give me your hunches and instincts. I want your human intuition, not just data from the computers.'

It was a game she'd played at conferences before, when you first meet everyone and the person who is leading the day gets you to do an ice breaker so you can get to know a bit about each other. Only this time, she wanted her team to get to know Cameron Platt better.

One of the uniformed officers volunteered to kick it off.

'Ma'am, I spoke to a prostitute that works the Berry Lane area. Showed her a photograph of Platt. She reckoned he used to come round about once a month. "Shifty little shit" were her words. Never wanted full sex, just hand and blow jobs and he wanted her to be fully clothed whenever she was doing it.'

'So he does like women, but from what we know about his religious background going to a prostitute was clearly not allowed. That cause him some psychological issues, Dr Lane?'

Harrison was in his usual spot, leant against the wall at the back of the room. He'd been listening. Thinking.

'Definitely. We know he has a love-hate relationship with the Church and Christianity. That's because of his father's behaviour and his own inner devil coming out. He knows he should be able to control it and banish it, but if he's going there regularly, he obviously can't. Repressed sexuality is important, but it's not the motivation for us.'

PC Deborah Fletcher raised her hand to speak.

'Ma'am, he was a loner. Never any sign of friends, let alone girlfriends according to the closest neighbours. One of them reckoned he'd barely left London all his life. Certainly never went on holidays.'

'So he has to be holding him somewhere local?' DCI Barker said, aiming her question to the back of the room again.

'If he's been upset by his father's death,' said Harrison, 'and I'm not talking upset because he's going to miss him, but because his father was a domineering individual who controlled most of Cameron's life even as an adult. If he's upset, he'll want familiarity and comfort. So yes, everything points to local.'

'A couple of the street sleepers reckon there's a new bloke bedding down around the big church on Fenton Road.' A young DC volunteered.

'Check it out,' said DCI Barker. 'He could also be sleeping in his van so make sure you keep an eye out for a post office van. Get the Specials involved, they might have better relations with those on the street. Ask them to see if anyone has seen anything or noticed a man and a boy in a squat somewhere.'

'In the lock-up, ma'am,' said one of the forensic team, 'we didn't find any teak oil. There were definitely traces on Darren's clothing.'

DCI Barker and the rest of the room stashed that information away. They also listened and noted down every other morsel that their colleagues shared with them. It took just half an hour, but it gave colour to a man who until a few hours ago hadn't even existed for them.

DCI Barker suddenly felt tired. The adrenaline from earlier had worn off and in its place was a weariness that came with expecting her mind and body to be on permanent full throttle. She gave a final rallying cry to her troops.

'I want a result. Don't leave anywhere unchecked. Ask every person you meet if they've seen him, a boy's life is depending on us.'

The gathering broke up without a crescendo of noise. The weight of responsibility had quelled that. Every man and woman in the room wanted a result. They wanted to find Alex Fuller alive.

DCI Barker waved Harrison over. Her bloodshot eyes looked at him from within dark circles. She looked beat, her skin dry and pale. Harrison knew just how much she put into her job and as a mother, just how hard cases like this were.

'Forensics have said you can go into the flat now. They obviously still want it kept intact as a crime scene, but the initial work is done, and Platt Senior's been removed. Can you get over there please? See if there's anything else you can determine about this man. Any clues in what he's written on the walls. We're drawing blanks, Harrison. We've searched everywhere we can think of. I need a miracle.'

29

Harrison loved how riding his bike cleared the anger from his bloodstream and freed his spirit. It wasn't easy in London, not like getting out on the open road, but just the feel of the bike beneath him and the fact he was in full control of a powerful machine, helped. By the time he pulled up to the Marion Estate flats, he'd calmed down about his disappointment with the Mannings. Harrison slowly rode around the area looking at the parking situation and decided that putting his prized Harley into an official car park was going to be a lot safer than pulling up and leaving it outside the flats. Besides, the walk would give him time to focus. He needed to get his head together. It irritated him how anything to do with Desmond Manning could wind him up and wreck his concentration.

High-rise flats were his worst nightmare. It was an attitude born of his mother's free spirit and the lifestyle they'd had when he'd been a child. To him they were claustrophobic cages. He struggled to live in London as it was. The people, the noise, the fumes, and the never-ending concrete. He'd only come here to study, but somehow, after his mother's death, he'd stayed. Perhaps it was because he'd nowhere else to go. At one point he'd toyed with the idea of going back to Joe in Arizona. He'd been the closest thing to a father to him, but he'd not wanted to impose. Joe had married and his wife was expecting. Harrison knew he loved him. There'd been nobody else in the world who would have flown thousands of miles to the UK to hunt Harrison down and get him back on the right track. He knew he owed Joe his life, and he never forgot that.

Once he'd got his own head sorted, that had been the catalyst to him wanting to study psychology. Trying to understand the human mind and what drove people like Desmond Manning became an obsession to him. He'd excelled at it. Stints at various prisons and correctional institutes soon led to his reputation spreading. It was his knowledge of cults and religions which gave him such unique experience. One thing led to another. He'd ended up being recruited by the Met Police because they'd got the budget and the need, but he'd found himself going all over the UK of late and that suited him just fine.

It was all a long way from his childhood. They'd lived with Joe on an Indian reservation. Before then his mother had wandered from one commune to the next, trying out Buddhism, earth living, and all manner of alternative religions, in an attempt to find her spiritual awakening. She'd lived on a Greek island and travelled to India, and somewhere she'd met his father and he'd been born. Harrison had no idea who his father was, or where he was from. His mother and he drifted from place to place, looking for whatever it was she was seeking. Her desperate need to fill a void and find a place where she felt at home was what drove her. He thought she'd found it in America. They'd stayed there longer than she'd ever stayed anywhere, and they'd been happy years. A time where there were no boundaries to anything—a huge great land full of learning and opportunity.

He never understood why it had all gone wrong. Neither did Joe. One day Harrison had been running through the hot desert tracking snakes and gophers, and the next he was on a plane to the cold, wet, miserable UK. He'd arrived home to find his mother sobbing, packing their belongings, and pleading with Joe to understand. Even at a young age, he'd been able to see that Joe couldn't. He couldn't either. They'd gone back to live in the commune run by Desmond and Freda Manning. His mother left more than Joe behind. She also left her smiles and laughter in America. They were dark days that had ended her life and nearly ended his.

Harrison pushed those thoughts from his mind. This was not what he wanted to think about right now. What he needed to concentrate on was the search for a little boy. He had to get under Cameron Platt's skin, work out what motivated him and where he might have gone.

The front door of the flat still showed traces of the grey aluminium dust forensics used to gather fingerprints. It also sported a new enhanced lock fitted to prevent any trophy hunters or media from gaining access. Last thing they needed was the caretaker or someone giving ghoulish tours to anyone who would pay. Harrison put on the full forensic suit, gloves, and overshoes, and used the key that DCI Barker had given to him.

The floor of the flat was no longer crunchy underfoot from the flies, but their squashed bodies lay everywhere, testament to the weeks that the corpse of John Jacob Platt had sat in his armchair. In places there were stepping plates protecting the areas that SOCO deemed important evidence.

The curtains were open, probably to allow the team to air the room after the initial analysis and the body was gone. Or what was left of the body. Harrison had seen the photographs. The natural decomposition aided by fly maggots had done a good job. The stench of a body in decay still lingered, soaked into the carpets and the upholstery of the chair he had sat in. The putrid rot of cadaverine and putrescine, with the sickening egg stench of hydrogen sulphide and a hint of sewage from the skatole. Just some of the gases and liquids produced during the putrefaction of a corpse.

He'd tried the light switch but got nothing. Stood to reason that they'd been cut off. Who would have been paying the bills? The open curtains allowed a pale wash of illumination into the room. The surrounding flats, streetlights, and general white light which leeched from offices, ensured enough visibility for him to reach the lamps forensics had rigged up.

Before he ventured out of the hallway, Harrison stood still and grounded himself. He needed to concentrate, needed every one of his senses working and focussed. He had to put himself into the mind of Cameron Platt, see what he saw without his own personal take on it all. Harison stood for five minutes, feet planted, getting his breathing and consciousness under control. Clearing his mind. Only when he felt the power of all his faculties alive and working together, did he open his eyes and look around him.

He stepped forward into the living room.

SOCO had marked various things in the flat with yellow numbered markers. Where the body had sat in the armchair, was a black stain that seeped into the carpet around it. Harrison wasn't interested in the chair. He looked first at the surrounding carpet, crouching down and using his iPhone light to look in detail at the carpet fibres. He knew this room had been full of forensic officers all afternoon and into the evening. There was likely to be very little in the way of signs for him to be able to read, but he found some.

It was probably helped by the fact the carpet was filthy, years of dust and dirt stacked between the fibres provided a cushion to crush. What was blatantly clear to Harrison, was that a path had been trodden and worn around the armchair. It was definitely around the chair in its current position, which was not its original placement. First, nobody would plonk an armchair in the middle of a room facing a door with his back to a window, and second Harrison could see the marks embedded in the carpet from where it had originally sat for what was probably decades before. This position and the path around it were new.

He stepped back and surveyed the entire room. The walls were covered in crucifixes, pictures of the Virgin Mary and Jesus. They hung on a faded pale green and white wallpaper that looked like it had once depicted fronds of plants and maybe even flowers. The pattern of the wallpaper was barely visible, because where there weren't religious pictures or icons, there was graffiti quoting passages from the *Bible*. Written in black marker pens, the writing had a fervour to it. Jagged points on the upper loops of the letters, but not the straight slashes of temper. The letters were small, which indicated Cameron's reclusive nature and they mostly slanted to the left. He'd clearly used a fair amount of pressure to write the words. These weren't hastily scribbled, they were placed carefully with passion.

'Fear not, for I have redeemed you; I have called you by name, you are mine. When you pass through the waters, I will be with you; and through the rivers, they shall not overwhelm you; when you walk

through fire you shall not be burnt, and the flame shall not consume you.'

'For all who are led by the Spirit of God are sons of God.'

Harrison could imagine it was when his father had just died. They were all messages of redemption and the passage into the afterlife with God and Jesus.

The writing wasn't uniform, though. As Harrison looked at each section, there was a clear deterioration. There were whole passages where the letters would slant both left and right within the same word. To the untrained eye it looked like the writer had perhaps struggled to control the pen on the awkward to reach surface, but to Harrison they showed a person who was losing their grip on reality. Other letters also showed a tremor, an indicator of the stress Cameron's mind was under. Where the writing deteriorated, so too did the tone of the *Bible* passages.

'You are of your father the devil, and your will is to do your father's desires. He was a murderer from the beginning, and has nothing to do with the truth, because there is no truth in him. When he lies, he speaks out of his own character, for he is a liar and the father of lies.'

'Flaming fire taking vengeance on them that know not God, and that obey not the gospel of our Lord Jesus Christ: Who shall be punished with everlasting destruction from the presence of the Lord, and from the glory of his power.'

As Cameron ran out of wall space he was cramming in as much as he could. *'Children, obey your parents in everything, for this pleases the Lord.'* And *'The rod and reproof give wisdom, but a child left to himself brings shame to his father.'* Harrison was sure that last one had been doctored slightly, that it should say *mother*.

He took some photographs. He'd run the writing by a graphologist, but from what the passages said and how the writing changed, it was a clear indicator of the state of Cameron's mind.

Harrison could imagine Cameron Platt, walking around the body of his dead father, quoting passages from the *Bible*, hour after hour, day after day, week after week, until maybe the stench got too much; or because he had another purpose.

Cameron's mental deterioration was clear to see, but why take the boys, and where to?

This room couldn't have been more different to the two homes he'd visited over the last couple of days. In both, he'd seen love and warmth. Surfaces that carried images of happy family life. Colour and joy. Here it was a bleak monochrome facsimile of a home, stripped of its humanity. If this was the life Cameron was brought up in, then he would have had a lonely childhood. Harrison knew his mother had left and his father was strict and loveless. That in itself would have led to the potential for psychological harm. It was well documented that those who were abused as children, were more likely than those who hadn't, to either be abusers themselves or to graduate towards abusive relationships. This flat screamed emotional neglect. Harrison felt some pity for Cameron Platt, but he doubted he was a particularly likeable personality. Now, he could at least understand his mental struggle.

That still didn't explain why he chose Darren and Alex. If they'd both come from broken homes, then perhaps it could have been that he thought they needed a father figure, but that wasn't the case. Harrison needed to keep looking.

There were two bedrooms leading off from the sitting room. He went into the one on the left first. It was devoid of character. More pictures of Christ and the Virgin Mary, and just one photograph—the first he'd seen of the living —a rotund, balding man shaking hands with a man in a suit, who was giving him something. Harrison looked closer at the image. It was outside a factory and it looked like he was being handed a glass plate. He took his own photograph of it.

Elsewhere in the room there was little else to see. A well-read *Bible* on the bedside cabinet. A couple of pairs of shoes. On a chair, a pile of clothes which had obviously been worn and were dirty. With his gloves on, Harrison looked through drawers and the wardrobe. His sense was of a man devoid of human emotions and needs, a man who lived just for his God. His God was a cruel God, the God of the *First Testament*, of fire and brimstone and an eye for an eye, not the forgiving gentleness of Jesus. The character of the father was clear to see in this bedroom.

Across the other side of the lounge was another identical sized room. Again sparsely furnished, nothing to give away the character of the person who had lived there. There were no photographs on these walls and no *Bible*. He knew one had been found in the corpse's mouth and it made sense that if Cameron had been using it to read from that it was his which was now in the forensics lab. There was, however, one other book on the bedside table. It was a Haynes manual for a van, the same make and model as the post vans. Harrison picked it up and flicked through it. He shook it. Nothing fell out, but when he held it again, it fell open on a diagram of the chassis. Cameron must have planned to snatch the boys. Worked out how he would disguise the van and carried out the work on it at the lock-up while still living at the flat.

What did that do to a human mind to return home each day and be greeted by the rotting corpse of your father?

The wardrobe contained very few clothes. It didn't look as though Cameron had taken many, if any, with him—wherever he'd gone—because there weren't even empty coat hangers left. Shoved on the top shelf, he found overalls covered in paint from his days at the paint shop.

There were no aftershaves, no deodorants. There was barely anything at all on top of the chest of drawers in the room, besides a hairbrush and a mug which had once held a cup of tea but now displayed a scientific extravaganza of mould.

Harrison stood for a moment and looked around, then he lifted the mattress.

Nothing.

He was about to let it drop back when he noticed something. There was a piece of loose thread at the end of a faint line in the mattress material. Could that be a slit sewn up? It was barely noticeable.

Harrison tipped the mattress up and felt the area. Underneath the fabric, he could feel something solid. He took a photograph with his phone for forensics and then pulled at the thread so the faint line became a gash in the material and gaped open.

They were slightly mildewed, but inside was a selection of old exercise books with the name 'Cameron Platt' on the front covers. There were seven in total. Harrison looked through them all and every single one was filled from cover to cover with writing, but it was the same sentences. 'I am evil.' And 'I must renounce Satan,' written over and over and over again. Where he hadn't said this, he'd copied out passages of the *Bible*.

Harrison took more photos with his phone and then left the books with the mattress. He'd let Tanya know to send someone from her team to log them.

Harrison checked in the other usual places that people

hide things, but the investigators had already done that and nothing else came up.

It was a sad room. No mark of its former occupant at all apart from that writing from childhood. Was it instigated by his father or was it just Cameron who believed himself evil?

Harrison carried on his tour, this time into the open-plan galley kitchen area.

The cupboards were mostly empty, barely any cooking or eating tools and not much at all in the way of food, bar some spilt pasta and a sachet of tomato ketchup.

The fridge was a similar situation, empty except for a mouldy milk carton that only had a tiny drop of milk in it, anyway.

Harrison peered into the waste bin. The first thing which caught his eye was a glass plate at the bottom of the bin covered in other rubbish. It was the plate from the bedroom photograph, only it had already been damaged. There were large, badly glued cracks across it. Clearly someone had broken it and then tried to mend it —badly.

The rest of the rubbish in the bin comprised old food cans, bread wrappers, and a couple of church newsletters. St Mary's seemed to be their preferred spiritual home. Harrison made a mental note.

Now he'd made his observations, Harrison needed to get into Cameron's mind and under his skin. He switched off the forensic lamps to return the sitting room to its dim, street lighting. For a few moments he stood in the gloom, allowing his eyes to get used to the darkness. Then he started to walk around the armchair in which the body had sat. As he walked, he looked at the graffiti on the walls, *'You are of your father the devil, and your will is to do your father's desires.'*

Round and round he walked, just thinking and soaking in the atmosphere of the flat.

He looked at what Cameron had seen. Listened to the silence. The distant tinny sounds of other people living their lives. TVs on, people laughing, shouting, and talking. The loneliness. The fear. Fear of the God who could at any time strike him down and send him to the pits of hell. He had no one to talk to except a rotting corpse. As the days had worn on, the putrefaction of his father's body would have seemed like evil at first, seeping from his eyes, nostrils, and mouth, and then bursting out from within. The dark clouds of flies were the Devil's host arriving to feast on his soul. What would Cameron be thinking? A lonely child in a loveless family environment. His forays to the prostitute would be preying on his mind. He had sinned. God saw everything. Perhaps at the end he was also hungry. He would have avoided human interactions. His own stomach would have felt empty just as his father's bloated.

Cameron was a man seeking redemption. Trying to put right some of what he had done wrong in God's eyes.

It was while he stood there in the gloom, thinking through Cameron Platt's possible whereabouts, that he heard footsteps approaching the front door.

He stopped breathing as he strained to hear. There was a jangle of keys, then one was inserted into the lock.

His heart jumped.

Could Platt have returned to his home, come back to his father?

Harrison was about to lunge towards the door to confront him, when it started to open. In that split second, reality returned, and he realised it couldn't be Platt because they'd changed the locks. In the next split second, he realised he was going to give whoever his colleague was, a mighty big fright because he was stood there in the dark.

Harrison lunged towards the forensics lamps to turn them on, just as the silhouette of Dr Tanya Jones was lit up in the doorway. His mind split in two. One half transfixed by her attractive figure, while his other half attempted to prevent the woman from having a heart attack.

Harrison managed to say, 'Tanya, it's me Harrison,' just as she let out a scream at the sight of a ghostly white silhouette in the middle of the sitting room where earlier she'd had to endure the ghastly remains of John Platt.

The forensics lights burst into life and Harrison rushed forward towards the door so that she could see him better.

The realisation it wasn't either of the Platts hit Tanya and as he reached her, she wobbled with shock.

'I'm so sorry,' Harrison said. He saw her wobble and instinctively put his arms around her to hold her up.

'Oh my God, I thought, I thought…' she garbled. She was breathless with the fright and would have just sat on the floor if it hadn't been for the big arms that had wrapped around her holding her steady and upright.

'What were you doing?' she squeaked at him.

'I was looking around the place, trying to get a sense of who Cameron is. I'm sorry, there're no lights. No electricity. I didn't expect anyone else to be here at this time.'

Harrison could feel her heart banging inside her chest. He was holding her tightly to him. Her cheek on his. He could smell her hair, her perfume, and moisturiser. He wanted to taste her too. He longed to kiss her.

'I'm sorry,' he said again, more gently and instinctively caressed the back of her head.

He felt her breathing relax and her heartbeat slow.

If he'd been able to see her face properly, he'd have seen the colour return to her cheeks.

Tanya didn't know whether to cry or laugh hysterically at this point. Either would have done.

As the shock dissipated, embarrassment replaced it, and despite feeling like she could stay wrapped in his arms for the rest of the night, she pulled away.

'Sorry, I'm not usually so…'

'No, really, it was totally my fault. It would have given anybody a shock.' He found himself still trying to hold on to her, his hands on the top of her arms. His turn to be embarrassed.

They broke away.

'I came to check something,' Tanya said. 'The pathologist found a blade mark on John Platt's rib bones. We think he was stabbed post-mortem, I was coming to look for any knives in the flat, see if they were the weapon used.'

Harrison was eager to help her forget his momentary overfamiliarity.

'I'll help you,' he replied.

'Oh no, I don't want to disturb what you were doing.'

'It's okay. I was done.'

'Have you worked him out?' she asked.

'I certainly have a much better sense of his state of mind. Now I need to read all the interview transcripts of those who knew him. Piece it all together.'

The pair of them talked work, both relieved to distract each other from their embarrassment and their own minds from the other thoughts which the encounter had created; that being held and holding onto each other had been a decidedly pleasurable experience. Harrison held the evidence bags open while Tanya searched through the kitchen drawers and took out three knives.

She'd just put the last one in when there was the sound

of shouting and raised voices from outside. It was a woman's voice.

'Alex, Alex, are you here? Alex?'

Harrison Lane knew that voice. He recognised the emotion in it. It was Sally Fuller, downstairs in the street below.

'That's Alex's mother,' he said to Tanya. 'What's she doing here?'

He looked at Tanya's face and again found himself momentarily pulled away as he stared into her eyes. This woman was not good for his concentration.

'You'd better go to her, see if you can help,' Tanya said. 'I'll lock up.'

'Thanks,' Harrison replied, sense returning. 'And you'll find some exercise books in Cameron's bedroom. I found them in the mattress.'

With that, and before Tanya could ask him anything else, Harrison left the flat, pulled off his white forensics suit and headed downstairs where a small crowd had gathered watching the commotion. Sally was still shouting for her son while her husband, Edward, was holding on to her.

'Sally, stop it. Just stop it,' he was pleading with her. It was clear neither of them cared about the crowd of people watching. What Edward cared about was the acute distress he could see on his wife's face, and he had no idea how to help her.

Harrison walked over and stood in front of them.

'Mrs Fuller,' he said.

Her glazed eyes registered his face.

'This is where he lives, isn't it? He could be here somewhere. Somebody must know something.'

Sally spun round to the crowd.

'One of you must know where my son is. Where is he?'

she screamed at them. Some of them drew back and melted away, ashamed to be witnessing her grief and trauma. Others stood tight, transfixed by the spectacle. A couple of them were filming the proceedings, no doubt hoping to get a few likes and views on whichever social media channel they were about to post it to. No thought or empathy for the traumatised woman they were using. Harrison tried to block their view with his bulk, but Sally was erratic. It was hard to protect her.

'She found out through Facebook,' Edward said to Harrison by way of explanation. 'She's been trawling it all day.'

As they spoke, the blue lights of a police car came into view and the crowd instantly thinned.

'We need to get her home,' Harrison said to Edward.

'Sally, what you're doing will not help Alex. The more attention we draw to this, the more likely his abductor will go to ground.'

'But I have to do something. I need to look for him. He has to know that we care. I care.' She threw a look at her husband.

'I said I needed to go back to work for the money,' Edward explained to Harrison, 'Truth is it's also because I just don't know what to do. I can't get through to her.'

Harrison looked at Sally, the pain on her face was palpable. She was unrecognisable from the woman in the photograph she'd given him.

'Sally, you need to be at home with your daughter and husband for when we bring Alex back. Please trust me, leave this to us. I'll find him, Sally. I will.'

She looked into his eyes, and the fire in hers dimmed. She started to wilt. All her fight left her. As she physically collapsed into her husband's arms, two police officers walked up to them from the patrol car.

'What's going on here then?' one of them said to Harrison.

He pulled out his ID.

'It's okay, we're done here.'

Harrison and Edward Fuller supported Sally back to their car and strapped her in. He watched as Edward drove off, both of their faces pale, strained, almost ghostlike in the streetlights. He hung his head as they disappeared around the corner. The weight of their pain on his shoulders.

He knew families grieving and coping with a trauma together weren't always the best support for each other because they coped with it in different ways and at different speeds. He hoped that Sally and Edward's relationship could survive the stress.

'What's this to do with Platt then?' a woman in her forties appeared next to Harrison, 'Her son's gone missing ain't he? Platt taken him?'

'I'm sorry. I can't…'

'Did he knock off his old man? Wouldn't surprise me if he had. Nasty piece of work, that one. Surprised he put up with him that long. Miserable old bugger.'

Harrison turned to look at the woman. She'd dyed her hair a fashionable purple. It had obviously been black once. She was confident but not cocky, with a kind face. He reckoned she'd have children of her own.

'You knew them well?'

'Went to school with Cameron. He was all right at first, till his mum left. Not surprised she bailed. I wouldn't have put up with that crap, but would never have left my kid behind, mind. My mum reckoned she wouldn't have neither, that 'er old man done 'er in and got rid of 'er body somewhere. Never let my kids anywhere near either of them. His dad was always shouting religious stuff at us and quoting the *Bible*. He told Cameron that she'd left cos of 'im. Said it was his fault. Went weird after that. Always felt right sorry for 'im I did, but not if he's snatched a kiddy.'

'Have you spoken to a police officer? Given a statement?'

'Na. Don't live round here no more. I was just back visiting me mate. We moved about five years ago.'

'So his dad, he blamed him for the mother leaving?'

'Yeah. It weren't his fault. He was just a little kid.'

'What was their relationship like? Cameron and his dad?'

'He was nasty. My mum offered to sit 'im but his old man weren't having none of that. Said people were interfering.'

'Would you give a statement to the police? Tell us what you know about the family, it could help us find her son.'

The woman shrugged.

'Guess so, if you think it will help. Got a photo on my phone here, look. Dug it out when I saw the post on Facebook. It's from when we woz in the school choir together. We woz only seven. That was just before his mum left.'

The woman turned her mobile phone around and showed it to Harrison. There on the screen was a little boy who bore more than just a passing resemblance to both Darren and Alex. Harrison had found the root of Cameron's motivation.

30

H arrison was about to head to his bike and leave the Marion Estate flats, when he saw Tanya walking towards him. His mental survival instinct told him to go, but desire won over and as she came to a halt in front of him, his stomach did a nice warm somersault as the memory of holding her washed through him.

'I don't suppose you could spare half an hour, could you?' she asked. 'I kind of need your advice, which would also give you an explanation why I was so jumpy earlier.'

'No explanation needed,' he said, and watched her face drop a little, 'but of course, you're welcome to ask me anything.'

She smiled, but it wasn't a reassuringly happy smile. There was a tension in her mouth. 'Thanks, I know a good wine bar not far from here. We could pop in there for a quick drink.'

Harrison didn't bother with his usual *I don't drink* routine. First, she'd realise he wouldn't be drinking because he was on the bike, and second, whether or not he liked it, he'd rather spend half an hour in a wine bar with her drinking water, than on his own in his flat.

The wine bar turned out to be a small place with painted grape vines adorning the walls and small, French-style tables around its edges. It was only half full. Perfect for them. They wouldn't need to shout to be heard and could find a table to sit at.

They sat down, opposite sides of the table, and instantly felt embarrassed. Seeing each other totally outside of the work environment made them both feel a little vulnerable—even if they were there through choice.

Tanya knew Harrison was a man of few words and so she broke the ice first.

'Look, I'm really sorry for overreacting back at the flat. That place had given me the creeps after the way we found Platt Senior's body, and I've been a bit jumpy of late anyway.'

Harrison leant across the table and put his hand on hers. His touch surprised her, but in a nice way. It surprised him too.

'Seriously, the second I realised it was one of us coming into the flat, I knew I was going to frighten you. I was standing in the near darkness, in a room which still stank of death and had until recently contained a rotting corpse —and you weren't expecting anyone to be there. If you hadn't jumped, I'd have been more surprised.'

At last Tanya's face curled into a smile. 'It must have looked pretty funny. It's at times like that I wish I'd had the video recorder going.'

Harrison smiled along with her. He'd quite enjoyed the post-shock part, that's for sure.

The two of them had both ordered sparkling water, much to the annoyance of the guy behind the bar who'd eye-balled them like they were trying to steal the money from his till. They both sipped at their glasses slightly awkwardly as their minds remembered their earlier embrace.

'I hope you don't mind me asking,' she began. 'But I was kind of wondering if it's unusual for people to imagine they're being watched and to believe it.'

'What do you mean?'

'Well, in the last couple of weeks, I've had the feeling that someone is watching me and following me. I've tried to catch them, but I don't see anyone. Is there some kind of psychological explanation?'

Harrison sat back and looked at Tanya.

'Do you have a suspicion of who it might be? An ex-boyfriend or someone who has a grudge to bear through work?'

'No, my ex and I parted amicably, it's definitely not him. Who knows with work, but I can't think of anyone.'

Harrison felt an uncomfortable trickle of envy filter through him at the thought of Tanya with her ex-boyfriend.

'Do you really think there's someone there?'

Tanya was silent for a little while and then nodded with a sad, worried look in her eyes. 'I know we're scientists and we should base our conclusions on clear evidence, but I feel it. I can't explain it.'

'There is a scientific explanation for that,' said Harrison, 'gut instinct exists, it's real. We have an extensively complicated communication system between our stomach and our brain. Our gut system contains something like 100 million neutrons, and if something isn't right, it tells our brain that. Our brains use all our senses to analyse situations, but sometimes our brains are too slow or too busy elsewhere—especially in today's modern world— to notice something that's going on. Your gut senses it, though. It will alert you even if you haven't registered seeing something happening.'

'Okay.' Tanya nodded but looked slightly upset.

'Sorry, have I made it worse?' Harrison asked, realising that maybe what she'd wanted was him to tell her she didn't need to worry, it was just her mind playing tricks.

'No,' she said, looking up at him and into his eyes. 'You've told me the truth. You've confirmed what I know really, but just didn't want to face up to.'

'I'm not saying there is definitely someone watching you,' he clarified. 'We also all have active imaginations, and all it would take is for the suggestion of something and for that suggestion to be reinforced by what may be random coincidences, for you to then interpret it as proof.'

'I know. You're saying that my body's early warning system might have detected someone, but it could also be my imagination. But I know that—not counting tonight— I'm usually the kind of person who just isn't spooked. I live alone. I can watch horror movies and still go to bed without seeing shadows. I just don't get easily scared. Perhaps it's part of being a scientist and part the job we do. But lately, I've felt spooked. I have definitely sensed as though someone is watching me.'

'Have you reported it?' Harrison asked, he was getting concerned for her.

'Reported what?' Tanya said, 'the invisible man? I think the best thing I can do is take some precautions, put up some CCTV, and get some kind of personal alarm. If the cameras catch someone, then maybe I could get help. But you know how tough it can be to get anything done about stalkers.'

'You can always call me if you're ever frightened, think someone's there. I'm pretty good at getting through the London traffic fast.'

'Thank you.' She smiled into his eyes.

'Would you like me to see you home tonight?' Harrison asked. 'I can follow you on my bike and make sure you get in okay.'

'No, seriously don't worry. I've got to take those knives back to the lab first, and then I'll head home. I'll be fine. Thank you, but I'm going to listen to my gut instincts though.'

Harrison's gut instincts were telling him he should ask the beautiful woman across the table from him out on a proper date, but his brain overruled. He had to keep focussed on Alex Fuller. There was no room for distractions, no matter how pleasant they seemed.

31

D CI Barker loved her job, but there were days when she wished she'd followed her school career teacher's advice and become a physiotherapist instead. Today was one of those days. Most cases were two steps forward and one step back, but sometimes the stakes were a lot higher, and when there was a young boy's life on the line, well that was well near to being top of the list and it exhausted her. Every cop had to have a thick skin. First, there was the abuse that got hurled at you daily. Not only did you have to learn to ignore it, but five minutes later you might have to forgive your abusers as they became people who needed you. Second, it was the things you had to see. The scenes of death like she'd had to witness in just the last forty-eight hours. Things that human beings were capable of doing to each other. The cruelty, the greed, and the hatred.

As she pulled into the parking area outside their home, she knew that the lateness of the hour would ensure her family would be in bed asleep. Sometimes that was a good thing. There were many nights when she came home drained with nothing left to give anyone. All she craved was solitude and peace for her mind to recover from the day, ready to do it all over again the next morning.

Other times she needed to talk to them, to make contact with the people she loved, and chat about silly unimportant things, or have the kids show her some silly meme or video which could make her giggle—anything which could ground her back into the real world, the world away from being a copper.

They had left the hallway lamp on for her and it illuminated the evidence of teenage existence. Football boots dumped on the floor next to a row of trainers. Sam's black leather shoes carefully placed together, marking out who was the grown-up. A quick look into the sitting room and an abandoned electric guitar and saxophone showed she'd missed out on some musical fun. No doubt Raff's latest masterpiece, penned with the fuel of lovelorn angst that dominated his age group's thoughts. She remembered those days.

She felt what she'd missed in her gut, an empty longing which groaned through her and sent her eyes to the photographs on the mantlepiece. In reality, she wouldn't have been able to take part even if she'd been there because she was about as musical as a cat with its tail in a vice. The kids had inherited their father's musical genes. She envied him that. With his music he was never alone, although he barely saw his wife some weeks. She used to watch him, lost in a piece of music, far away from the real-world stresses, and she longed for that escape. He saw the world in a completely different way to her. He looked upon it as an artist, hearing music in the trees and the melody of voices, the wind, and even the most mundane acts of everyday life. She saw it as cold hard facts. A crime scene or potential crime scene. A raised voice that could lead to an attack, or a gesture that betrayed a hidden menace. Some officers found their release in art or writing. She had found nothing artistic that she could do. Her drawings turned out looking like a five-year-old had done them, and her writing was too clinical and official. A staccato account of exactly what happened, without nuance or imagination. That's why she and Sam made such a great team—they say opposites attract. Balanced parenting.

In the kitchen she ran a glass of water for herself from the tap. She wasn't always the best at watching her hydration levels. There would be times when she'd go for hours without a drop to drink, and it would only be when her throat and mouth were too parched to talk, that she'd remember she had drunk nothing. She'd also not eaten anything, besides chocolate, since lunchtime and it had now gone 11 p.m. Sam had long ago given up on texting her to ask if she'd be home for dinner. They'd come to an agreement that if she turned up then great, dinner was always between six-thirty and seven-thirty, and if she hadn't appeared by then, he would make a plate up for her. When she looked in the fridge, her dutiful husband had done just that. A portion of what looked like steak pie sat with some new potatoes and vegetables. When Sam had first started doing this for her, the plate had just been covered with a sheet of cling film, but as the months had turned into years, he'd bought her a special lid, a bit like you get on a hotel room service dinner.

Sandra Barker took her dinner out and looked at it before replacing the lid and returning it to the fridge. She'd take it into work tomorrow and have it for lunch instead, she was too tired to eat.

Slowly she climbed the stairs, being careful not to disturb anyone. The door to their bedroom was slightly ajar, and so she peeked into the dark room. She could see

Sam sleeping, hear his slow rhythmic breathing. She would sleep in the spare room again tonight, avoid disturbing him. Only who was she kidding, it was less spare room and more *her* room now. What had once been an occasional occurrence had become the norm. It wasn't that they'd fallen out of love, or that their relationship had gone wrong. It was just he'd got used to her not being around. Besides, Sam snored, and that was a recipe for disaster when it came to getting a much-needed good night's sleep.

Then there were the nights when her day job seeped into her dreams. The violence. Bright reds and harsh lights crashed around inside her head and prevented her from resting. She would wake at the slightest noise. Heart pounding at a thousand knots, with a sweat on her skin. The day haunting the night. On those occasions, she'd need to turn on the bedside light. Sometimes she'd have to get up and go watch a bit of inane television before her brain could switch off again. It was hard to do that when you were in the same bed as someone without disturbing them. This arrangement worked for them both.

By the time she'd been to the bathroom and changed into some pyjamas, Sandra didn't care about anything except putting her head onto the soft pillow in front of her. She hoped sleep could bring her some respite and get her ready for another busy day ahead.

Across town in the Docklands, Harrison Lane was still not in bed. Guns N Roses were playing, Sweet Child O' Mine, accompanied by the rhythmic pounding and whirr of his treadmill. Harrison was pushing himself hard. Sweat poured from his naked torso, his muscles bulked and accentuated. His skin shone and his breath came and went in ferocious bursts. There was a look of steely determination on his face. He didn't drop his gaze, just kept running and running and running.

In front of him were two photographs. The first was the woman in the flowery dress, his mother, and the second was the one that Alex Fuller's mother gave to him.

He kept running, even pushed up the speed on the treadmill. There was pain on his face, his chest heaved with the exertion, but still he kept on pushing.

It was only when he'd nothing left in him, when his muscles threatened to betray him and trip him up, that he slowed to a walk before bending over, hands on knees, and tried to find his breath. His entire body grasping for oxygen. At last, he knew he would be able to sleep. He stretched his muscles and finished the bottle of water. Then, with one last glance at the two photographs, he flicked off the lights, headed to the shower, and ultimately bed. He was asleep within fifteen minutes.

Running until exhausted helped Harrison. Perhaps it was the sheer physical shut-down that took his body into reset mode and allowed him to brush aside clutter. Or maybe it was the quality of sleep which gave him clarity. Either way, it worked. Harrison woke up the next morning with a clear vision of the way forward in his mind. He knew where Cameron had gone.

32

I t was early, not quite 8 a.m., but DCI Barker had already called a team briefing with her lead investigators. DS Salter, Sergeant Evans, DCs Oaks and Johnson, were all in her office at the conference room table. In front of them was a pile of croissants and takeaway coffees.

Sandra thought Jack looked slightly better this morning. Still had the bags under his eyes, but he looked a little less haggard than he had of late.

'Good night?' she asked him, without going into any detail in front of the rest of the team.

'Much better, thanks,' Jack replied. It had been much better too. Marie was trying to communicate now, to express what she was feeling, and they'd both felt more relaxed than they had done in weeks. Perhaps the drop in tension had been picked up by Daniel, because he'd slept through as well. His alarm had woken Jack up for the first time in ages, rather than the baby monitor or Marie getting out of bed because she couldn't sleep. The relief was palpable.

Tanya hurried into the room.

'Sorry I'm a little late. Got held up by a problem on the Tube,' she explained.

'We've not started yet.' DCI Barker smiled at her and noted that even she looked more tired than usual. This case was taking its toll on all of them. She hated to think what state her own face was in. 'Help yourselves, you lot.' She gesticulated at the croissants and coffee. 'You're not usually so shy.'

'I was waiting to see if the new evidence involved John Platt and his remains first,' said Jack. 'I'd rather have my croissant *after* looking at any images of him if that's okay. Still haven't got the smell out of my nose.' He said it with humour in his voice, but they all understood the sentiment. After attending a body like that, it usually took a couple of days for your nose to forget the stench. It permeated into the membrane of your nostrils and wouldn't budge, no matter how many times you blew your nose or took a shower.

'So, what have you got for us?' DCI Barker addressed Sergeant Evans now. He'd texted her late last night to say something had come to light in the evidence they'd collected from Cameron's flat.

'Well,' smiled Evans in his warm Welsh lilt, as he reached for a croissant, 'I might have to keep you in suspense until I've eaten all the croissant.' He had a box next to him and he opened its lid, taking out several bagged items of evidence. He put them on the table in front of them and took a bite of his croissant while the rest of the team took them in.

DCI Barker picked up what looked to be a woman's purse. It was old-fashioned, not something you'd get in the shops now, and it had cash in it and an old credit card. Then she looked at another bag, a passport with the name,

Joyce Elizabeth Platt, on the front. She opened it to see a thin, pale woman staring back. She didn't seem to have an ounce of joy in her face, DCI Barker saw nothing but sadness staring back at her.

'The wife's?'

Evans nodded with his last mouthful of croissant. DCI Barker passed the items round the table.

'We found her passport, purse with her driving licence, all hidden at the back of John Platt's wardrobe. Tanya's team has already gone over them, just his fingerprints and that of an unknown. Nothing from Cameron.'

'So what you thinking?'

'We're thinking that it's mighty odd for her to have left all her money and ID behind. Would have been more difficult than it is nowadays to get replacements, and we don't think she had any work, or a career with which to support herself. We can't, in fact, find any trace of Joyce Platt, or Joyce Wilson as she was, after 1976. No medical records, no renewed passport or driving licence. She simply disappeared off the face of the earth.'

'What about parents or siblings?'

'She was an only child. Father was an alcoholic and looks like the mother had enough to deal with. Both now deceased.'

'I interviewed a woman last night,' interjected DC Oaks. 'Dr Lane had spoken to her. She was at school with Cameron Platt when his mum disappeared. She said that her mum, now unfortunately in a care home with dementia, always maintained that John Platt had killed his wife and got rid of her. Said that was a widely held view at the time, but nothing ever happened.'

'No police investigation?' DCI Barker questioned.

'I've checked and there was an anonymous tip-off received. They looked into it, but there was no evidence that a crime had been committed. John Platt said she'd left him for another man, and that was that. They marked it down as malicious gossip and dropped it,' added Evans.

'And we're absolutely sure that she hasn't just surfaced, that Cameron isn't with her somewhere living under an assumed name.'

'As certain as we can be, Ma'am, I've tried every database I can think of. Unless she assumed a false identity.'

DCI Barker sat back in her chair and let the latest information soak in.

'Okay, so we have a potential cold case to look into and the prime suspect is also dead. We have to park that one right now, the priority has to be the living and most particularly young Alex Fuller.'

'Indeed, but it could help explain his state of mind though?' suggested Jack.

'Any evidence that he'd seen this stash of his father's?' DCI Barker asked Evans.

'Obviously can't be sure but as there were none of his fingerprints on it and they were found well-hidden at the back of the father's wardrobe, I'd say not.'

'Ma'am,' said DC Oaks, 'what the witness did say, was that Cameron told her his dad said his mum leaving was his fault. There'd been some argument the day she disappeared, and it involved Cameron. She couldn't quite remember, but felt that his parents argued quite a lot about him. His father was very strict and his mother less so. She used to defend him when his dad got too heavy. Wasn't averse to knocking her around either.'

'That tallies with her medical records, which show a couple of times when she allegedly fell down the stairs,' added Sergeant Evans.

'After the argument between his parents, Cameron

woke up the next morning and his dad said his mum had left because she couldn't stand having to deal with Cameron's bad behaviour any longer.'

'That also fits with something Harrison found at their flat last night,' Tanya spoke now, and then realised that she'd just admitted she'd seen him last night. That made her colour slightly at the thought of their meeting. She pushed it out of her head and tried to remain professional. 'Sewn into Cameron's mattress were several exercise books which look like they date back to when Cameron was at school. He kept calling himself evil.'

'The father put it all on him.'

'And that's not all,' said DC Oaks. 'Take a look at this photo of Cameron. It was at a school event just before his mother disappeared.'

He showed an image on his phone to the rest of the team.

'So he's definitely picked boys that resembled him,' DCI Barker said. 'We need Harrison in here to give us an idea of what this could mean.'

She took her mobile out of her pocket and tapped in a text to Harrison, while her team reached for the rest of the croissants.

'What about forensics on the flat?' she looked to Tanya now.

'So, going to be difficult to determine cause of death with John Jacob Platt. It looked like cut and dried natural causes with the cancer diagnosis, despite the bizarre way in which the body was dealt with post-mortem. However, Dr Aspey found some marks on his rib cage that are consistent with him being stabbed in the chest. We've got the knives from the flat and are cross-referencing those with the blade marks on the ribs. Going to be incredibly difficult to tell if they were caused before or after death. We might simply never know. Estimated time of death is around four to six weeks. We should have a slightly better idea in the next twenty-four hours or so. That ties in with his doctor's prognosis for the cancer. Obviously don't yet know if either Darren or Alex's DNA is in the flat, but there's no evidence so far that they were there.'

'Right so, where are we on the search?'

Sergeant Evans cleared the evidence bags back into the box and opened up a laptop.

'We're nearly done with all the places we had on the list. Nothing. No sightings, no CCTV, no sign of the van, or Cameron and Alex. Nothing since the day Alex went missing.'

Everyone in the room had frustration etched on their faces.

'He could be bloody anywhere by now, who's to say he would have stuck around the area once he knew we found Darren?' Jack looked downcast.

'Where else would he go?' his boss asked, less to him and more as an open question to herself.

The sound of strident footsteps heading towards her office door made her look up. Dr Harrison Lane was coming their way, and he looked like he had something to say.

'That was quick,' she said to him.

He didn't bother with any perfunctory greetings or to explain he'd already been on his way over before she'd texted him. He just launched straight in.

'We've been focussing on the wrong man,' he announced, 'ensuring all the officers in front of him gave their full attention. 'It's the father who's the key to where Cameron is now. The writing on the wall in the flat, the *Bible* pages we found with Darren, all about his relationship with his father.'

Harrison had some papers in his hands and started to quote from them. *'You are of your Father the Devil, and your will is to do your Father's desires.* That's what he got Darren to write out time after time. He stayed with his father's body for weeks in that flat after he'd died.'

'How can you be sure about that?' asked Salter, always one for the facts.

'From the wear on the carpet around the corpse, he'd been walking round and round him repeatedly for what must have been hours, days on end. Plus, the food wrappers in the bin—the last use by date was about two weeks ago and before that there had been consistent food waste.'

Tanya nodded in agreement.

Everyone was silent, not because they disagreed, but because they were allowing the information to sink in. Tanya was looking at the imposing figure of Harrison with another thought on her mind. His handsome face was the most animated she'd seen it. Usually it didn't communicate any emotion or the slightest inkling of what he was thinking, but this morning it had lit up.

'He chooses the boys because they represent his seven-year-old self,' Harrison continued. 'He believes he is evil, that he drove away his mother, it's what Platt Senior had told him. He's teaching the boys like his father taught him, trying to cleanse their souls and save them. He doesn't want their lives to be ruined like his was. Doesn't want them to turn to sin, like he did. It was a love/hate relationship by Cameron towards his father. He probably feared him, but also craved his approval. He tried to rebel against the overbearing strict upbringing which came from John Platt's more extreme religious views. Hence why he ended up with a *Bible* in his mouth. Part of Cameron hated his dad and the religion he adhered to. Part of him believed every word. He's torn, but for him it's like he's helping his seven-year-old self by taking the boys.'

Harrison looked around the table at the faces which stared back at him. He lingered a moment longer on Tanya's. Her eyes seemed to draw him into her. She looked beautiful this morning and was wearing a fuchsia pink top that accentuated her colouring. Harrison forced his eyes away from her face.

'We were just coming to a similar conclusion with regard to why Cameron had taken the boys,' said DCI Barker, who hadn't missed the look between Tanya and Harrison. She'd think about that a bit later. 'We also think the father may well have killed his mother. But how does this lead us any closer to finding where they are?'

'We need to be looking at something connected to his father and Cameron's childhood, not to his adult life. The death was the catalyst, but there is something from his past, something that has driven him back to his childhood while he sat alone with that body.'

'Wait a minute... Alone...' Jack was suddenly animated and dashed out of the office to his desk where he looked something up on his computer.

The others waited. Harrison stayed standing but he could feel Tanya's eyes on him and it took all his willpower not to turn round and look at her.

'There was an interview with a former neighbour,' Jack said as he walked back in the room. 'Used to live next door but moved across to another block. Mentioned something about his dad working security in a factory on night shifts and Cameron being left on his own. They used to hear him crying every night. Yes, here it is. A woman who had lived next door for a few years but asked for a transfer because she disliked Platt Senior so much. Shame she didn't try to help his son,' he added then quoted from the interview transcript. ' "He used to turn the electricity off, so the boy was completely in the dark. Said he'd left the lights blazing all night and it was costing him a fortune".'

'The electricity was off by the time we entered the flat, find out when that had run out, but it's possible he'd have been alone in the dark with that body,' added DCI Barker. 'So he's regressed to childhood, hates the dark, again how does that help us? We know why, but we are still no closer to finding out where, and we're potentially running out of time.'

'Where did the father work?' asked Harrison.

'We're still waiting on information from HMRC, but I think the neighbour mentioned it somewhere.' Jack scanned the interview transcript. 'Yes here, he worked at the Holden Furniture factory for over thirty years.' Jack looked up at them.

'That's it. It's the only photograph that isn't religious in the entire flat,' Harrison said, scrolling through the images he'd captured on his phone. 'It's in John's bedroom, him receiving a long service plate from the MD of Holden Furniture. Clearly meant a lot to him. The long service plate was broken and in the bin.'

As they talked, DC Oaks had googled the factory.

'It's been closed since the late nineties,' said Oaks 'but the site is still there, derelict but standing.'

'What kind of furniture did they make?' Harrison asked.

'Nice wooden framed stuff, the kind that became too expensive when cheap imports flooded the market from Asia, and IKEA arrived.'

'That could fit with the teak oil found on Darren.'

All of them could feel their adrenaline levels notch up.

'Where is it?' DCI Barker asked.

Oaks squinted at the tiny map on his phone. 'Just outside of the area we'd been searching.'

He looked up, excitement on his face.

'It makes sense. This could be it. I'll take this straight to Robert, get warrants and the Territorial Support Group on board. In the meantime, pull as many of our officers together as we can spare. I'll find out who the security company is that's looking after the site and call them.'

It didn't take long for DCI Barker to telephone the security company, which had been employed by the site's new owners to keep it secure and squatter free while they went through the planning process. The affronted man on the other end of the phone assured her that nobody could possibly be at the site, but she cut him short and told him to have a man at the gate in an hour to let them in. In her experience, a security job like that was an easy number. A couple of drive throughs each day to ensure there wasn't any unusual activity or kids weren't getting in, and that was it. Things could be missed. People went totally unnoticed. Murderers hid out of sight.

33

The atmosphere in the car was a ferment of adrenaline, nerves, and anticipation. DCI Barker sat in the passenger seat, her dark blonde head in front of Harrison. She spent the entire journey on one phone call after another, talking with Chief Inspector Graham McDermid and ensuring they had forensics and medics on standby.

Jack drove. Harrison saw his face in the rear-view mirror, serious and concentrating on getting to their destination as fast as he could. Bushy eyebrows furrowed together. There'd been a noticeable step-down in his antipathy towards Harrison over the last couple of days. He was relieved. It meant they were able to get on with their jobs rather than focus on a petty rivalry that didn't exist.

To Harrison's right was DC Oaks. He could almost feel the adrenaline pumping out of the young officer. Harrison estimated he was about twenty-six, a serious career head on the young man. He reminded him of the singer Will

Young in looks, a slightly large bottom jaw with an overbite and a smile which curled up at the corners like a cartoon cat. His dark brown hair was always immaculate and his suits well-fitted. He was good looking, but definitely more interested in Sam Smith than Taylor Swift. Harrison liked his attitude, he was keen to learn, and would hedge a bet that in a few years' time he would sprint up the ranks.

Nobody said a word apart from DCI Barker and her constant one-way conversation on her mobile. All of them were mentally preparing to do battle with whatever they were to find at Holden Furniture.

Harrison was glad when they neared their destination, sprinting and weaving through the London traffic in the back of a police car made him feel nauseous at the best of times, but with the anticipation somersaulting round his insides, he was looking forward to being in the fresh air.

They reached the Holden Factory site boundary long before they got to the entrance. It was a big area. It was obvious that the land was worth far more than the business ever was, but Harrison wondered if the owners had benefitted or if they'd had to sell their family business at a loss, and some lucky property developer was sat ready to cash in. Some of the permitter was walled, in other places it was six-foot railings. It wasn't an easy place to get into, but definitely not impossible.

When they finally reached the entrance gates, they found huge wrought iron throwbacks which spoke of the success the business had once been and an age when British manufacturing had been in its heyday. Holden Furniture was spelt out across the top in metalwork. Harrison could imagine the pride Cameron's dad would have felt at being a part of this mini empire.

'Bloody hell, this place is huge, we're going to need

more officers and dogs too,' Jack proclaimed as he peered through the windscreen at what lay beyond the gates.

'Territorial Support will be arriving any moment. They've only got a small team available for the next couple of hours because there's a big drugs operation going on at the docks today. It's pulled a lot of officers away. Graham can't lead, it's going to be Inspector Summers. I've also asked for the helicopter. Heat sensors might come in useful.'

'Don't hold your breath, and James Summers is a pain in the arse,' Jack declared. 'He's too methodical and slow, plays everything by the book.'

'I get that,' Sandra replied, 'but you know protocols.'

As they'd pulled up to the factory gates, two men who had been waiting in a Zebra Security van, got out.

One was in a security guard uniform and the other a suit. Before she was introduced, DCI Barker had already sussed out that the suit was the manager she'd spoken to on the phone.

'Detective Chief Inspector Barker?' queried the suited man. His manner was defensive, which wasn't unusual. A lot of people took that approach when the police called them.

'Yes, Mr Wilson?' she countered.

He stepped forward and shook her hand.

'I can assure you that nobody is living within these premises. My men complete regular checks, as our client has stipulated. We patrol the site and there is nobody here.'

'I'm sure, but we would like to take a look around please, Mr Wilson, we're not trying to get anyone into trouble. We have reason to believe that this site may have a connection to a suspect we're looking for.'

The man was obviously panicking about what the client might say if the police found someone had been living on the site under their noses. Especially if the media then got involved.

DCI Barker was relieved that the Detective Chief Superintendent was so keen to get the case wrapped up that he'd rushed through their warrants.

'I have all the necessary search warrants, and any delays could risk the life of a kidnapped child. We would appreciate your cooperation and that will be reflected in any report.'

The man nodded to her and then at his colleague, who turned to unpadlock the gate.

'This the only way in and out by vehicle?' DCI Barker asked.

'Yes.'

Behind them a navy van pulled up with blue and yellow stripes and 'Territorial Support Group' written in white writing on its side. An officer in a pale-blue baseball cap and black all-weather uniform jumped out.

'Ma'am. Inspector Summers, I'm here to assume command of the search operation.'

'Inspector.' Sandra smiled at the officer but secretly just wanted to tell him that she was in command as senior officer. She knew their unit had been assigned the search detail, but she was itching to get in there herself.

Harrison had got out the car and was looking through the gates at the site beyond.

'The vans you use, are they all like this one?' Harrison asked the Zebra Security manager.

'Vans? Yeah, why,' Wilson looked at Harrison as though he'd asked him to do the Tango.

'So every one of the vehicles that would come in here are of this type?'

'Yes. We have a fleet of about thirty. We're not a bunch

of cowboys, you know, we have a good reputation. Been going twenty years.'

'That wasn't what I was asking—or inferring,' Harrison replied brusquely. He was onto something and he wanted facts, not emotion. 'You always use the same tyres on your vans?'

'Yeah. We have a programme of maintenance and unless one of the guys had a puncture and so had to use the spare, we would keep them all consistent. I don't get why you're asking me that?'

Harrison turned to look at the man directly in the face. Mr Wilson stepped back a little as he came under his scrutiny.

'I asked because even from here I can see that there is a well-travelled path of tyre tracks that seem to match your van, but over there are another set. A different vehicle has come through those gates and it has not only got different tyres to yours, but its tyres don't match. So you see, it's important.'

DCI Barker, Wilson, and Inspector Summers, all turned to look where Harrison was pointing, but none of them could see what he referred to. The road into the factory was covered in dust and debris, decades of neglect, while the owners had waited for property prices and planning to catch-up with their expectations, and the outer edges of London's sprawl to reach them.

'Is there ever a time when these gates aren't padlocked?' DCI Barker asked the two Zebra Security men, looking from one to the other.

'No, of course not. We keep the site secure,' Wilson replied.

'Perhaps when you're carrying out your rounds?' Barker prompted the man in uniform next to her. He

flushed and instantly looked nervous. Eyes jumped from
Barker to his boss and back again.

She raised her eyebrows at him questioningly. She'd get
tougher if she had to.

'Well... maybe,' the man finally stuttered out. 'When
we go inside, it's difficult to have to lock the gates behind us
so we tend to just close them and drive round, locking
them when we leave. But no one would come in, not while
we're here,' he added with one eye on his boss.

'So yes then,' DCI Barker qualified. 'Someone could
have driven in while you were out of sight somewhere else
in the grounds.'

He nodded sheepishly, aware that his boss was glaring
at him.

'And do you ever check the buildings, or do you just
drive round?'

'We don't go into the buildings because it could
endanger our staff.' Wilson was back on the defensive now.
'Some of the buildings contain asbestos, some are falling
apart. They're mostly sealed up. Kids break into the site
occasionally, but usually it's just to find somewhere to meet
and drink and then they'll smash some windows,' the
manager continued, he was trying to find excuses now, for
anything that the next hour or hours might uncover.

'It's a big site,' DCI Barker reassured him. She realised
he was getting more dejected and nervous, and she wanted
his cooperation.

'Where do you think would be the most likely place for
someone to stay if they were in there?' Inspector Summers
spoke now and addressed Wilson.

'The main building. It's the most comfortable and least
damaged.'

'Then that's where we'll start,' he said, without a
second glance to Harrison.

He walked back to the Territorial Support van and jumped in. Harrison and DCI Barker watched them head through the gates.

'Sandra, they're going the wrong way,' he said to DCI Barker. 'There's just six of them and they're going in the wrong direction. It could take them hours to search at this rate.'

'You sure?' she asked.

'I'm positive. I don't know where those tyre tracks end, but they definitely did not go in the direction that he's just gone.'

It was all the excuse she needed.

'Okay, let's follow your tracks and see where they lead us then.'

As THEY DROVE through the entrance gates, Sandra Barker was feverishly visualising finding a little boy unharmed in one of the buildings in front of her. She was also reciting a prayer in her head. Perhaps this time it would work.

'This way,' Harrison said to Salter. He had his head out of the rear window and was staring at the ground as they travelled. 'Go slowly.' His eyes searched the dust and debris on the track. Jack didn't question him, he turned slowly in the direction he indicated.

They weren't travelling on the main road directly into the factory complex, that was the way the TS team had gone, but were heading off to the left side.

'Are those the same tyres as we saw at Felton Woods?' DCI Barker asked him.

'Yep,' Harrison replied. He was curt, but not out of rudeness, it was because he was concentrating on the ground. The tracks weren't new. The wind had caused disturbances and the imprints of animal trails criss-crossed them. He didn't want to make a mistake. Cameron Platt was here, of that he was certain.

The factory complex gradually loomed towards them. It was a huge, sprawling single-storey building, built in the 1950s and added to in the 60s, when buying British had meant something and there were the craftsmen around to build the furniture. Most of the roof was of the large, corrugated type, probably asbestos, which is why the current owners had the place sealed up. It was a simple brick-built structure and, as had been mentioned by the security manager, most of the windows they passed were smashed or already boarded up. Here and there windows were intact, reinforced with wire for security, but you could see the marks of the stones and other missiles on the glass where frustrated vandals had tried repeatedly to finish the job.

They drove past a small cluster of buildings, heavily sealed with a series of 'Asbestos keep out' signs all over.

It had the feeling of riding into a ghost town, Jack half expected a tumbleweed to roll across their path as he drove through.

'Down there.' Harrison pointed to a narrow alley that ran between two buildings. Salter didn't question him, but turned down it. As they drove, they saw the TS team right the way across the other side, getting out in front of where the factory reception had once been. Above the door hung an old wooden sign, its paint peeling but still just legible, 'Holden Furniture, proud to be British'. Harrison recognised it. That was where John Platt had proudly stood, shaking the hand of his MD, and receiving a glass plate for his thirty years' service.

'Okay, stop,' Harrison said and jumped out the car. He was like a bloodhound. They watched as he walked, eyes to the ground, first to the left and then the right. Then all around the area. He shook his head, mumbled something, and walked back to the car.

'Have we lost him?' DCI Barker asked.

'Yes, and no. I think he's gone into one of these loading bays.'

The four of them stopped and looked in front of them. A series of six large loading bays and delivery areas ran the full length of the building. Each bay had a large roller door, and each one was padlocked shut. The bays faced the River Thames at the far end of the site. DCI Barker knew it would take well over an hour before the Tactical team arrived to search these buildings. They had to act now.

'How's he got in?' Barker asked.

Harrison scanned the padlocks. They all looked the same. He'd hoped to see a shiny new one.

He checked in front of each one, but the area was like a wind tunnel, even now leaves were being picked up and swirled around and the breeze was slight. It meant the ground had been disturbed and getting any clear answers this way was going to be impossible.

'He wouldn't be the first one to figure out how to pick a padlock,' Jack suggested.

'No, you're right, and these are heavy duty but not high tech,' Harrison said, inspecting the mechanisms.

'You think the van is behind one of those?' asked Barker.

'Definitely. But which one I don't know.'

'Okay, we'll let the TS team start on the far side while we go in here. I'll let Summers know what we're doing and that we need these padlocks cutting off asap.'

'He won't like it. TS like to do it their way.'

'Well, he's just going to have to put up with it,' DCI Barker replied. 'We don't have time for arguing and this is my operation. Let's get moving.'

Harrison and Jack scanned the building's facade. At the end of the row of loading bays was a door. It was unlocked, forced open a long time ago so that the weather had got in and warped the wood, preventing it from being able to be closed. They jogged quickly round the back. It was a dead wall, no windows, no doors. That made things a little easier. The only way in and out was going to be at the front, through the bays, or through that one door. The windows, which sat like dark square patches on the brick facade, were protected by metal bars. While in most cases the glass was broken, there was no way anything, but a mouse was going to get out that way.

When they got back round to the front, Barker had finished talking on the radio to Summers.

'We need to get in that building now, but be careful, it's derelict and there could be asbestos so try not to disturb walls and coverings or stir up broken debris. If it looks like it's too dangerous, we don't go on. That clear?'

'Yes, Ma'am,' they murmured.

'The only way in—or out—is this side,' said Jack. He was slightly breathless, not through exertion but adrenaline.

She nodded and turned to look once more at the building in front of them.

'He's going to hear us coming. Be vigilant. He could try to make a break for it in the van. David, you stay outside here as liaison, I need eyes and ears covering the outside. Any sign of trouble you call for back-up immediately. No heroics.'

DC Oaks nodded. His heart had sunk initially at the thought of being stuck outside instead of going in and searching, but he knew it was critical to keep an eye on the outside and the DCI had trusted it to him.

Sandra Barker was nervous. She was a cautious

woman, and she didn't like taking her officers into a situation without a clear plan and protection, but she also knew that speed was critical right now. Platt could decide to kill the boy at any moment, especially if he heard them coming for him. She turned, gave one last look over her team to make sure they were ready, and gave the signal to start.

34

D S Salter led Barker and then Harrison into the building. He shoved at the excuse of a door. It was clear that despite what the security company said, kids had also not found it too hard. There was evidence of all of humankind's favourite pastimes, vodka bottles and beer cans, used condoms, and even the odd pile of human excrement. It also stank of human urine. The three of them picked their way through the debris using powerful torches to check exactly where they were treading.

Once through the initial entrance, the bravery of the vandals had clearly petered out. It was pitch-black inside the corridor, and while there were occasional bits of debris and rubbish on the floor, it became easier to move forward. The air improved slightly too. A blessing provided by the vandals who'd broken the glass in the windows.

The corridor seemed to lead all along the back of the building. Now and then, shafts of light crossed the darkness in front of them. Daylight coming through the windows of the offices which interspersed the loading bays.

In the corridor, Barker motioned for Harrison to lead

the way. She knew he'd be able to spot any signs that someone had been there. He was eager to get on and jumped at the opportunity to lead them forward. Harrison trained his torch on the floor and walked.

They came to their first office on the left. Its door was closed and carried a sign, 'Security'. Jack pointed to the sign. Could this have been where John Platt came to work every night? Could this be where his son was hiding?

Barker motioned for Harrison to stay back. Harrison Lane was not a police officer and so he was to follow up the rear. She and Jack went into operational mode, taking a side of the door each and communicating only through signs and facial expressions. They counted down, three, two, one, and then opened the door.

Daylight filled the room that they entered and streamed into the corridor where Harrison stood, creating a beam of dancing dust. The second they were both inside the office, he followed them.

The office window was smashed, its blinds ripped down and dumped in a tangle of plastic and string on the floor, but apart from that and the broken glass, there was very little else in the room. Dust and bits of ceiling tiles covered the dirty brown carpets, and here and there were pieces of paper. The walls were painted cream and still carried the 'Rota Board' with names as initials. Jack pointed out the initial 'JP' on the list. Elsewhere on the walls a couple of faded colour posters of women, half naked, still clung to the wall. Evidence of the advancements in equality and political correctness since the factory had closed. They scanned every inch. There was nowhere for anyone to hide.

Barker turned to Harrison and whispered, 'Any signs?'

He had already started to scan the ground where they hadn't already trodden, looking for evidence of recent activity. He searched, his feet scrunching through the broken the glass.

Everywhere was covered with dust, but there were no footprints, no disturbances. He shook his head.

They returned to the corridor, the beams of light from their torches swinging from side to side. They should reach the loading bays soon. If Harrison's calculations were right, the first one would be off on the left in about fifteen yards.

His heart was pounding in his chest, his whole body ready for fight or flight. All he could think about was finding Alex Fuller and getting him to safety. Platt had to be here. He could feel it.

The door into the first loading bay was closed but unlocked. They followed the same pattern of action, Salter and Barker in first, Harrison following up the rear.

This time there was no light from windows to help them. They entered a dark, cavernous area with only their torches.

They worked as a team, taking a section of the bay each, shining light into each of the corners. There were some cardboard boxes on one side. They didn't look promising, but they checked them out anyway.

Harrison searched again for any signs of life. He saw nothing but rat trails and decades old rubbish.

One thing was certain, there was nothing in the bay that could hide a boy, let alone a van.

Harrison was itching to run ahead. He was like a dog told not to chase a ball. He knew he had to be restrained and follow procedure. This was a police operation and if he didn't follow orders it would be his last. They had to do things properly, and he didn't want to endanger anyone's life—or the chance of a conviction. But it was tough.

It was as they crept towards the second loading bay door that he heard him.

Harrison was up front. His senses on high alert, eyes scanning, ears straining, and they heard something.

He held his hand up for them to stop.

Nothing.

For a moment he thought he'd been mistaken, perhaps heard one of the other police officers outside.

Then it began again, a low mumbling voice of a man.

At first Barker and Salter couldn't hear it. They looked quizzically at Harrison, who motioned for them to listen. All three of them crept forward towards the door.

A few more steps and they all heard it.

DCI Barker brought them to a halt. She turned away from the door and bent her head to whisper into her radio with her hand cupped over the microphone.

'Sounds of a man's voice in loading bay two. That's second bay in from the entrance—and second from right if you're outside. We are going to go in. Everyone on standby. We may need reinforcements.'

DCI Barker double-checked her body camera and took several deep breaths. She looked at the two men with her. Their faces were alive with expectation. This was the moment they'd been working towards for days. She knew their hearts would be in their mouths, pounding and their stomachs tight with tension. She knew this because hers were.

Like before, DCI Barker and DS Salter were to go into the room first. If this had been America, they'd have gone in with their handguns cocked and ready, but it wasn't. They had Tasers and truncheons, but DCI Barker also knew she had some back-up in Harrison Lane who she wouldn't like to pick a fight with if she was a bloke.

She counted down, hand on the door handle. Three —two—one.

DCI Barker pushed open the door.

The first thing they saw as soon as the door opened, was the flickering yellow light coming from a small bonfire in the middle of the loading bay. Behind it was the post office van, and walking around the fire was a small, dishevelled man.

'Cameron Platt, stay where you are. On the floor. You are under arrest,' shouted DCI Barker.

She and Jack worked a pincer movement, coming at Platt from either side of the bonfire. He didn't look at them and made no move to get on the floor, or to try to run. His eyes were glazed.

Harrison didn't care about Platt, he was frantically scanning the room for Alex.

This loading bay had pieces of furniture stacked, boxes and wooden crates, some of which had made their way onto Platt's bonfire. Harrison clocked each of these. Near to the fire was a crate upturned with paper and a pen and another box that clearly functioned as a seat. This was where Platt must make Alex write. But where was Alex? There was no sign of him.

Besides the smoke, Harrison could smell other odours, which took him a moment to place.

As he moved further into the bay, he saw several rusted cans of linseed oil and teak oil which had been used on the furniture. It looked like Platt had used some to get his fire going. Both of them highly flammable.

Perhaps the most surprising thing was that Cameron Platt didn't seem all that concerned at their arrival. The man was clearly unhinged.

'Now is the judgement of this world; now will the ruler of this world be cast out,' he shouted at them, standing above the fire on a small crate like a demonic preacher, his face glowing in the flames.

'The Gospel according to John,' replied Harrison. Cameron looked at him for the first time. His pupils dilated.

'Cameron Platt, we are arresting you on suspicion of murder and abduction. You do not have to say…' DCI Barker tried to read him his rights, but he ignored her.

'And he seized the dragon that ancient serpent, who is the Devil and Satan, and bound him for a thousand years —Revelation,' Platt continued, staring at Harrison. He didn't seem to register Barker or Salter as they closed in on him.

Jack moved forward with his handcuffs.

'Where's the boy?' he asked.

Platt said nothing, staring at Harrison still.

His eyes had returned to their vacant look. He didn't seem to be in the room at all.

'Where's the boy? Where's Alex?' Jack repeated, louder this time as he grabbed Cameron's left arm and put a handcuff on his wrist.

'Mr Platt, we have found the body of your father. We also know that you killed Darren Phillips. Don't make things any worse, please tell us where Alex is? Is he alive?' added DCI Barker.

At the mention of his father, it was as though somebody had flicked a switch on. Cameron Platt's face changed from one of passive disconnection to hardened evil. His eyes almost seemed to grow darker. DCI Barker saw the change and Harrison noticed her muscles tense, ready in case of attack. Salter, who was behind Platt putting the cuffs on his right arm, didn't see his face.

'He has been saved,' was all Platt said to her, almost

spitting out the words. Then he looked back to Harrison, triumphant, goading.

'Where is he then?' DCI Barker pushed, 'is he dead? Where is he?'

Cameron Platt slowly turned back to look at her, Harrison moved towards them nervous that he was about to do something. While Jack was holding him and Platt was no match for his size, there was something else, an inner strength that worried him. It was the strength of the desperate and the mentally deranged, that extra reserve of power and surprise which could give a person superhuman energy.

'We'll find him, so you might as well do yourself a favour and tell us first,' Jack said to his captive.

'Over there.' Platt nodded behind them to where a door led into the next bay. DCI Barker instantly moved towards it as Jack and Harrison also turned. It was all that Platt needed. He lurched from Jack's tight grip, not completely, but enough to reach the metal cans of oil which were sitting by the fire. His hands were cuffed, but his legs weren't and before Jack could even react, he had kicked the cans over, sending a torrent of linseed oil towards the fire. It ignited instantly as the highly flammable fluid hit the flames. Jack yanked Platt backwards as the fire leapt up, red and angry. They almost fell, Platt banging into Jack.

'And the Devil that deceived them was cast into the lake of fire and brimstone, where the beast and the false prophet are, and shall be tormented day and night forever and ever!' Platt shouted.

DCI Barker was on her radio in an instant. 'Get the fire brigade here now, we have a fire in cargo bay two. We've found Platt, but not the boy. Keep searching for the boy. We need all officers here now.'

Jack regained his balance and pulled Cameron Platt further away from the flames. The bottom of his trousers had caught light and so he knocked him to the floor, rolling him on the ground to quell any flames.

Harrison had just one thought on his mind, finding Alex Fuller. The boy had to be in the building somewhere, whether he was dead or alive, and if they didn't find him quickly, he would definitely be dead.

DCI Barker disappeared through the door Platt had pointed at, Harrison rushed over to the van.

He yanked the driver's door open and looked in the cab. In the passenger seat footwell he saw a child's coat. It was agonising. Alex was here. Somewhere he was here. But where?

He rushed to the back of the van, convinced he would open it and find the boy tied up. The door was unlocked, but the rear of the van was also empty. Nothing. Not even any evidence at all that anybody or anything had been in there.

Harrison could hear DCI Barker shouting Alex's name next door and he too called out to the boy.

Jack had managed to secure Platt to a railing and was attempting to put out the fire. It was ferocious. With the oil it had spread fast, and the tinderbox dry old wood and cardboard became ready fuel. The smoke was starting to hit the back of their throats and sting their eyes.

He looked for fire extinguishers, but the brackets were empty. There was nothing to dampen down the flames, Jack was forced to give up and instead joined the search for Alex. They pulled crates and sheets of wood away from the walls, hunting for a frightened, young boy.

Jack and Harrison had just finished their trawl of the loading bay when DCI Barker returned. She looked at them expectantly and shook her own head. The whole bay was beginning to fill up with smoke and the fire was spreading fast.

Harrison saw the same desperate expression on Jack's face as he felt inside. They couldn't get this close and not save Alex. He had to be here somewhere.

There was the sound of others in the corridor outside and a blue capped Tactical squad officer peered in through the door. They were searching all the other bays and offices.

'Anyone seen any signs of the boy?' Barker shouted into her radio.

'Negative, Ma'am,' came back the replies.

'Where is he?' Salter had marched up to Platt and grabbed him by his top, just under his chin. 'Where is he?' he shouted again.

'He is destined to burn in the fires of hell for all eternity,' Cameron replied.

'Harrison, is he lucid? Does he know what we're asking him?' Sandra asked. Her whole face was pleading for an answer, something they could work with.

It was virtually impossible to tell at this point, Platt was almost certainly having a psychotic episode, but whether he could understand their question, work out the consequences of his actions, was hard to tell. The events of the last few weeks had sent him over the edge.

'I don't think he has any concept of reality right now,' he replied.

'Perhaps I can help him,' said Jack.

He dropped his grip and pulled his arm back to swing a punch, Harrison was too quick for him, he grabbed his arm and stopped him.

'Don't, he's not worth it. It could end your career.'

'We need to get out of here,' DCI Barker shouted at them. 'Get him out.' She motioned at Platt.

Any longer and the fire would block their exit. They were going to have to go back the way they'd come.

Salter and Harrison dragged Cameron Platt down the corridor. Even that was starting to fill with smoke. Sandra was on her radio telling everyone to evacuate.

As they reached the exit, DC Oaks opened the door and helped them haul Platt out of the building.

'He needs medical attention,' said DCI Barker, 'possible burns to his ankles. Where's the fire brigade?'

'On their way, Ma'am.'

'And any sightings at all of Alex Fuller?'

'No.'

'We need to carry on looking,' said Salter.

Inspector Summers ran up to them. 'We've searched the whole building. He's not in there. We need to fall back until the fire's under control and carry on looking over the rest of the site.'

'Okay, you carry on, Inspector, thank you.' Sandra nodded to him. He jogged off, barking instructions into his radio. 'David, can you escort Mr Platt to the car, please.'

Harrison's mind was racing. There was no way that Platt would have kept Alex in another building. He wouldn't leave him alone, he needed him close to teach him.

'He's in there,' said Harrison. 'I know he is.' And he turned on his heels and ran straight back into the building and down the dark corridor.

'Harrison, get back here now,' DCI Barker shouted after him.

'Give us five minutes,' Salter said to her as he too spun round and headed after Harrison.

35

J   ack hoped Harrison had a plan. Both of them knew
    they'd have just a few precious minutes before the
    smoke would become too thick and they'd be
overwhelmed.

They couldn't get back into the loading bay the way
they'd gone before because the flames were licking around
the door frame. Instead, they ran into the next-door office
and entered via the side door.

Both of them checked over the van again, pulling up
the spare wheel cover, shouting out for Alex to respond if
he could hear them. Nothing.

Then they looked around the bay itself. Harrison willed
every one of his senses to work together. He blocked out
the immediate danger of the fire and focussed on one thing
and one thing only, finding that little boy.

The top half of the bay, near the door they'd come
through earlier, was an inferno. If he was there, it was
already too late, but there was nothing in that area which
could possibly hide a child.

'Alex, this is the police, we are here to help you. Shout

so we know where you are,' Jack yelled to the cargo bay, and they both stopped for a few moments—ears straining for any sound. 'Bang or kick, Alex, if you can't shout, anything.' They stopped and listened again for something, anything that could indicate where Alex was. Nothing.

'We need to check every crate again. Darren was held in an enclosed space,' Jack shouted to Harrison above the sound of the fire. It was getting louder, and the smoke meant visibility was becoming so poor, they were in danger of being disorientated. With each breath, the heat and smoke were getting into their lungs, slowing them down, making them cough. They knew it was almost too late.

They both ripped at crates, pulling them from against the walls, ripping at any with lids.

'Alex, Alex. Please can you hear us?' Jack shouted in desperation, his hands splintered and cut.

They would have to leave or risk passing out and dying in there.

Jack was behind the post office van, Harrison round the front, when there was a cracking sound and part of the ceiling fell down. It crashed onto Jack, who fell to his knees as the debris covered him. It wasn't so heavy as to crush him, but he was done in. All out. Hacking with the smoke and dust. For a moment he thought he was going to pass out, then he felt the strong arms of Harrison Lane pull him from the floor and hoist him back into the next-door office out of the bay.

Jack wasn't injured, but he needed air, and his head was spinning. For a moment he blacked out, coming to as they reached the end of the corridor and daylight.

The pair of them emerged coughing and spluttering, their faces blackened with the smoke.

'You bloody fools. The fire brigade is coming. Thank God you're out.' Barker didn't need to ask if they'd found

Alex. Her face was thunder, but she couldn't hide the relief in her eyes when she'd seen them emerge.

'Get those cargo bay locks off ready for the fire brigade,' she shouted to one of the TS team.

Smoke was now pouring out of the smashed windows in every one of the offices.

'We need to fall back. There could be asbestos in there.' Barker waved to Oaks to move away from the burning building. He was by the car. Inside Platt sat watching the flames and smoke, mesmerised.

Salter and Lane were both bent over double, coughing up the smoke.

'Have the other bays been searched?' Jack asked DCI Barker.

'Yes. Nothing. The whole building has been covered.'

'But Platt said about him burning in hell, he has to be in there somewhere.' Jack's face was pleading, as though his boss could somehow miraculously find the little boy.

'Platt is not mentally stable, we can't trust a word he says,' was all Barker replied. She didn't want to think about the consequences if he'd been telling the truth. Not now. Not yet.

Jack looked at her face and back at the burning building behind him.

'Perhaps he's not in there at all. Maybe he's in one of the others on the site.' But even as he said it, he knew it was just his brain trying to make him feel better.

'That's what I'm hoping,' replied Barker. 'We've got officers searching right now.'

Jack nodded, but his face didn't look convinced.

'Come on, we need to move.'

Harrison watched them. It couldn't end like this.

He went to follow them, but the smoke in his lungs hit him again, making him bend over and cough. As he did so, the photograph of Alex and his parents fell from his jacket pocket onto the ground in front of him.

He stared at it. Anger and frustration mixed with desperation on his face. Where could the boy be? Harrison looked over to see Platt staring at him from the back of the car. The intensity of his gaze reminded him of the photographs he'd seen of his father's corpse. It took him back to the flat, images of Cameron walking round and round his dead father's body. Of him as a young boy left alone at night while his father worked here. Their flat, devoid of character and life, no warm photographs of family memories, no mementoes of summer holidays, or even bookshelves and ornaments—just one book—a *Bible*. Only, there wasn't just one book, was there? In Cameron's room, there had been the Haynes manual on his bedside table. Harrison's mind focussed on the moment he had opened it. It had fallen open at a page that had obviously been well read. He remembered…

'The van. He's in the van.'

The second the words were out of his mouth, he knew he was right. Platt's face changed.

Harrison hadn't ever been surer of something. He ran back towards the burning building.

'What? No. We looked. We all looked,' Salter shouted after him.

'It looks empty,' was all they heard him say before he disappeared back through the smoke-filled door.

'Harrison, don't be stupid, the fire…' But DCI Barker's words were wasted.

From behind her came the voice of Cameron Platt, shouting in the police car, 'As smoke is driven away so drive them away. As wax melteth before the fire, so let the wicked perish at the presence of God.'

DCI Barker turned to the prisoner.

'If you don't shut it then the fires of hell are going to seem like a picnic by the time I've finished with you.'

She turned back to the building. There was no sign of Dr Harrison Lane.

'Harrison, you fool, what have you done?'

'I'm going back in.' DS Salter had picked himself up and was heading back towards the entrance. 'He might need help.'

'No, you are not. And that is an order.' DCI Barker was quicker this time. She grabbed his arm.

'Think about Marie, about Daniel. They need you.'

The dilemma was on his face.

'I'm the boss. If anyone's going in it's me,' she said to him, her face hardening with the resolve that clutched at her insides.

'What about your family?'

'They stopped needing me years ago. I can't leave him alone in there.'

DCI Barker started to run towards the entrance, when the huge cargo door in front of them started to move. Within seconds they saw the bottom of Harrison's legs, splayed apart. He was hauling the heavy door up with the chain.

'Quick, don't just stand there, help him,' she shouted to the men behind her.

DC Oaks, Jack, and one of the TS officers rushed over, and as the smoke poured out from the gap, helped heave the heavy door upwards.

'Stand back,' Harrison shouted at them.

At first, they weren't sure what he meant, but at the sound of the van's engine, the penny dropped. The door was only just high enough to fit underneath, but that didn't stop him. He revved the van and crashed through into the car park, scraping the roof and shattering the windscreen.

Harrison almost fell out of the driver's door, coughing. For a few moments he couldn't speak.

'He modified it. We looked but didn't see…'

He staggered to the back of the van and flung the doors back, then he started to rip at the floor. They'd already pulled up the spare wheel recess, but it was behind there that he searched.

'There has to be something…' he said, his hands running all over the floor.

Behind him, the building groaned and crackled as the fire consumed its core.

'We need to fall right back. Get that prisoner out of here,' DCI Barker shouted to Oaks and Jack. DC Oaks reluctantly got in the car and drove a safe distance away, but Jack wasn't budging.

Harrison sat up. There was nothing. How could he be so wrong? He was sure Alex was in the van. He couldn't have judged it so badly.

'I don't understand. I'm sure he's modified it. He has to be here,' he said to DCI Barker. Behind her Jack's shoulders sagged.

'Harrison,' she said, 'we have to go. The fire brigade will be here, then we can go back in. We need to move back.'

He sat staring at the van. What was he missing? His head was pounding from the smoke, his eyes streaming. His senses were deserting him.

'Dr Lane!' DCI Barker commanded now. 'We need to move.' She put her hand on his shoulder and he turned.

Harrison looked at Sandra Barker and she saw the disappointment she felt reflected on his face. They had failed the boy. Failed his parents. Was Alex now lying somewhere trapped inside that burning building?

'We've got dog teams and specialist equipment on its

way,' she said to him. 'We will search this whole complex. We could still find him. Come on, Harrison, we have to move.'

But even as she said the words to reassure him, she knew that he saw through her bravado.

Harrison was beat. Everything hurt. He'd been so sure. So convinced.

The spare wheel was halfway out of its recess, and he kicked it in frustration.

That's when he saw it.

A small lever at the back of the spare wheel recess. It was shiny metal, too new and clean to be original.

Harrison lunged for it. As he pulled it, there was a popping sound and the back of the driver's cab inside, moved. He hadn't modified the floor, he'd created a compartment inside.

DCI Barker watched, amazed, as Harrison scrambled inside and yanked at the now loose panels. He flung them to one side and there in front of them was a small boy, bound and gagged, his eyes closed. He was curled up in the tiny compartment barely large enough to fit him, with just holes in the floor for air.

'Alex, Alex.' Harrison grabbed him, pulling the child from his prison and into the main compartment. He'd been terrified that his body would be cold and stiff, but it wasn't. He was warm. He was alive.

DCI Barker was in the van with him in seconds, Jack right behind her. They pulled the gag from Alex's mouth and she shouted into her radio for an ambulance.

'He's breathing, but it's shallow,' said Harrison, feeling for Alex's pulse. 'He'd have been taking in smoke, he needs oxygen, fresh air.'

Harrison Lane picked up Alex Fuller in his arms and ran with him. His chest screamed in pain, his legs felt like wet concrete, but he had to get that little boy away from the smoke to clean air. Behind him he heard DCI Barker shouting into her radio, relaying instructions. In the distance, the sound of sirens heralded the fire brigade. For all Harrison cared, the building could burn to the ground now. They'd found what they'd come for.

36

DCI Barker stood listening to the grey-haired doctor in front of her. Her eyes were bleary with tiredness and the effects of smoke, but she could see that his face was reassuring and positive. It was good news.

'The fact the air holes were near to the floor probably helped save him. There appears to be no permanent smoke damage, and apart from dehydration he is remarkably okay. We will need to keep him in a couple of days for observation, but otherwise, I'm positive about his physical outcome.'

'Thank you, doctor,' DCI Barker said. 'And psychologically?'

'Not my area, but we've booked him in for a full assessment tomorrow. Not today, he's too tired.'

DCI Barker nodded. Her mind thought about the weeks and months of nightmares ahead for Alex Fuller, but at least he was alive and back with his family.

'And my officers?'

'They'll be fine. We've given them both oxygen and dealt with a few minor burns and scrapes, but after a couple of days' rest, we're not foreseeing any long-term damage. We're lucky there didn't appear to have been any particularly noxious chemicals on site.'

'No, just plenty of wood and furniture oil,' replied DCI Barker ironically. 'And thankfully, no problems with asbestos either.' She'd become paranoid about developing asbestosis in the hours since the incident. When the fire officer on command had rung up to tell her the building hadn't contained any asbestos after all, she'd been mightily relieved.

The doctor returned to his busy round and DCI Barker went to check in on the Fullers for one last time before going home. Their prisoner, Cameron Platt, had already been in and patched up, and was on his way to a custody cell at Lewisham where a mental health expert was ready to assess him.

When Barker arrived at the room where the Fullers were sat around Alex's bed, she found Harrison had beaten her to it. She didn't go in straight away. Instead, she watched through the observation window in the door as Harrison crossed to Alex's bed and tenderly took the boy's hand.

Did Alex know he'd saved him?

The parents certainly did because Sally Fuller stood up and hugged him. DCI Barker smiled at the sight of their hero, looking decidedly awkward and embarrassed at the closeness of the embrace. She really was going to have to find him a good woman. He deserved a chance at love and a happy family life after what he'd been through with his own. He might come across as cool and aloof, but she knew he had a lot to give. Perhaps she could help engineer something with Tanya. They seemed rather taken with each other.

She was just about to go into the room when she saw

Harrison reach into his jacket pocket and pull out what looked like a photograph.

The photo of the smiling Fuller family was a little creased and scuffed now, and there were smears where black soot had gotten from his fingers onto the photograph, but that didn't matter. Harrison held it out to Sally Fuller and smiled.

'I don't need this anymore. I wanted to return it to you.'

She took it, tears coursing down her cheeks. Edward stood and shook his hand and put his arms around his wife to comfort her. They had their family back together again.

37

Harrison slept for ten hours solid. He didn't even remember how he'd got into bed. Sandra had arranged for a taxi to take him home because his bike was still in Lewisham, and quite frankly he wouldn't have trusted himself to ride it without causing an accident, anyway. He knew he'd had a shower, drunk about ten pints of water, and then that was it. He'd hit the pillow and was out. His sleep hadn't been without dreams, some of them violent and vivid, but he'd battled through them and slept from nine in the evening until seven the next morning.

He felt the after-effects of the fire. His chest, lungs, and throat were sore, raw, almost like he'd got a bad chesty cold. He could feel the inflammation in all his airways, and he'd got the ghost of a headache still, as though the smoke had settled in his brain. He hadn't anticipated just how tired and heavy his limbs would feel. It was going to be a quiet day for him while his body caught up with the exertion and lack of oxygen.

He felt at peace, though. The weight of responsibility

had lifted—for now at least—until the next one. There was always a next one.

He allowed himself the luxury of another shower and then a leisurely breakfast, lounging on his sofa in front of the big bank of windows. It was a nice day outside. The sun sparkled on the River Thames as it slowly meandered past. He loved watching the river. It was officially the second longest in the UK, after the River Severn, but Englishmen would argue that the Thames was the longest, because the River Churn fed it, which some said should be unofficially included in its length. Harrison didn't care about its size; he loved the life in its waters. So much history on its banks and in its silt.

He felt for it, though. The Thames was a captive animal, unable to evolve and escape. If London hadn't grown up around it, with concrete banks restricting its course, then the meanderings would have turned into oxbox lakes by now. As it was there were already over eighty named islands along its length. The free spirit of the Thames was constricted, but it breathed on. A twice-daily tidal ebb and flow that allowed the river a slow intake and exhalation.

Harrison closed his eyes and slowly breathed in and out. Seeking to repair his mind and awaken his senses, just like the river.

As his head slowly began to clear, his thoughts turned to Tanya, and her fear that she was being watched. He should text her, check if she's okay.

He'd avoided picking up his phone so far, but now he'd thought about her he needed to see it through. He kept it short, to the point. *'Did you manage to sort the cameras and alarms okay? No developments?'* he wrote.

There was a text on his phone from Ryan too. Could be something important so he read that.

'Morning, great news re Alex. Managed to discover some interesting things about your Nunhead location. News story about a woman being found stabbed in 1993. Case never solved. Witchcraft or Devil worshipping involved. Have emailed details.'

Harrison's heart lurched, and he felt sick. It was true. That image he'd seen in his head was a real memory. The night he and his mother had been there a woman died. But who was she? It explained why his mother had been so scared. Flashes came back into his tired brain. Pale skin, red blood. The stone.

He had to find out more. Now he had two murders to solve—but he was pretty sure there was only one killer.

38

The next day, the incident room was like a pressure cooker with its lid lifted, the atmosphere had lightened, and officers were smiling and chatting, the urgency gone. There was still plenty to do, the case would need to be sewn up for the Crown Prosecution Service and Cameron Platt was still being interviewed, but they'd taken a dangerous man off the streets and put a boy back with his family. They'd also given answers to Louise and the Phillips family, and a closure of sorts. That wasn't a victory, but it was the best they could do in the circumstances.

Some of the team were off after their endless overtime, and already DCI Barker was working on a new case. Jack Salter was trying to type his report with bandaged hands. It was a slow process. He looked up as Harrison came out of DCI Barker's office. The door had been closed.

'Everything okay?' he asked him.

'Yeah, fine. There'd been an enquiry from one of the papers after the incident with the photographer at the Phillips' house. She's managed to make it go away.'

'I knew she'd take care of it. She's like a lioness when it comes to her team.'

'Yeah, but she's making me do an anger management course...' Harrison replied.

Jack smirked at him and Harrison smirked back. Two naughty schoolboys who'd just bonded.

'This was handed into front desk for you,' he said, holding out a brown A4 envelope.

Harrison looked at it. He'd no idea who it could be from, so he tore it open. Inside was a single photograph. He pulled it out. It was of two people, the man in black witch's robes, standing next to the young woman, his mother, in his photograph at home, only this time she was also wearing black robes. There was something in her eyes, a sadness. Loss. Someone had drawn on the photograph with a black felt-tip pen. There was a noose around her neck.

'Who's that pair of weirdoes?' asked Jack, peering at the photo in Harrison's hand.

'My mother,' he replied.

'Sorry.' Jack looked embarrassed. 'What's with the noose, is everything okay?'

'She died some time ago. It's okay.'

'That your dad?'

'No. Her murderer. I haven't quite caught up with him yet, but I will.'

'Murderer? Has he been convicted, or under investigation?' asked Jack.

'No, it's fine, I'm going to deal with him my own way.'

Jack didn't know what else to say, but he needn't have worried because Harrison had already had enough of the small talk and started to walk off. He frowned after him, turned round to his computer and jotted a note onto his pad. If it was an unsolved murder, then he couldn't let that just rest. He'd look into it himself.

DCI Barker came out of her office and walked up to Jack's desk.

'So who's for the pub?' she addressed the room and saw Harrison just about to exit. 'Harrison! You're not sneaking off, are you?'

Harrison stopped and turned back to her.

'I don't drink.'

'Have an orange juice!'

'Sorry, it's youth Taekwondo night, they'll be expecting me.'

Jack raised an eyebrow quizzically at Barker.

'Blackbelt, I told you he was handy. Teaches at some club for teenagers, reckons the discipline helps them. Jack, you'll come?'

'Sorry, Ma'am, I need to get back home, check on Marie, you know I would normally.'

'Right pair of party animals you two are. Fine looks like it's just me and this rabble then.'

She watched Harrison wander out the room, looking at a photograph in his hand.

Close behind him went Jack Salter, staring at his phone.

DCI Barker turned and walked up to the incident board. Someone had drawn devil's horns on the photograph of Cameron Platt. She gave it one final look over, lingering on the face of Darren Phillips, and then headed back to her office for her bag.

A WORD FROM GWYN

Firstly, a huge thank you for choosing to read **Preacher Boy**. I hope you've enjoyed being introduced to Harrison and colleagues. This series has been several years in the making and it's been an exciting but nerve-wracking experience bringing it to the world. I would really appreciate it if you could leave a review on the Amazon book page. Reviews mean a lot to authors, they tell us that people are reading our work, and help guide other readers.

If you'd like to read a FREE short story about Harrison and DCI Barker's first case together, then you can sign up for my Readers Club for free. I'll not bombard you with emails, but I'll keep you updated with release news, competitions, offers and more. Visit: GwynGB.com/readersclub

Plus if you'd like to read more, you might like to try **The Horsemen**, the second in the series. Thank you again, I really do appreciate your support.

Best wishes, Gwyn

THE HORSEMEN

BOOK 2 IN THE HARRISON LANE MYSTERY SERIES

Behind the glamorous world of horse racing hides a dark secret…

A Herd of wild horses stand guard over a body on the Cambridgeshire Fens.

A mysterious secret association within the world of horse racing.

Only one man can untangle the truth...

Psychologist, Dr Harrison Lane, Head of the Ritualistic Behavioural Crime unit is called to the Cambridgeshire Fens where a promising young horse racing jockey's body has been found in mysterious circumstances. Is black magic behind the murder? Harrison starts to investigate, but there's someone else on his mind...

Back in London, Forensic investigator Tanya Jones is being stalked, but she has no idea who or why they're watching her. Harrison is worried for her safety because he knows exactly what kind of man is lurking in the shadows...

ACKNOWLEDGMENTS

Every book relies on a team of people and so I'd also like to say a few thank you's to those who have helped bring Harrison to you. For the cover work, thank you to Adrijus from Rocking Book Covers. For his advice on policing, which helped to inject some reality into my fictional world, thanks go to Graham Bartlett at Police Advisor. A huge thank you to my editor, Emma Mitchell at Creating Perfection who came to the rescue after my first editor fell seriously ill with Covid. Sending best wishes to Angela Brown for a full recovery.

Then, there are those in my life who support me in my writing passion: Fellow Blonde Plotters, Deborah Carr and Kelly Clayton, who have been waiting to meet Harrison after hearing so much about him. Plus my husband and boys who have brought me cups of tea and tried not to get jealous of the time I am spending with Dr Harrison Lane; and last, but not least, my constant fur girl writing companion, Molly, who had to wait patiently (or not so patiently) some days for her walkies.

Faithful, but nagging, writing companion, Molly

ABOUT GWYN GB

Gwyn GB is a writer living in Jersey, Channel Islands. Born in the UK, she moved there with her Jersey-born husband, children, dog and geriatric goldfish.

Gwyn has spent most of her career as a journalist, but has always written fiction in her spare time and is now a full time author.

You can connect with Gwyn online:

Website: https://www.gwyngb.com

 facebook.com/GwynGBwriter

twitter.com/gwyngb

instagram.com/gwyngb

ALSO BY GWYN

DI CLAIRE FALLE SERIES

Someone's watching. Someone's Lonely. Someone's going to Die. Could it be You?

LONELY HEARTS

Meet Rachel, she loves animals and works at a dating agency bringing lonely people together – only somebody is watching her every move and she's scared…

Neil didn't see who killed him – but his murder brings DI Claire Falle on the case. What she uncovers leads her to discover a serial-killer is preying on the clients of the dating agency where Rachel works.

Can Claire work out the connection between all the deaths before Rachel becomes the next victim?

What is it in Rachel's past that haunts her?

As DI Claire Falle investigates the lives of the dating agency staff and clients, she is pulled into a tangled web of loneliness and deceit which will have devastating consequences for someone…

What readers are saying about Lonely Hearts

'What a twist! It absolutely had me on the edge of my seat.'

'Brilliant. If you want to get completely lost in a page-turner with an amazing twist, then Lonely Hearts is the book for you.'